WILD FOR YOU

THE WILDS OF MONTANA

KRISTEN PROBY

&

AMPERSAND

PUBLISHING, INC.

Wild for You

A Wilds of Montana Novel

By

Kristen Proby

PROLOGUE
REMINGTON

"Sir?"

Numb, and not a little lost, I turn from the window that looks out to Bozeman, to the woman standing behind me. "Yes?"

"I know this is an incredibly difficult time, but would you like to meet your daughter?"

My daughter.

Our *daughter*. Mine and Jessica's.

"Oh, of course. Yeah."

"Right this way." She gestures for me to follow her and leads me down a long, stark hallway lit too brightly with fluorescent lights. Behind closed doors, I can hear people talking, some crying.

And all I can think is, *get me out of here.*

"I understand that the circumstances are, well, different, but I have to ask you some questions."

"Sure, just let me see the baby first, okay?" Yeah, my

voice is harsh and short, but for fuck's sake, I haven't even met my child yet.

"Of course," she says and leads me into a room.

A recovery room.

"This is where your wife would have been—" She breaks off and clears her throat. "Go ahead and have a seat, and I'll wheel your daughter in."

I nod and sit in the one uncomfortable chair opposite the empty bed.

That's where Jessica should be, not on her way to an operating room to—

"Here she is," the same nurse says as she walks back into the room, wheeling the hospital cradle to me.

I look inside, and there's my little girl.

"Six pounds, four ounces," the nurse says, "and eighteen inches long. She's perfectly healthy, Mr. Wild."

"Yeah." I have to clear my throat as I gaze down at the baby. "She's beautiful."

"What's her name?"

I reach in and scoop her up, then lift her to my face and breathe her in. She smells like baby powder and, ironically, *hope.*

"Mr. Wild?"

I kiss my daughter's cheek and then look up at the nurse, raising an eyebrow. "Yes?"

"What's her name?"

"Holly," I reply, looking down into the face that looks so much like Jess's. "She wanted to name her Holly."

"That's lovely. I'll leave you be now. The doctor will be in shortly."

I nod but don't reply, and when it's just Holly and me, I let out a long breath. The baby's eyes are open, and although I know she can't see me, she's looking up at me.

"You are the most beautiful, amazing girl ever born," I whisper. "And you and your older brother are going to be best buds."

I swipe at a tear running down my cheek as Holly opens her tiny mouth and searches for her fist.

She's hungry.

"Don't worry, okay? We're going to make this work. I mean, this isn't my first rodeo, and my parents live close by. Heck, you have three uncles and an aunt close by, too, so there are plenty of grown-ups to take care of things."

I sigh and lean in to press my lips to her forehead.

"But, my sweet girl, your mama didn't make it. I'm so sorry."

I swallow hard and cuddle Holly against my shoulder as I wonder what in the hell I'm going to do.

"I'm so damn sorry."

CHAPTER ONE
ERIN

"You're changing the sign!"

I grin up at the man who's screwing in the new sign.

Welcome to Bitterroot Valley, Population 8,746.

"The population changed again," he calls down to me, and I nod.

Yeah, I am one of the new residents who has changed the population from 8,731. I moved here in December, and since then, three babies have been born, along with a couple of new families that moved to town.

Just in the past four months.

"How often do you change it?" I call back.

"Once a year, when it's warm enough to climb up on a ladder without freezing to death," he informs me. I nod, look at the sign once more in satisfaction, and then keep walking, on my way to work.

It's official. I'm a citizen of Bitterroot Valley, Montana. I mean, sure, I've technically been that since

December when I came here with all my cousins for a vacation and decided to stay, but it feels extra official now, and I couldn't be happier. I knew as soon as we landed here that this was my home.

With a little more bounce in my step, I make my way down the sidewalk. It's finally springtime, which means that the bitter cold from winter seems to be over. We still have a little snow on the ground, and I've been told that the mountains will have snow until early summer, but it's finally warm enough to walk to my job at Bitterroot Valley Coffee Co.

I *love* my job. I've met so many people already, thanks to the coffee shop. I have my regulars who never miss a day, and the best part is, I'm still meeting new people all the time. I've never really considered myself to be a social butterfly, but I admit that it was hard to move away from my huge, loud family to a place where I knew absolutely no one. But I've started to weave myself into the community, and it's only made me love this little town more.

Not to mention, my new friend, Millie Wild, works with me. Actually, she worked there first and helped me get the job. We became fast friends, and now I can't imagine my life without her. We're roughly the same age, and it's as if we've been friends forever.

I tip my head back and take a deep breath, pulling in the crisp spring air, and smile.

Yeah, this is exactly where I'm supposed to be.

Before long, I've crossed the imaginary line from residential to downtown blocks, and I walk into the warmth of the café. The smell of freshly ground coffee meets me, along with a wave from Millie.

"Good morning." I grin at her and walk behind the counter, hurrying to the back to stow away my things. Once I've grabbed an apron and tied my hair back, I return to the counter and take in the number of people already sipping coffee, having conversations, or typing away on their computers all over the space. "It's busy in here for a Thursday morning."

"I know," she replies with a sigh and wipes her forehead with the back of her hand. "I should have asked you to come in earlier."

"I totally would have. Why didn't you?"

She turns and gives me a grin. "I know how much you like to sleep in. Besides, it's not normally like this, especially in the middle of the week. Anyway, there seems to be a lull now. How are you?"

"I'm *great.*" I tell her about the population sign change, and she laughs, shaking her head at me. "What? It's a big deal."

"You're just so cute. I love how much you *love* living here, Erin. It reminds me to be thankful for it, too. I guess I forget, since my family has been here for more than a hundred years."

"It's my home." I shrug a shoulder, but I mean it with every fiber of my being. The bell over the door jingles, and Millie grins.

"What do *you* want?" she demands, her voice full of humor.

"An oil change," her brother, Chase, says with a grin as he saunters in. "And maybe a haircut."

"You won't get either of those things here," Millie replies, rolling her eyes. She reaches for a to-go cup to start making her brother's favorite coffee.

"How's it going, Erin?"

"I'm great, thanks. And you?"

Chase smiles and leans on the counter. I've met two of Millie's brothers so far, and they're both *gorgeous*. Chase has a smile that could likely melt all the snow on the ski mountain. Not to mention, he's a cop, and that uniform is *hot*.

"I can't complain."

"Have you arrested anyone today?"

Chase shakes his head mournfully. "So far, everyone has been law-abiding. Well, except for Mrs. Wilburn, who refuses to drive the speed limit on her way into town."

"Is she a speeder?" I ask.

"No, she won't drive above twenty-five," he says with a pained expression. "*Anywhere*. So, she backs up traffic and they call me."

I press my lips together, trying not to laugh, but I can't help it.

"It gives you something to do," Millie says as she passes her brother his coffee. "Do you want a muffin? Jackie Harmon brought some fresh huckleberry-lemon ones in this morning."

"I don't pass up Jackie's muffins," Chase says with a nod. "I'll take two."

"I've got this," I assure Millie and, with tongs in hand, gently place the enormous muffins into a bag for Chase. When I pass the bag to him, his fingers brush mine, but there's no spark there.

Too bad. Chase is definitely a sexy guy.

"Well, ladies, it's been real. Call if you need anything. I'm walking down the block to check out the new restaurant going in."

"What kind is it?" Millie wants to know.

"Italian," I reply before Chase can. "I walked by last night and spoke to the owner. It's called *Ciao*. I guess it's a sister restaurant to one of the same name in Cunningham Falls."

"That's kind of cool," Millie decides. "Do you know when it's opening?"

"I didn't ask. Do you know, Chase?"

"Next month," he confirms with a nod and sips his coffee. "It's always good to have something new come in. Well, I'm out of here to keep order in our little town. Have a good day."

Chase walks out, and I grab a rag to wipe down the espresso machine.

"Do you have a crush on my brother?" Millie asks without hesitation. "If you do, it's okay, but I saw the way you two kind of flirted and smiled at each other, and I just need to know so I don't roll my eyes incessantly whenever you flirt with him."

I laugh, shaking my head. "No, definitely not. Don't get me wrong, he's really handsome, and who doesn't love a man in uniform?"

"I mean, usually, yeah. But he's my brother."

I laugh again. "No, there's no spark there. But it's fun to flirt a little, you know?"

"Sure, I get it. I've had to deal with friends or just people I know crushing hard on my brothers all my life, so it's nothing new for me. I guess that happens when you have four of them, and they're all, from what I'm told, *hot*."

"I've only met two of them," I remind her. "But yeah, Chase and Brady are both hot as hell, so I get it. Also, I grew up surrounded by a family of beautiful people, and I guess it just doesn't make me go all stupid and gooey, you know?"

"I get that," she says with a nod. "I guess it's the same for me. I wish you could meet Ryan, but he's never in town."

"He doesn't live here?"

"He has a house here, but he travels a lot for work. We haven't seen him in a couple of years. And then there's Remington, the oldest. Getting him off the ranch for anything is like trying to pull teeth out of a shark. He's as dedicated as it gets to that place. But I'll take you out there sometime because it *is* kind of cool."

"But you don't live out there."

"Are you kidding? Hell no. It's way too far out of town for me. I want to be where the action is, and I'm not really needed out there. I do spend a few days there in the spring, when it's time to brand and castrate the calves."

I turn and blink at her. "That sounds...horrible."

Millie chuckles and tucks her dark hair behind her ear. "I'm just used to it. Been doing it all my life. Anyway, that covers everyone in my family. Tell me about yours."

I open my mouth, but then a group of about eight people hurry inside to order coffee and food, and we're busy for the rest of the morning.

SINCE MILLIE HAS the early shift at the coffee shop, she gets off work early, and I stay by myself for the last two hours to close on my own. On our off days, the other two girls, Candy and Marion, who happens to be the owner, work the same shifts.

At first, I was surprised that there were only four employees, but given that the café is closed on Mondays, it works out well for us. We all get along and keep the place running smoothly.

I enjoy the couple of hours by myself in the afternoon. By then, things are usually pretty quiet in here, so I can clean and mop without too much interruption.

Until *he* comes in. Every single day. Right about...*now*.

The bell over the door dings, and I glance up to see my least favorite customer walk through the door. He's tall, probably in his mid to late thirties, and always wears a baseball cap. Today, he's in a denim shirt with the sleeves rolled just below his elbows, with dark blue jeans and boots. And my, oh my, how he fills out those jeans. Not to mention the way his muscles bunch in his forearms when he reaches for the wallet in his back pocket.

Everything about him *screams* cowboy, that's for sure.

And he's handsome as hell. Just looking at him makes my blood heat.

I mean, if you like the grumpy, surly type.

"Hello." I greet him with a forced smile as I lean the mop against the wall and walk behind the counter. I've never asked his name because he's never been talkative enough to make conversation. "What can I get for you today?"

"Coffee, black," he says. He always orders the same thing.

"Sure. We have huckleberry-lemon muffins today. I have three left, if you'd like one. They're popular."

I smile, but he doesn't smile back. He does, however, eye the last of the muffins in the case.

"I'll take them."

"All of them?"

He levels a look at me, and those eyes—brown? No, too light to be brown. Hazel eyes—stare into my soul. "Yes. All of them."

"Okay. You must be hungry." I happily ring up the muffins and coffee into the computer, and while he does his thing with his credit card, I bag up the treats and pour his coffee. "It's sure a nice spring day out there today. You know, for as cold as it got this winter, I'm surprised by how quickly it's warming up. Still plenty of snow in the mountains, though."

"Hmm," is all he says in reply as he taps the screen on the computer, finishing the sale.

"Okay, well, here you go. I hope you have a nice afternoon."

"Yeah." He grabs the brown paper bag and his coffee and turns to go. "You, too."

The door closes behind him, and I let out a long breath. I can usually get a smile out of people, especially if I meet them more than once, but this guy is impossible.

Grouchy cowboy.

I shake my head and get back to work. Before long, it's time to lock the door and set the alarm, which Marion put in just this past winter, and set off for home. I like to walk through town, taking the long way back to my place. I found the cutest apartment above the garage of an elderly guy in town. I like to take him soup and a cookie from Mama's Deli just down the street. He always tells me that I shouldn't bother, but I can tell by the way he lights up that it's his favorite part of the day.

I never see anyone come to the house to visit him, and he reminds me of my grandpa back in Seattle.

"Hello, Erin," Jeannie, the manager of the deli, says when I walk in. "I have his favorite today. Beef with barley."

"Oh, that'll make his day." I smile at the other woman as I pull out my credit card, but she shakes her head.

"It's on me today. It's Mr. Sherman's birthday."

My mouth drops. "It *is*? Well, shit, I didn't know that."

"Of course, you didn't. How could you?"

"How do *you* know?"

Jeannie sighs, then shrugs. "I never forget a date, and my parents must have mentioned it at some point. Before he died, my dad and Mr. Sherman were friends."

"Jeannie, does Roger have any family here? I never see anyone come to see him."

"No." Jeannie shakes her head as she adds an extra cookie to the bag. "Roger and Sue never had any kids, and Sue's been gone, jeez, twenty years now, I guess."

"That's so sad. He's a really nice guy."

Jeannie looks over at me in surprise and then laughs.

"What? He is."

"Well, he may be nice to *you*, but he's always been kind of a grumpy old man. He's your typical *get off my lawn* type of guy, you know?"

I shake my head. "No, I've never seen that side of him. That's so funny. Hey, throw in a chocolate cupcake, and I'll pay for it."

"That's sweet. I even have a candle you can have."

"That's awesome. Thank you. Well, I'd better hit up one of the shops for a gift for him on my way home. Thanks, Jeannie."

"You're welcome, honey. Go enjoy that weather."

I nod and, with the hot soup and cookies in one hand, set off across the street to a shop that sells both women's and men's clothes, and find Roger a nice scarf. It's blue and will be handsome on him.

With that finished, and content because they offered to gift wrap it for me, I hurry home and make Roger's house my first stop, before going into my apartment.

"Hello?" I call out as I open the door. Roger told me a while ago that I didn't have to knock, since I come over so often. "It's just me."

"Oh, hello, dear."

He says it that way every day, as if it's a surprise to see me, even though he sees me every day. His eyes light up when he sees the wrapped box in my hand.

"You didn't tell me that it's your birthday." I set the bag of food on the table and hold the wrapped box out to him. "But thankfully, I have my ways of finding things out."

"It's just another day," he begins, but I shake my head.

"No, sir, it's your *birthday*. You've been incredibly kind to me since I moved here, and you're one of my closest friends. I celebrate my friends on their birthdays."

His eyebrows pull together as he stares down at the box, and then he looks up at me with soft brown eyes.

"Thank you," is all he says.

"You're welcome."

"Now, since it *is* my birthday, I'd like you to stay for dinner. Jeannie always packs enough soup for two."

"It's your favorite today," I inform him. I don't personally love beef with barley, but for Roger, I'll choke down a small bowl. "What did you do today?"

"I took my morning walk," he says as I bustle about his kitchen, pouring our soup and getting us settled at the table. "They changed the sign again."

"I saw it! I was so excited because *I'm* one of the new people they added."

"Too many people moving into our town," he grumbles as he sits at the table with me. "Now, you, I don't mind, but we have too many move-ins trying to change our town. Make it bigger and what they think is better. If they want Bitterroot Valley to be like California, they should stay in California."

"Maybe you should run for mayor. Or city council."

Roger scoffs as he takes a bite of his soup. "Been there, done that. Many years ago. No one wants to listen to the opinions of an old man."

"I do. Here, open your present."

I notice the slight tremor in Roger's hand as he tears the wrapping paper. I've noticed the tremors getting worse for a while now. When I first moved in, he didn't have any shaking at all, and now his right hand is never still.

If he *was* my grandfather, I'd ask him if he'd been to the doctor, but he's not my grandpa. And it's none of my business.

"Now, what did you do here?"

"It's just a scarf," I say with a smile. "I thought you'd look handsome in it on your morning walks. Until summer, anyway."

He immediately wraps it around his neck and smiles over at me like a kid at the best birthday party ever. "I love it. Thank you."

"You're welcome."

I spend a few hours with Roger, helping him plan some gardens for his backyard, and we even watch an episode of an old TV show that he likes. After surprising him once more with the cupcake and the birthday candle, I head over to my apartment above the garage.

It's just a one-bedroom space with a tiny kitchenette, but it's what I can afford without dipping into my trust fund.

And I'm determined *not* to dip into that at all if I can help it. My dad was so mad at me when I wouldn't let him buy me a fancy house on the ski mountain or in a gated community. But I didn't want that.

I want this, to live within my means, *in* the community.

I want to do this on my own.

And, speaking of my parents, it's time for my weekly video call with them. So, I change into comfier clothes and settle on the couch with my phone.

Mom answers on the first ring.

"There you are," she says with a smile. "I wondered if you were going to call tonight."

"I'm only a half hour late," I reply and shake my head. Then I look closer. "Mom, do you have *pink* in your hair?"

"Yep." She turns her head so I can see it more clearly. "I used to put colors in my hair all the time before I had you girls, and I've decided I want to do it again. How are you, baby girl?"

"I'm great. I *am* sorry that I'm late. It's Roger's birthday, so I spent some time with him after work."

"Is it wrong that I kind of love that you've befriended an old man in this new town of yours, and I don't have to worry about some man your age?"

"It's not wrong. Roger's sweet. Anyway, what's Dad up to?"

"I'm here," I hear him say from somewhere else in the room. "I'm coming."

Suddenly, they're both on the screen. Dad might have a couple more gray hairs mixed in with the dark brown, and I'm sure that's all thanks to me and my move to Montana.

"Hi, Daddy."

"You look good," he says. "Are you exercising?"

"Of course." I can't help but laugh. Leave it to my dad, the former professional quarterback, to worry about that. "It's even warm enough to start walking to and from work again. I'm on my feet all day. What's new with you guys?"

"There's always *something* going on with the family," Mom says. "You know how it is."

"Yeah, everyone's been great about texting me updates. But what's new with *you*?"

They look at each other, and I frown.

"Are you getting divorced?"

Dad laughs, and Mom just stares at me in shock. "What? Why in the world would you ask something like that?"

"I'm as obsessed with your mother as I was the day I married her," Dad assures me.

"You look...serious. Is Zoey okay?"

"She's great," Mom says. "Dad and I are thinking about selling the house and moving into something just a little smaller. We're empty nesters, and we don't need this huge house anymore."

My heart pings at the thought of them selling the house I grew up in. All of my firsts live in that house.

"At least it's not divorce," I reply with a forced smile.

"But it makes you sad," Mom guesses correctly. "I know you."

"It makes sense for you. If that's what you guys want to do, I say do it. Buy something fancy and modern, but a little smaller. I can't wait to see it."

"Zoey had a harder time with the idea," Dad says. "In fact, there were tears and threats."

"She'll get over it." I sigh and then yawn. "You don't have to save my old stuff. Donate it or toss it."

"That's my sentimental girl," Mom says with a laugh. "I miss you, baby."

"I miss you, too. When are you coming to see me?"

Dad's eyes narrow. "Maybe sooner than you think."

CHAPTER TWO
REMINGTON

"Your mother wants to retire." My dad and I are sitting on horses, almost ready to pack it in after a long day of checking calves.

"You're already supposed to be retired," I remind him. "That's why I'm in charge now. Yet, you come to work every day."

"Hell yes, I do. I get to enjoy the ranch without any of the responsibility for the first time since before you were born. I'm having a hell of a time. Am I in the way?"

I can't help but laugh at that and shake my head. "Of course not. I don't know what this place would do without you. So, what does Mom mean, exactly?"

"*She* wants to retire," he says, stressing the *she*, and I nod slowly. "She's been taking care of the books for this place since we got married, and she's damn good at it. But she'd like to pass the torch to someone else."

"We tried." I rub my hand over the back of my neck. "We've been through several bookkeepers, but they're never up to Mom's standards, and we end up letting them go, and Mom goes back to business as usual."

"I know," he says with a sigh. "Maybe it's time we look for another one and see if that one sticks. Joy wants to travel, and you know as well as I do that I could never tell that woman no."

"She wants to travel?" I stare over at him in surprise. "She *hates* to fly. She's always sworn that she wouldn't get on a tin can with wings."

"She's changed her mind." He shrugs. "Maybe it's hormonal. How in the hell should I know? Anyway, I wanted to let you know so it's on your radar."

Great. One more thing on my already overloaded radar.

"No problem. I'll see to it. I heard from Ryan the other day."

Dad's eyebrow wings up. "And?"

"He's coming home next week. He was just giving me a heads-up. We'll want to do a big family dinner, I suppose."

"Your mother would like that," he agrees. "You know, you and Ryan need to figure your shit out."

I smirk and shrug a shoulder.

"I'm serious, Rem. You two may be as different as they come, but he's your brother."

"I don't dislike him."

Okay, that's a lie. I *do* dislike my brother. He's only a year younger than me, and we were always as close as we could be. Best friends. Planned to live our lives on this ranch, the way our dad and *his* dad had done before us. Then Ryan got a taste for money. Venture capitals, and all of the shit involved in that that I don't understand or care about.

But it's made Ryan a billionaire before he's thirty-five.

"You don't *like* him," Dad points out.

"We want different things."

Dad nods thoughtfully. "That's for sure. When do the kids get out of school?"

I check my watch. "In about an hour. I should get back to the house and clean up before I head to town to pick them up."

"The school bus has a stop right at the end of our driveway."

I shake my head as we turn the horses and start back to the barn. "I don't want my kids sitting on that bus for two hours after school. That's not fair. I'll get them."

"Maybe you need a nanny," Dad suggests, and I shake my head again.

"I'm doing fine by my kids."

"You're doing fantastic," he corrects me. "Doesn't mean that you couldn't use some help. If your mother and I do start to travel, we won't be here to help as much."

I've thought of that, of course. I admit, I depend on my mom for a lot when it comes to the kids. If she's gone, I'll just have to utilize my ranch hands more to cover the work I can't see to.

And that doesn't feel right either.

"Something else to think about," Dad says with a smile.

I FEEL a little guilty that whenever I go into the coffee shop in the afternoons, on my way to get the kids, my sister is already gone for the day. I hardly ever see her now that she's moved into town and is doing her own thing. As annoying as she could be when she was little, I'll admit that I miss the hell out of her.

But I don't have time to come into town any earlier than this. Hell, I'm lucky if I make it off the ranch in time to stop in for the coffee at all.

Some days, Marion, the owner, is here, and she tries to chat me up. Marion has always been chatty. She's nice enough, but my mind is usually elsewhere.

Today, the other afternoon woman is here. I don't know her name. I assume she's new to town because I only started seeing her around Christmastime.

She's pretty. Okay, pretty is a fucking understatement. She's gorgeous, from head to toe. Rich, dark hair is twisted up in a bun at the base of her neck. She's wearing a green Bitterroot Valley Coffee Co. T-shirt, a black apron, and some jeans that hug her ass in a way that makes my dick twitch, and she's wielding a mop when I walk through the door.

She looks up, and her friendly smile dims, replaced by a fake one.

"Hello," she says happily and sets the mop aside before walking behind the counter to wait on me. "Man, it's been raining all day."

Just when I'm about to tell her that it hasn't rained a

bit at the ranch, she starts to sneeze uncontrollably. She steps away, sneezing into the towel she picked up off the counter. It's not a feminine sneeze, the way some women let out a tiny little *achoo.*

No, hers is loud and sounds like a linebacker's.

It's actually kind of cute.

"Oh, man, sorry about that. There must be something in the air right now, with it being spring and everything. I've been sneezing like that all day." She walks over to wash her hands before walking back over to me.

"Allergy meds," I say simply, and when she looks up at me in surprise, I raise an eyebrow. "They help, you know."

"Yeah, I'll pick some up on my way home." She tucks a stray piece of hair behind her ear and returns to the cash register. "Now, what can I get you? Did you like the muffins the other day?"

"Yeah." The kids thought they'd died and gone to heaven when they got into my SUV and I passed them each one. "What do you have left?"

"Let's see." She bites her lip and studies the glass case. "We have some chocolate chip cookies and a huckleberry Danish."

"I'll take it all," I reply. "And a coffee. Black."

She nods, tapping my order on her screen, then turns it to me so I can tap my card while she fills the order.

I like to watch her bounce around back there. She's cheerful and even hums while she works. Her movements are efficient and graceful.

Hell, she's sexy as fuck.

Not that I have time to think about sexy women, even someone as interesting as this one. She reminds me of the seven dwarfs that Holly loves to watch so much.

I've seen her happy, which is most days. In the beginning, she was bashful. Then one day, I came in, and she was practically asleep on her feet.

And today, she's sneezy.

Obviously, I watch too much TV with my five-year-old daughter.

She crosses to pass me the bag of cookies before pouring my coffee. But when she turns to hand me the hot brew, she sneezes, and a bit of the coffee lands on my hand, scalding me.

"Holy shit, I'm *so* sorry." She rushes to grab an ice cube and grabs my hand, placing the ice cube on the small burn. "This should soothe it."

"It's fine."

"It's *hot*," she retorts. "I don't want you to burn."

"Honest, it's fine," I repeat and wipe the coffee—and melted ice—with a napkin. "There isn't even a mark."

"Okay." She blows out a breath of relief and then smiles at me. "I hope you have a good day."

"Thanks, Doc." It just slips out, but I can't say that I'm sorry. Especially when she looks back at me with a frown.

"Huh?"

"Like the dwarf. Doc. You've been happy and sneezy and even dopey that day you said you had a blonde moment. Then you tended to my burn."

Now those green eyes narrow on me. "So, that would

make you Grumpy."

I can't stop the bark of laughter at that, and when she smiles, it makes my blood hum in a way that it hasn't in years.

"Wow, you can smile. And apparently *talk*, since this is the most you've said to me in the four months that I've worked here."

She sets the coffee in front of me.

"Guess so." I take a sip and turn to leave. "See you around, Doc."

Before the door closes behind me, I hear her say, "Peace out, Grumpy."

Satisfied that *that* interaction went well, I get into my SUV and drive over to the elementary school, snagging a parking spot in line. I learned early on that if I want a good spot at pickup, I have to get here early.

While I wait, I drink my coffee and catch up on emails, check beef prices, and contact vendors. I actually get a lot of office work done from the driver's seat in the pickup line at school.

And today, I munch on a Danish while I do it.

Before long, I hear the bell ring, and kids almost immediately come rushing out the doors of the small elementary school. *My* kids rush to the car, hand in hand, with smiles on their little faces.

God, I fucking love them.

"Hey, Dad," Johnny says as he jumps into the back seat and scoots over to make room for his sister.

"Hi, Daddy," Holly echoes.

"Hi, guys. Did you have a good day?"

"Yeah, but I have a project due tomorrow. I forgot to tell you," Johnny says as I pass them cookies from the café. "Yay, chocolate chip!"

"What kind of project?" I ask as I wait my turn to pull out into traffic.

"I have to make a poster all about me," he continues, licking chocolate off his fingers. "You know, just use some pictures and stuff. It'll be easy."

"Sure, except we don't have any of the supplies at home," I mutter and pull away from the school, headed for the nearest craft supply store. "You really need to tell me about these things, buddy."

"You got an email from Mrs. Holt," he says with a shrug, and I mentally sigh. I likely did but didn't pay attention to it.

Jesus, I'm tired.

By the time we choose materials for Johnny's project and get back out to the ranch, it's dinnertime. Thankfully, my mom has a pot of stew on the stove, waiting for us when we walk in.

"There's bread cooling on a rack, as well," she says and kisses my cheek. "I have to go. I have a book club meeting in just a little bit."

"Thanks for making dinner," I reply. "Really. It's a big help."

"You're welcome. We have to keep our babies fed."

She kisses each of the kids, and then she's off for the evening, and I get to work, serving dinner and getting the kids bathed so they can enjoy some TV or reading time before bed.

"I want to go to the barn," Holly announces. "To see the new baby horses."

"Me, too," Johnny agrees.

"Sorry, we have to do your project." I shake my head as they both frown. "That's what happens when you wait until the last minute. Come on, let's dig in. You can see the horses tomorrow."

"I didn't wait until the last minute," Holly grumbles. "That's stupid that I can't go."

"You're not going by yourself," I inform her. "So, you can help us, or you can grab a book to read or watch something on TV."

"She can't help us," Johnny argues, and I sigh as my kids start to fight.

"Enough." My voice is deep and sharp, which makes them stop swiping at each other. "Holly, go find something to do while we work on this."

She stomps out of the room, and I turn to my son, who's scowling. "This isn't your sister's fault."

"She's a busybody."

"Where did you hear that phrase?"

"From Grandma."

It's late when I finally get the kids into bed and sit down to eat some stew myself. I'm hungrier than I realized and go back for seconds before sealing up the leftovers and popping them into the fridge.

With two fingers of whiskey, I sit in my leather chair in front of the fire and sigh.

Today would have been Jessica's thirty-sixth birthday.

I didn't mention it to anyone. Johnny was only two when she died, and he has no memory of her. Jessica's family moved away from Bitterroot Valley after her death because they said it was too painful to be reminded of her all the time.

So, there's no one here to remember her with me.

Jess wasn't the love of my life. We married because she was pregnant, and we were friends. I *liked* her a lot, and we did well as co-parents. We were a good team.

But was there love? Passion? Not really.

And I never felt guilty about that because it was the same for her.

But it feels wrong that today, on her birthday, it's just another day. Hell, I didn't even *remember* until I had tucked Holly in and passed by Jess's picture in the hallway.

Blowing out a breath, I lift my glass in salute. "Happy Birthday, Jess."

"I can't find Holly."

I turn and scowl at my son. "What?"

Without waiting for him to answer, I rush upstairs, with Johnny right behind me.

"She's not in her room," he says. "I don't know where she went."

"Holly!" I yell her name as I search every room on the second floor and do the same downstairs. "Shit, Holly!"

"Did she die?" Johnny asks, tears filling his eyes. I turn to him and scoop him into my arms.

"Definitely not. She's just hiding." I kiss his cheek and pull my phone out of my pocket, just as it rings.

It's my senior ranch hand, Lucky.

"Yeah."

"Your little princess is in the barn, boss," he says in my ear, and I deflate in relief. "Found her petting the filly."

"I'm on my way." I hang up and set Johnny on his feet. "Get your stuff for school, and I'll grab Holly's."

We drive to the barn, and I rush inside and find my daughter giggling as the filly sniffs at her neck.

"Holly Wild."

Her gaze snaps up to mine, and there's guilt in her eyes.

"Get out of that stall *now*."

"Daddy, I just wanted to see the babies."

"You know you're not allowed in the barn by yourself." I pick her up and head for the SUV. "Thanks, Lucky."

"You bet, boss."

"It's a good thing you're dressed, or you'd be going to school in your pajamas."

"Why are you mad?" she asks as I set her in the back seat. "It's just the barn."

"You're *five*," I remind her. "I make the rules here, and you know you're not allowed to wander around the property by yourself. We have animals out here, Holly. You saw the big bear we had last fall."

"He looks friendly," she says.

"He's *not* friendly." I start the car, and then Johnny gasps. "What?"

"I forgot my poster."

I close my eyes and count to ten, then drive back to the house and run in for Johnny's project before returning to the car to take them to school.

"You won't be in the barn for the rest of the month," I inform Holly. "You're grounded from it."

"But, the babies!"

"You should have thought of that before you broke the rules. And you don't get to go to Kayla's birthday party on Saturday."

"But we already bought a present!"

"That's the consequence, baby girl."

Holly sniffles in the back seat. "I'm really sorry, Daddy. I didn't know any better."

But rather than fall for that old trick, I laugh. "Oh, yeah, you did. You're just stubborn, and you made a potentially dangerous choice today, so you'll have to pay the price for that. I'm not kidding when I say I don't want you walking around alone."

"I'm not a baby!"

"Yes, you are," I shoot back. "You're *my* baby, and you'll do as I say for as long as you live in my house."

"I want to move in with Grandma."

I snicker and shake my head, not willing to participate in this conversation any longer.

Damn it, maybe my dad's right. I need some help.

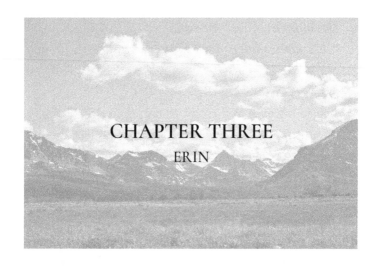

CHAPTER THREE
ERIN

"What are you doing right now?"

I sigh and lie back on my couch, exhausted but happy to hear from my sister. "I just got home from work, and I'm dead on my feet. It's spring break here, and we're full of tourists."

"Interesting." My baby sister, Zoey, who's actually less than two years younger than me but I always call her the baby, called to chat. Because she misses me. Of course, just when we were starting to get along better after a childhood of being at each other's throats, I moved away. "So, you feel a big difference there during tourist season?"

"Yeah, a lot, actually. And I've noticed that when people vacation, they kind of lose their minds."

"What do you mean?"

"They're stupid. They ask really stupid questions that, when they're at home, I'm sure they would never ask. Like, 'Do you wear bear spray to repel the bears?' or 'Where do you keep your horses?' It's so weird."

"Now I want to come hang out there and listen."

"You should. Spend one day in the coffee shop, and you'll get an ear full. Anyway, enough of that. How are *you*?"

"I'm fine. I went shopping with Haley and Chelsea yesterday, and we all ended up at a tattoo parlor, and the next thing we knew, we had matching tattoos."

I pull my phone away from my face and frown at it. "Seriously?"

"Yeah, they're really pretty. I'm surprised you didn't see our posts on the 'gram about it."

"You *know* I don't do social media. Definitely not after what happened when I was in college." This makes me feel left out and like I'm missing *everything* back home.

"Erin." I can almost hear her rolling her eyes. "The stalker thing happened more than five years ago, and you know that Dad took care of it. I understand that you don't want to have a huge social media presence, but just make up a fake profile so you can lurk and comment on our stuff. You're too far away to be alienated from all of us."

I sigh and rub my hand over my eyes. I get that Zoey thinks she understands, but she's not the one who had a psycho following her every move. "I know. I'm not really homesick much, and I know that I made the right decision when I decided to stay, but I do miss all of you guys a lot. I miss getting together all the time and being able to find out what everyone is up to. Cousin parties are the best."

"We hosted one that was *wild* last weekend," Zoey says with a chuckle. "Yeah, get on the 'gram, okay? Just text the group text so we all know it's you."

"I'll think about it."

"Erin—"

"I know you think I'm being silly, but what happened was really scary, and I don't want to chance going through it again, okay?"

"I get it. I do. Just think about it because I want you to be privy to all the fun things happening around here. I mean, you'll be here for the important stuff, but the day-to-day is still important, too. Oh, did you hear that Haley is going to go to school for sound healing and Reiki?"

"Is that, like, energy work?"

"Yep," Zoey confirms.

"No, I hadn't heard, but that sounds right up her alley. I have to say, though, isn't the herbalism taking up all her time?" Our cousin has been into all things crystals and herbs for as long as I can remember.

"Yeah, for sure, but she wants to do this stuff, too. It's fun to be her guinea pig. The next time you're home, you need to have her make you her special teas. They're delicious."

"I'll remember that."

It's not lost on me that she called Seattle *home*, but I think of Bitterroot Valley as home now.

Not that I'll say that to Zoey because it'll just hurt her feelings.

We spend about an hour talking about all the cousins, which is a *lot* of them, and what they're up to. When I finally hang up with her, I'm freaking *starving*.

"I don't want to cook," I mutter as I stare inside my small refrigerator. I'm so tired, and every muscle in my body is just...*sore*.

I want to curl up on my small but cozy sofa and watch a true crime show. With pizza.

So, I pick up my cell and call Old Town Pizza.

"OTP, this is Heather."

I smile at the sound of the owner's voice. "Hi, Heather. I'd like to place an order for delivery, please."

"You betcha. Hold on; let me grab a pen. Is this Erin?"

I blink in surprise. "Yes, how did you know that?"

"I have a knack for names, but it also came up on the caller ID."

I laugh in response. "You had me really impressed there for a minute. Okay, I'd like a medium pepperoni and pineapple on hand-tossed crust, and let's also do some hot wings. With ranch."

"Got it," she says slowly. "What about any breadsticks?"

"I'm tempted, but no thanks. This will do me. I'm above Roger's garage."

"Okay, honey, this will be on its way to you in about thirty minutes."

"Perfect. I'll just pay with cash when it gets here, if that's okay."

"Fine by me. Thanks, Erin. I'll see you at the coffee shop soon."

She clicks off, and I smile as I set my phone down. There are so many places in Seattle that I order from or eat at all the time, but they don't know me by name like this. And it's not just Heather. It happens all over town.

And I kind of love it.

With a renewed spring in my step, I decide to take a quick shower and get comfy while I wait for my delivery. And it's just the right amount of time because, as I walk out of my bedroom, there's a knock at the door.

Fully expecting to find a teenager delivering pizza, I'm thrown for a loop when I find a *very* angry Millie on the other side of the door.

"Hey, come in."

"Thanks." She moves past me and starts to pace my small living room. "I'm just *so* pissed off, and I need to vent, but I can't do that in an empty apartment."

"Obviously not. What's going on?" Suddenly, there's another knock on the door, and I hold my finger up. "Hold that thought. That's food."

I swing the door open, and this time, it's a lanky, awkward teenage boy standing on my stoop, loaded down with boxes.

"Hey, Miss Erin," he says and clears his throat as he blushes bright red. "Heather threw in the breadsticks, even though they're not part of your order."

"She didn't have to do that." I pass the cash to him and accept the boxes. "But tell her thanks. You can keep the change. Have a good night."

"Thanks, you, too."

I close the door and bring the boxes directly into the living room and set them on the coffee table.

"Okay, we have pizza, hot wings, breadsticks, and wine. We are totally set up for a major vent sesh."

Millie sighs. "I'm sorry. I shouldn't have just shown up to your place like this, out of the blue, when you're about to eat dinner."

"Why not?" I frown up at her as I open the bottle of wine. "I have a million cousins and a younger sister. This is what we *do*, Mill. Now, let's eat and talk."

"I really *am* hungry," she admits and bites her lip. "Are you sure you have enough?"

"I can't eat this whole pizza, that chicken, *and* an order of breadsticks by myself. You'll be doing me a favor by helping me eat this."

"Well, I *am* all about being there for my friends." She sits on the floor by the coffee table, takes a hot wing, and bites into it. "Okay, this is good. I'll have energy for all the bitching I'm about to do."

"I can't wait. Give it to me." I pass her some napkins and dig into the pizza, then sigh in happiness.

Old Town Pizza rivals *any* pizza I've had in Seattle.

"Okay, so I was hanging out at The Wolf Den, just having a glass of wine at the bar and chatting with Belinda, the bartender. I didn't want to be by myself at home tonight, so I thought I'd be social, you know?"

"Sure." I take another bite. "That's a fun bar. I like it in there."

"Same. So, I'm just minding my own business, sipping my wine, and because it's a freaking tourist week, in come these complete idiots who are here to hike for the week. They're pissy because it's still too early in the season to actually hike much, since the snow hasn't melted all the way in the mountains, and they didn't bother to actually do some research to see if this is a good time for outdoorsy stuff."

"So, they're morons."

"*Total* morons," she agrees with a vigorous nod. "Like, if you're going on vacation somewhere, wouldn't you do some research to see if what you want to do is even a thing at that time of year? Anyway, I'm just sitting there, not engaging with them at all. I might have rolled my eyes at one point because holy shit, were they ever whiny, but I was keeping my opinions to myself. And I have to tell you, I was proud of that because I could have really unloaded on them."

"I'm proud of you, too."

"Thank you." She reaches for a slice of pizza and takes a bite, chewing thoughtfully. "So, the holding it in didn't last long."

I can't help but laugh at that, and Millie narrows her eyes at me, so I stop, clear my throat, and hide my smile behind my wine glass.

"Sorry. Go on."

"Well, they were talking shit about my town. Calling us all country bumpkins and how we're too stupid to figure out how to hike in the snow. It was disrespectful as fuck."

"Yeah, that's not cool at all."

"So, I turned around on my stool and proceeded to

let them know that if they didn't like it here, they could just go on home. We wouldn't miss them. Maybe they'd learn to actually research their vacations in the future."

"And they didn't like that."

"No. They didn't." She takes a deep breath, then reaches for another slice of pizza. "And I didn't care. I ended up standing nose-to-nose with the leader of their little gang, and then he pushed me."

My eyes come up, wide. "He *pushed* you?"

"Yeah, and he had his fist reared back to punch me in the face, but then *he* was suddenly punched in the face, and several guys kicked all four of them out of the bar."

"Good, what a bunch of assholes."

"But that's not all." She shakes her head and then stands and begins to pace my apartment once more. "No, it gets much worse."

"They were waiting for you outside, and you had to kick all of their asses?"

"I wish. That would have been better." She finishes the last of her crust and then turns to me. "The person who just *had* to jump to my rescue was freaking Holden Lexington."

"Who's that?" I frown up at her, trying to search my mind for that name, but I don't know it.

"He's the oldest child and only son in the fucking *Lexington* family. You've heard the story of the Hatfields and the McCoys?"

"I guess. Rival families, right? Somewhere back east?"

"Yeah, they hated each other. It's the same here, but

it's the Wilds and the Lexingtons here. Our families have fought for generations."

"Why?"

She waves her hands in the air and begins to pace faster. "Because we have property next to each other, and there's *always* something to fight about. Our two families pretty much originally settled Bitterroot Valley. Holden's about Remington's age, and they've always hated each other. In fact, all of us siblings hate each other."

"That's a lot of hate," I comment and then frown. "Wait, so, there are five of you Wild siblings? How many siblings are in the Lexington family?"

"Five," she says with a sniff. "But where we're four boys and a girl, they're one boy and four girls."

"So fascinating," I murmur, sitting back on the couch. "And I gather that it was bad that Holden came to your defense?"

"*Yes.*" Her voice is getting more and more shrill with frustration. "Of *course,* it's bad. I don't want Holden to jump in and try to save me. Do I *look* like I can't hold my own against some stupid tourists?"

"No, you could handle it, but he pushed you."

"And he was about to get a kick to the gonads, I'll tell you that. But I didn't get to do that because Holden decided to be the goddamn hero. Figures."

She shakes her head in disgust.

"And *then* he, like, tried to smile and placate me, and just because we slept together once does *not* mean that I want him to do that."

"Whoa." I hold up a hand. "You *slept* with him?"

"Once," she spits out. "*One* time. Because Holden is fucking beautiful in every way. It's just so unfair that he's so hot because that can go nowhere. Our families hate each other, remember? Remington would kill Holden if he ever found out that Holden had his hands on me."

"But, was it fun? The handsy sexy time?"

Millie blows out a breath and scrubs her hands over her face. "Hell yeah. It was damn good sex. But it cannot happen again, and it *won't* happen again, even if Holden thinks he can defend me against tourists. Although, it was kind of hot when he punched that guy."

"I bet. I wish I'd been there to witness it."

Millie narrows her eyes. "I'm not going to think about Holden and his hotness anymore. He's not sexy. He's annoying."

"Sure, you just keep telling yourself that."

She looks at me now, and it seems the worst of her anger has worn itself down.

"You look like shit," she decides. "Did something happen to *you*? Oh, my God, I'm a horrible friend because I just had diarrhea of the mouth this whole time, and you have issues of your own that I haven't even listened to."

"I'm okay," I reply, shaking my head. "I'm just really tired. It was a long day. And then I talked to my sister, and she was telling me about some stuff that's happened back home, and I'm missing it. I don't want to go back to Seattle; I just hate that I'm missing out on some fun stuff with her and my cousins. She said that I wouldn't miss as much if I'd just get on social media, but that's not a good idea."

"You're not on social media?"

I shake my head again. "I had a stalker a few years ago, and it originated on socials. It scared me."

"Okay, Boomer, but you can totally have a secret account that you just use to interact with your family."

"That's pretty much what my sister said." I smile and pour more wine into our glasses. "I guess I could do that if I don't have to use my real name or pictures of myself."

"You totally don't have to," Millie insists. "Download the app on your phone. I'll help you set it up."

"Right now?"

"Absolutely. This is taking my mind off the Lexington family. One member in particular."

"Okay." I shrug and tap the screen of my phone. "Which one should I do?"

"Just Instagram," she replies.

"Okay, it's downloaded. Now what?"

"Now we have to come up with a name *and* a username for you."

"I can be Erin McBride. That's my mom's maiden name."

"Perfect. It's easy for you to remember," she says as I type the name into the app. "Okay, now a username. What about SexyCoffeeGirl69?"

I blink at her and then shake my head. "No. Definitely not."

"CoffeeVixenXO."

"No."

"BigSkyRideorDie."

I smirk. "Hell no. Why do we have to die? Absolutely not."

"This is fun. I'm on a roll." Millie sits again and nibbles on the end of a breadstick. "Okay, how about—"

"Hold up." I lift a hand and smile. "I have it. BigSky-Barista. It's generic."

"I like it. Now, what will you put as your profile photo?"

"I have a picture that I took of a latte I made at work the other day." I bite my lower lip as I scroll back and select the photo of a foamy-topped latte. "There. I have an account. Now I just have to text the cousins and let them know that it's me."

"Perfect." Millie smiles sleepily. "Now you won't miss out on anything."

"Do you want to sleep here tonight?" I ask her. "You're about to crash from all the excitement."

"Yeah." She sighs. "I think I do. But that couch is small."

"I have a king bed. We'll both fit."

WITH THE FLOOR ALL MOPPED, and all my other end-of-day cleaning duties finished, I'm ready to close the coffee shop for the day. I'm *so* ready to go home. I get the next two days off in a row, and I plan to sleep, clean my apartment, and help Roger in his garden.

The tourists have exhausted me.

Before I can make it over to the door to lock it, in

comes Grumpy.

Great.

But I paste on a smile. "Hey there. You're later today, so I don't have a ton left."

"Coffee," he says shortly, even more curt than before. His handsome face is drawn in a dark scowl. "Black."

"Oh, I don't have any more brewed coffee, but I can make you a latte or something."

His eyes narrow into slits. "You don't have any more brewed coffee?"

"Well, no. We close"—I check my watch—"one minute ago. I was just about to head out for the day. But I don't mind making you the latte. I even have a couple of scones that I'd just boxed up, if you want those. On the house."

Grumpy mutters under his breath, and I have to take a deep breath of my own to keep myself from snapping at him.

"Never mind," he bites out and turns on his heel to march out the front door.

"See you, Grumpy," I say, loud enough for him to hear, but he doesn't turn around to look at me.

For fuck's sake, everyone has been so *moody* today. My cousin Haley would say it's because of a moon phase, or Aries is in Jupiter, or some such thing.

Whatever that means.

Personally, I think people are just pissed off. Why? I have no idea. But for the first time since I started this job, I'm ready for a few days off so I don't have to be around people.

CHAPTER FOUR
REMINGTON

"Jesus, you've been in a shitty mood all fucking week."

I turn to glare at my brother, Brady. "So?"

"So, what's wrong with you? I mean, you're usually a grumpy fuck, but you're not typically an asshole on top of it. What crawled up your ass?"

Leave it to my brothers to call me out on my shit.

We're repairing some fence line on the edge of the property to the south, but I take a minute to take my gloves off and rub my eyes.

"It's been a shit week." I sniff and look over the pasture to the mountains beyond. We own that *whole* mountain.

Sometimes that stops me in my tracks.

"Why?" Brady asks. "The kids are on spring break, so you haven't had to run them to school and back, and Mom's been hanging with them all week."

"Yeah, but Holly's pissed off because she's grounded

from the barn after her little stunt last week. Then, on that same day, I got a call from Johnny's teacher, and she told me that my boy is failing math."

Brady scowls. "How does a second grader flunk math?"

"I asked him that. He told me he hates it, so he doesn't care about it."

"I mean, *I* hate math," Brady says with a grim nod.

"Don't tell him that. Anyway, between the kids, losing that filly yesterday, *and* having a mountain lion on the property killing my beef that I can't seem to catch, it's been a shit week."

"Fair enough," Brady says.

"When do you start rodeo stuff? I'll need to hire another hand before you go."

Brady shrugs. "In about a month or so. Shows start in May. I can still work here; I'll just be in and out through the summer, as usual."

"Yeah, but I want to make sure I have the coverage here so you don't feel like you have to hurry home. I know what your first love is, and it's not the ranch."

"I do love that rodeo ring," he says with a grin. "She can be a bitch of a mistress, but I can't get enough of her. You never have issues finding hands. Especially with that new bunkhouse. It's fucking *nice*."

"The old one was falling apart. I want our guys to *like* living here. Besides, we're making a shit ton of money now. The ranch should reflect that."

Brady nods and then changes the subject. "Speaking of a shit ton of money, I spoke to Ryan this morning."

I concentrate on pulling my gloves back on. "Yeah? I think he flies in tomorrow morning."

"He does. Mom wants to do dinner on Friday night at your place, since it's the biggest. That okay with you?"

"Sure. She cooks dinner almost every day at my house anyway."

"Are you ever going to stop being pissed at Ryan?"

"I'm not pissed." I grab my tools and walk down the fence, not at all interested in discussing our brother. "Let's get back to work."

"Right. You're not pissed, and I'm a vampire."

"Is that so? Maybe you're the one killing my beef."

"Ha. Ha. You're a regular comedian."

"Hey, Mom, is everything okay at the house?"

"Of course, it is. I'm just out in the garden, getting things ready for some flowers to brighten it up this summer. The kids are inside. They helped me for a while, but then they wanted to go in and play some video games, and I didn't see the harm in it."

"I'm glad it's been uneventful. I'll be home in about thirty. We're just finishing up a few things."

"Sounds good. I'll see you when you get here, honey."

I hang up and have a quick meeting with my guys, setting up a game plan through the weekend. The week has gone by fast.

Hell, every week goes by fast these days.

"My niece's birthday is Sunday," Bruiser says. He's a

big guy, about six-foot-seven and all muscle. And he's all gooey when it comes to his niece.

"Then I guess you'd better take Sunday off," I reply with a nod.

"Thanks, boss."

"There's something on this property killing my beef. Keep an eye out. We have wildlife cameras set up, but so far, we haven't caught anything."

"We saw bear tracks," Lucky says, looking up from his notebook.

"I know, but this feels more like a mountain lion to me," I reply and turn to Brady. "What do you think?"

"Could be a wolf, or a pair of wolves," Brady says. "Hell, it could be any of the above."

"We'll keep an eye out," Lucky says, making notes in his ratty old notebook. He's had the same small spiral notebook tucked into the pocket of his work shirt since I was a kid.

At least, it's always *looked* like the same notebook.

After a few more minutes of catching up, I break the meeting and head for the house.

My kids have been on break all week, and I've hardly seen them. Tomorrow's Friday, and I didn't spend any time with them at all.

I'm a fucking jerk.

Tomorrow, I have to take Holly to the eye doctor for a checkup, and I figured I'd take Johnny with us and spring for lunch when we're done.

They'll like that.

"Hey, Mom," I call out when I see her gathering some weeds and tossing them into a trash bin.

"Hi, honey. How did it go today?"

"It was fine. Want to come in for some iced tea?"

"Actually, I'm meeting your father in town for dinner in just a little while. I'd better get on home and change out of these dirty clothes. I have some lasagna in the oven for the three of you. Have a good evening."

"Thanks. You can leave that. I'll clean it up. Maybe later, I'll light a little fire outside and roast marshmallows with the kids."

"Oh, they'll love that. Have fun. And I'll take you up on cleaning this up for me."

She pulls her gloves off, then reaches up and cups my face.

"My boy. You always were the quiet, serious one. Don't forget to have a little fun."

"Thanks, Mom." I bend down and kiss her cheek. "I'll see you later."

"Bye, now!"

She waves and sets off for home. My dad had a house built for them less than a mile from my place, and I like having them close by.

"You're going to be in so much trouble!"

Welcome home, I think to myself as I hang my hat in the mudroom and slip out of my dirty boots.

"No, *you* are. I told you not to pour it like that."

"What's going on?" I ask as I walk into the kitchen and then stop cold.

There's milk spilled all over the countertop and on

the floor. Someone dragged a bath towel through the milk, smearing it all over.

"Is that chocolate?" I ask, pointing to the brown substance dripping onto the granite.

"I wanted chocolate milk," Holly says as her eyes fill with tears. "And Johnny spilled the milk all over."

"It fell," Johnny insists. His own voice is quivering. "The jug was full and heavy, and it just fell. I couldn't make it stop coming out."

"Don't be mad," Holly pleads, and I realize that I must be a real asshole if my kids are this scared that they'll get in trouble for a silly mistake.

"I'm not mad." I take a deep breath, surveying the scene. "It looks like you two need to go change your clothes because you got wet."

"Yeah." Johnny's voice is already much calmer. "It really splashed."

"Can we change into jammies?"

I raise my eyebrows at my daughter. "Before six in the evening? Sure, if you want to. Go get comfy, and I'll clean this up."

"Thank you, Daddy." Holly throws herself around my legs and hugs me tightly before running off to change.

Johnny, however, stays behind, his face totally serious.

"What's up?" I ask him as I reach for the paper towels.

"Thanks for not yelling." He shuffles from one foot to the other. "I mean, you don't usually yell *real* loud, but we don't usually mess up this bad, and you've been really mad lately. So, thanks for not yelling."

And with that, he runs off behind his sister, and I have to take a minute to myself.

Yeah, I've been mad.

I've been frustrated.

And as of right now, I'm going to stop taking it out on my kids.

"It's definitely a mountain lion."

I turn at the sound of Lucky's voice and raise a brow. "Did you catch it on camera?"

"Yeah, a few minutes ago, before the sun came up. She was out hunting and would have taken a calf if we didn't get there first. You're going to want to see this, boss."

I stand and grab my hat. "Show me."

He nods grimly, and we hurry out to the Jeep I bought last summer for times like this when we need to get somewhere on the property fast, and there isn't a road to take.

It's a bumpy-as-fuck ride, but before long, we see some of our guys standing around the carcass.

"I had to fire," Bruiser says, looking completely miserable. "She was about to take out that calf over there. I *had* to."

"Okay, I understand."

"She's a mama," Lucky says, and points to the tree line where three cubs watch us from the brush.

"Well, son of a fucking bitch." I immediately pull out my phone and call Chase. My brother is a cop, not Fish and Wildlife, but he'll know who to call for this.

"Yo," he answers.

"I need someone from Fish and Wildlife out here right away, and I don't know who to call."

"I can handle that. Where on the ranch are you?"

I give him our location and the gist of what's going on. "It's a fucking mess, Chase."

"I'll be out there, too. Give us thirty to get there. Don't touch those babies, Rem."

"We know better," I assure him and end the call, turning to my guys. "They're on the way. We don't touch those cubs."

"What will happen to them?" Bruiser wants to know.

"They'll probably go to a wildlife rescue." I rub my hands down my face. "Fuck."

"It's not poaching," Lucky insists. "We're entitled to protect the herd."

Of *course,* it's not poaching, and the fact that Lucky feels like he has to jump in to defend Bruiser tells me that he respects the other man, because we all know that Bruiser didn't illegally hunt that cat.

"No, no one's in trouble. It just sucks that she's a mom. Those babies aren't weened yet."

"Do you want us to stay here?" Bruiser asks.

"Yeah, let's wait so we can all answer questions. Just

be honest, you understand? You didn't do anything wrong, and you won't be in trouble."

Bruiser, looking like he's full of guilt, nods.

Just like Chase said, thirty minutes later, two vehicles drive out onto the pasture and park next to the Jeep.

Chase gets out of the police SUV, and two other men step out of the truck.

"Hey, Rem." Nathan Price extends his hand for me to shake. "I'm sure sorry about this."

"You and me both." I shake his hand and then turn to the other officer. I don't recognize him. "I'm Remington Wild."

"Cole Sutton," he replies and shakes my hand. "What happened?"

"I'm going to let Bruiser explain." I gesture to my ranch hand and step back next to Chase as we listen to him describe seeing the mountain lion on camera and then racing out here to the field.

"She was poised and ready to kill the calf. She's been killing cattle for about a month now, and we had to protect the calf." Bruiser wipes his hand over his face. "So, I shot her, and when I walked up on her, I heard them."

At his gesture, we turn to the tree line, and Cole says, "Damn."

"I have traps in the truck," Nathan says grimly. "We'll take them to a sanctuary. They might even be able to be released back into the wild at some point."

"Just far away from my ranch."

"There's going to be paperwork," Nathan warns me.

"Of course, there is." My phone rings, and I pull it out to find that it's my mom. "Hey, Mom."

"Hi, honey. Did you forget about Holly's eye appointment?"

I close my eyes. Yeah, I had forgotten it in all of this mess. "Shit, yeah, I did."

"I can't take her because I have a doctor's appointment of my own," she says. "I suppose I could reschedule."

"No, I'll figure it out. Just give me a minute."

I check the time and curse under my breath. I have less than an hour to get my daughter to her appointment, but I can't leave the ranch until this whole mess is figured out.

So, I call my sister.

"Hi, favorite oldest brother," she says in my ear.

"Remember that I'm your favorite, okay? I need some help. Tell me you're not working today."

"I'm not working today."

"Good. Can you come get Holly and take her to her eye appointment? I'm hung up here at the ranch."

"Uh, sure. Give me an hour."

I close my eyes. "I can't. She has to be there in less than that."

"Jesus, Rem, give a girl some notice. Okay, I'm pulling myself together, and I'll be there shortly."

"I'll let Mom know. I'm in the north pasture, so I won't be at the house when you pick her up."

"I'll talk to you later," is all she says before she hangs up.

"You good?" Chase asks.

No. I'm not good.

But I force a smile. "Yeah, great. Let's get this taken care of."

IT TAKES two hours to answer a million questions, get the babies trapped, and bury the carcass of the mother so she doesn't draw in other unwanted visitors.

By the time I get back to the house to return to some admin work in my office, Millie is just pulling in with the kids.

"I have to get glasses," Holly announces as she bounces out of my sister's car and runs over toward me. "Are the kids at school gonna call me *Four Eyes*?"

"Only if they're idiots," I reply and kiss her on the cheek.

"I helped her pick them out. She's going to be gorgeous in them." Millie smiles at both kids as they hurry inside.

It's a cold spring day today, so we trudge up the steps behind them.

"Rem, we need to talk."

"Hold on." I hold up a finger and find the kids in the family room, already settling in to play their game. "Are you guys good in here for a little bit? I want to chat with Aunt Millie."

"We're good," Johnny assures me. "We had McDonald's for breakfast on the way home. We got there just in time, before they switched to lunch."

"Grandma already fed you breakfast."

My son just smiles slyly at me.

"Right. Okay, we'll be done shortly."

I walk into my office and close the French doors behind me.

"Okay, what's wrong? Are you in trouble?"

Millie frowns. "Huh? No, why? What did you hear? It wasn't my fault. The stupid tourists were being assholes, and I just—"

She breaks off and tilts her head to the side.

"That's not what you meant, is it?"

"No, but now I want to know about the asshole tourists."

She laughs and shakes her head. "It's no big deal. I'm not in trouble, Rem. That's not why I wanted to talk to you."

"Good."

"Your kids miss you."

"Sorry, what?"

"Look, I've never been one to tell you how to raise your kids. Hell, I *was* a kid when Johnny was born, and you're a great dad. You really are. But your responsibilities here at the ranch are *huge* now, Rem. You bought ten thousand more acres to the west last year, which means more work. Dad decided that since the ranch is now bringing in seven figures every year in profit, he could retire, which is awesome for him, but that means way more work for you because now you're in charge."

"Thanks for the recap."

"You have a *lot* going on, and yeah, Mom helps out with the kids a ton, but even she can only do so much. I asked the kids today what you've done for spring break, and Holly said she's hardly seen you all week because you're gone before they get up in the morning, and you get home at dinnertime."

"Like you said, I'm running a business here, Mill."

"But you have kids, and this was their spring break, and they spent it playing video games and helping Mom in the yard. I'm not telling you this to make you feel guilty."

"Yeah, well, you *are* making me feel guilty." I rub a hand over the ache in my chest. "Shit, Millie, I'm doing the best I can."

"I think you need a nanny," she announces.

"How will hiring someone else to be with my kids actually give *me* more time with my kids?"

"You need help to get them to and from school. Taking them to appointments. Helping with homework and all the other little things that you don't have time for. Then, when you're here, you can just be with them, and not worry about all the shit you haven't done. You can spend quality time with them, Rem. They're craving that with you right now."

"Running a ranch isn't a nine-to-five job."

"I know that, and you know that. But they're just kids, and they miss you. You've taken on a lot more over the past year, and they're feeling it."

"I do need the help. Mom's spread thin, and she should get to enjoy her time with Dad anyway."

"Yeah, she should."

I sit back and tap my fingers on the top of my scarred desk. It used to be my dad's, and his father's before him.

I think about how rushed everything always is where the kids are concerned, and how I'm not able to enjoy them, or them me, because it always feels like we're running around with our heads cut off.

"Okay. I'll hire a nanny. But it needs to be someone reputable and trustworthy. Not a kid."

"Agreed," Millie says, nodding. "I'm going to keep my eyes and ears open, and I'll keep you posted."

"Do that, because the last thing I have time for is to find a nanny."

"I have time," she says with a bright smile. "Just leave it up to me."

"Deal."

CHAPTER FIVE
ERIN

"You have *got* to be kidding me." I lean forward and rest my forehead on the steering wheel in absolute despair. It's been too cold the past few days to walk around town for work or my errands, thanks to a spring storm that rolled through and reminded us that, although the season may have changed, winter is still hanging on with her icy fingernails.

But halfway home from the grocery store, my car decides to simply stop running.

It's dead. Deader than a doornail.

"Shit. Shit. Shit."

I have a trunk full of groceries that I need to get home, and I'm at least two miles away from my apartment. Glad that my dad insisted that I invest in the roadside assistance insurance, I find the card in the glove box and call the toll-free number.

"One hour," I repeat when I'm told how long I'll have to wait. "Well, at least my ice cream won't melt."

"I'll get someone there as soon as possible. The driver will call or text when they're on their way," I'm assured before the call ends.

I take a deep breath, blow it out, and frown because I can see my breath in the cold air. It's damn cold. The week started out pretty decent in regard to the weather, but now it just feels like February all over again. And, of course, I didn't bring any gloves or a hat with me, because I was planning to simply go from the car to the store and back again.

Just when I'm contemplating a two-block walk to a restaurant to sit and wait for the tow truck, my phone rings.

"Hey, this is Peter with A-1 Towing. I'll be there in about ten minutes."

"Oh, thank goodness. I appreciate it."

"No problem. See you soon."

My teeth have just started to chatter when the tow truck pulls up in front of me, and a tall, *very* handsome man steps out of the driver's side and walks my way.

I get out to talk to him and to get the circulation moving in my legs.

"I don't know what's wrong," I begin. "It just stopped, and I could barely get it pulled over to the side of the road."

"Interesting," he says, eyeing my car. "It's not a beater."

"No, it's only a few years old actually, but it doesn't seem to enjoy winter weather."

Peter grins. "Can't blame it. Well, I'll get it towed to

Brooks's Garage across town, and they'll get you figured out."

"I appreciate it. But I have groceries in the back."

Peter nods. "I'll take you to your place first, if that's okay."

"Really? That would be *amazing.*"

"Let's do it," he says, and before long, he has my car secured to his truck, and I'm in the passenger seat, giving him directions to my apartment. "You live above Roger's garage."

"Yeah, I do. Do you know Roger?"

"Of course, it's a small town. I'll help you get your groceries upstairs."

"Oh, it's okay. I need the exercise anyway. Let's just put the bags on the sidewalk, and I'll make trips."

Peter *seems* nice, but I know better than to let strangers into my house.

"Whatever you want," he says with a shrug and helps me get the groceries unloaded. I remember to grab my purse and the few personal things I have in the vehicle before Peter drives off, headed for the garage.

"Great," I mutter as I load up more bags than I should and head for the stairs leading up to my place. "Another expense. I hope this doesn't cost me an arm and a leg because I can barely make all the bills I have as it is."

After three trips, everything is upstairs, and I'm winded.

So, I lean on the counter and catch my breath.

"Okay, so I *do* need to work out more." I peel my sweater off and get to work putting my things away. Just when I close the cabinet door to what I've made the pantry, my phone rings.

"Hello?"

"Is this Erin Montgomery?"

"Yes, this is she."

"Hey there. I'm Brooks, down at the garage you had your car towed to, and I've had a look through your car."

"Wow, that was fast."

"Yeah, well, it wasn't hard to find. Are you sitting down?"

I blink and frown. "Should I be?"

"I would advise it, yeah."

Grimly, I drop down to the edge of my couch. "Okay, hit me with it."

"Well, it looks like you had a complete computer failure, which is honestly something I've never seen. Not to this extent, anyway."

"Great." I close my eyes and take a deep breath. "How much will this cost?"

He blows out a breath. "It's going to be a couple grand, at least. I'm still diagnosing other things, but yeah, a few thousand. I can have a more complete estimate for you by tomorrow, but I don't want to mislead you. You're looking at a lot of money here."

Of course, I am.

"Is it worth fixing?"

"I guess that's up to you, isn't it? If it were my car, I would probably fix it, yeah. But, if it were my wife's car, I don't know that I would trust it again. You *could* sell it for parts and buy another car."

Sure, if I had the money for a car payment.

"Okay, I'm going to think about that."

"I'll be in touch tomorrow with a more accurate estimate. Sorry for the bad news."

"Yeah, thanks."

I hang up and set my phone aside, rubbing my hands over my face. I do *not* want to use my dad's money.

But I need a reliable car. The weather is too flaky here to depend on being able to walk.

I'll just have to pick up a second job and make what I have stretch.

"Shit, it's cold." I rush into the coffee shop the next morning, rubbing my gloved hands together. "So, *so* cold."

"Did you walk here?" Millie asks with a frown. "For the love of Old Man Winter, Erin, you can't be walking around in that."

I glance back and see that the snow is falling *sideways*, thanks to the wind.

"I had to," I reply simply and hurry back to change out of my coat and boots and pull on an apron for work. When I return, Millie is slammed with customers, so I immediately jump in to help.

We stay busy through the lunchtime rush, and we switch back and forth between taking orders and filling them.

Finally, when there's a break, we both take a breath and survey the mess around us.

"Whoa." I blink at the crumbs, spilled coffee drips, and other debris on the tile floor. "It looks like there was a battle."

"There was," she says. "And we won. Good job."

Just as I'm grinning at Millie, the door opens, and in walks a group of guys. Millie stiffens next to me.

"The asshole tourists," she hisses, and I feel my eyes narrow into slits.

"I've got this," I assure her.

"*We've* got this," she replies as the leader of the group —sporting a bright black-and-blue eye—steps up. "How can we help you?"

"Shit, it's you," he sneers.

"Yep, it's me. Now, we can work this one of two ways. Either you and your friends can be nice, or you can go."

"Me? I'm always nice," he replies and blatantly looks Millie up and down in the creepiest way ever, then turns his gaze to me. "Now, *you're* hot. And not as mouthy."

I raise an eyebrow before I start laughing. I laugh so hard I have to hold my stomach. "Mouthy? Oh, honey, you have no idea just how *mouthy* I can be."

"Let's just go, man." One of the guys standing in the back taps the asshole leader on the shoulder. "We can get coffee somewhere else."

"Fuck that. Now it's the principal of it. What is it with the bitches in this town being little cunts?"

Without saying a word, I pull my phone out of my back pocket and dial 9-1-1.

"This is Erin at the Bitterroot Valley Coffee Co. We need assistance."

"Oh, please," he sneers, but he starts to back up a couple of paces. "Gonna *tell* on me? Jesus, what a bunch of sniveling babies. I guess you're not so brave when you don't have some asshole at the ready to fight your battles for you, are you?"

Several customers are standing, just waiting to jump in if this jerk takes it too far and lays a hand on us.

Which I kind of hope he does because I'd *love* to kick him in the balls.

"I don't need *anyone* to fight for me," Millie says calmly. "But I won't be harassed, here at my job or anywhere else. This is *my* home. These are *my* people. And you're nothing but an annoying little bug."

Just as he steps forward, the door flings open, and Millie's brother, Chase, walks in, his hand on his weapon and fire burning in those hazel eyes.

"What's the problem?" he asks.

"We'd like these customers to be escorted out," I reply as Millie continues to have a staring contest with the asshole in question. "They've been rude and threatening, and we don't want them here."

"I'm not rude," Asshole says with a smirk.

"You heard her," Chase says. "Let's go, guys."

"I have the right to be here," he insists. "We all do. This is a free country."

"*This*," Chase emphasizes, "is a private business, and you've been asked to leave. Don't make me arrest you for trespassing."

"You little bitch," he snarls at Millie. "You've done nothing but cause me trouble on this trip, and you're going to pay for it, you hear me?"

"Oh, my God," one of the others says with exasperation. "Why can't you keep your mouth shut?"

"On second thought, I believe I *will* arrest you for trespassing, disturbing the peace, and verbal assault. Do you want to press charges, ladies?"

"Yes," we reply in unison just as Asshole takes a swing at Chase, who easily ducks out of the way and twists Asshole's arm behind his back as Chase reaches for his handcuffs.

"Let's add on assault on an officer," Chase says with a wink for Millie and me. "We'll take your friends with us, so they can either post bail for you or leave without you. Either way, I don't care as long as you get the fuck out of my town. Come on, guys."

"You're such a fucker," the quiet guy says to the asshole friend as all of them walk out the door.

"Well," Polly, the owner of the cutest dress shop in town, says from the corner. "I almost came over there to punch that guy."

Polly's no taller than five feet, and can't weigh more than ninety pounds, but I can see by the look on her face that she's a force to be reckoned with.

"Chase must have been nearby," Millie says after she swallows hard. I know that bully put her on edge, and I hate to see that. "I'm glad he came quickly."

"You were handling yourself," I assure her. "He's nothing but a bully."

"Yeah, I know. I hope they go home and get the hell out of my town."

"Chase will run them off," another customer calls out. I glance over and see that it's Peter, the driver who helped me with my car yesterday. "But if you want someone to escort you home later, just let one of us know."

"Thanks, Pete," Millie says with a wink. "You're the sweetest. Okay, everyone, I'm going back to business as usual."

Taking her hint, everyone goes back to what they were doing before the incident, and Millie and I begin to clean up our mess from our earlier rush.

"Hey, I have a question," I say as I wring out a rag in the sink. "Do you know of anywhere that's hiring part time?"

Millie frowns over at me. "Why do you ask?"

"I need a second job." I sigh and wipe down the countertop by the espresso machine. "My car has decided to be dramatic and needs a *lot* of attention, so I'll need another source of income for a little while."

"Is that so?" Millie leans on the counter and smiles over at me. "I might just know of something kind of perfect, but first I have to ask if you like kids."

"Uh, sure? Why do I feel like this is a trick question?"

"It's not. It's an honest question."

"I like kids. I have cousins younger than me, and we were always babysitting and stuff. Is the school hiring or something?"

"I wouldn't know about that, but I *do* know that my

oldest brother, Remington, is looking for a nanny to help him out at the ranch. Holly and Johnny are the kindest, most well-behaved, and *amazing* kids on the planet."

"I'm sure they are." I can't help but grin at how proud Millie sounds.

"He's a single dad, and with the kids getting older and having more activities and stuff, he just can't manage it all by himself anymore. I finally talked him into hiring someone, and I *know* you. You're totally trustworthy."

"Do you know what the hours would be?"

"I'm not positive, but I'm sure you could work it out. I know he'd like to have help either in the mornings to get them off to school, or when they get out of school until dinner time."

"That doesn't seem too hard."

"I don't think it's hard at all," Millie assures me.

"I don't want to have to quit this job. I *like* it here, and the whole point is to have both income streams."

"Well, if he wants you to take afternoons, I'll switch shifts with you so you're off work before school lets out."

I chew the inside of my lip, thinking it over. "It would be nice to have that flexibility."

"Just go meet with him," Millie suggests. "You can get a feel for it, and if you like him and the kids, take the job. If not, no harm, no foul."

"I think that's a great idea."

"Awesome." Millie bounces on her toes as she pulls her phone out of her pocket. "I'm texting him right now to see when he's available for a chat."

"Wait. I don't have a car right now. I don't have a way to drive back and forth to the ranch."

"I have a loaner," Pete says as he dumps his trash into the bin next to us. "You can borrow it until your car is ready."

Stunned, I stare at Pete in surprise. "Really?"

"Sure. It's just sitting there. Probably needs to be driven. I'll park it out front here in about a half hour."

"Holy shit, you're all so nice to me."

"You're one of us now," Pete says with a wink and turns to walk out the door.

"Pete's hot *and* nice," I say to Millie as I turn around.

"I know," she replies with a sigh. "It's really too bad that he's married. Okay, Rem says he can meet with you tomorrow morning at around nine, but he's hoping you can come to the ranch because he has something to do out there afterward. Of course, he does."

Millie rolls her eyes, and I grin.

"Yeah, I can meet him at the ranch at nine, now that I have a loaner car."

"Cool, I'll tell him." Millie types out her message and then tucks her phone away. "I'll give you directions to the ranch. It's not hard to find, but it's out of town a ways. You're going to be driving a lot; I should warn you of that."

"Have you ever been to Seattle? It's all sprawled out, and if you want to go anywhere, you have to drive a lot. No biggie."

"Oh, my gosh, the kids are going to *love* you. I just know it."

Okay, so the car Pete loaned me is a little old and makes a couple of funny sounds, but it runs, and the heater works, so I'm not complaining. The highway out of town to the ranch is icy in spots, so I've been taking it easy.

The last thing I need is to put a car I don't even own into the ditch.

Finally, I see the sign for the Wild River Ranch that Millie described to me, and I turn into the driveway.

It's pretty out here, with lots of snow-covered evergreen trees and bushes. There's a family of three deer next to the driveway, watching me as I roll on past.

The storm has passed, and I'm hopeful for a warm day today to melt off the last of the ice and snow, but I have to admit, it's just so pretty out here on the ranch, all glittery with ice.

Following Millie's directions, I stay to the left when the driveway forks. She told me that if I went right, I'd run into her parents' new house and the tiny cabin that her other brother, Brady, lives in.

Remington and his kids live in the farmhouse, now that he's in charge of everything on the ranch and his dad has retired. Plus, their parents really wanted a smaller house to take care of.

Just like what my parents are thinking of doing.

I turn to the left and am met with a big farmhouse. It looks like something out of a Currier and Ives painting, so classic and...*sturdy*. The outside is brown with a big rock chimney. The shutters on the windows are red, and it looks like someone recently painted them over the summer.

There's a Jeep in the driveway, next to a big SUV that looks like it would easily fit six kids. To the right is a big garage, and since the door is up, I see that there's a truck tucked inside.

I can just picture this house at Christmastime, covered in lights and garland. The smaller evergreens along the driveway would be *gorgeous* with strings of lights on them.

And when I gaze out over the field and see black cattle, I grin.

It looks like we should be riding over the snow in a sleigh.

With a wide smile, I stride up the steps—steps that have been de-iced and shoveled very recently—and ring the doorbell.

Before I can even step back to wait patiently for an answer, the door swings open, and my heart stops.

"Grumpy."

CHAPTER SIX
REMINGTON

"Are you lost?" I don't know what it is about this woman, but my body fucking hums whenever I'm near her.

And I had no idea that *this* was the person Millie was sending my way to interview as a potential nanny.

Fuck me. How am I supposed to have her in my house all the time and keep my hands to myself?

"No," she says with a grin. "Do you *get* many people who are lost out here? Because that's a hell of a drive from town to find yourself lost."

"No, not many strays make their way out here. Come on in," I reply and step back, then close the door and catch her rubbing her hands together. "Are you cold?"

"A little," she confesses with a shrug. "I feel like I've been cold since I got here in December. It's okay, I'll adjust to the climate eventually. You have a lovely home."

I turn to look at the house I grew up in through her eyes. Aside from some new furniture here and there, and a coat of paint, not much has changed since I was a kid. The same chandelier hangs in the foyer over a worn rug. To the right is the kitchen and living room, and to the left is my office. I gesture that way and lead her inside, then close the doors behind us.

"Thanks for coming all this way." Taking my seat behind the desk, I watch her wander slowly to the chair across from me, her eyes gazing over my shelves, the paintings and photos on the wall, and the window to my back. Her green sweater hugs every curve of her body perfectly, leaving nothing to the imagination. I'm relieved to be sitting. "Have a seat."

"Okay. So, *you're* Remington. And here I thought your name was simply Grumpy."

"And you're Erin. Not Doc at all."

Those lips of hers tip up on one side. "Guilty. I'm Erin Montgomery, and I seriously love your sister."

I sit back and steeple my hands in front of me. "Everyone loves my sister. I guess I'll start by telling you what I need, and we'll go from there."

"Sounds great."

"I have two kids, and they're both in school. I'm finding it challenging to get away from the ranch to get them to and from school, take care of homework and meals, and still have fun with them, too."

"I can see that," she says, nodding slowly. "From what Millie tells me, your ranch is very busy."

"Yeah, that's an understatement. But I don't know how you can help me if you're not planning on quitting the coffee shop. You're still working when school gets out."

"I'll switch with Millie," she replies easily. "She already offered. I'll take the early shift and be off about an hour before school gets out. It'll be perfect timing for me to run home and change and get over to them. I don't think I'll be able to do mornings, though. So, if you need someone for both, it might not work for us."

I take a breath, thinking it over. Just having someone do the afternoon pickup would be a huge help.

"I think I can continue to manage in the mornings, if we decide this is mutually beneficial."

Erin watches me with happy green eyes as I outline the salary, what I expect, and what I absolutely won't tolerate. When I come to the end of my speech, her smile grows.

"I think that all sounds perfectly reasonable."

"Can you start on Monday? Of course, I'll have my brother run a quick background check to make sure there are no warrants out for your arrest, but as long as that checks out, you're hired."

"Awesome, but before I officially accept the job, can I meet the kids?"

"Of course." I stand, both happy and relieved that she asked to meet them before accepting. It shows me that this isn't just an extra paycheck for her. "Follow me. My mom is in the kitchen with them right now."

We walk through to the kitchen, where my mom is just starting the dishwasher.

"Grandma made us pancakes," Holly says with delight as she chews and turns to Erin. "I'm Holly. What's your name?"

"It's nice to meet you, Holly. I'm Erin. Those look like delicious pancakes."

"You can have some," Johnny offers. "Grandma makes the best ones."

"As tempting as that is, I'll have to pass for today. You must be Johnny." I like the way she smiles at the kids. She's warm and isn't fake about it.

You can always tell when people don't like kids and are only being nice because it's expected. And my kids know the difference, too.

"Hello, Erin," Mom says with a smile. "I'm Joy, Remington's mom. I'm about to get out of your hair, Rem. I'm off to the salon."

"Thanks for coming over, Mom," I reply and kiss her cheek before she bustles off.

"Where do you live?" Holly asks Erin.

"In town, in an apartment above a garage," Erin replies and leans on the counter, settling in to talk to the kids. "And I work with your aunt Millie at the coffee shop."

"I want to work at the coffee shop when I grow up," Holly decides. "I also want to take ballet classes. I have friends at school who do it, and it looks so fun. See, I can even do some of the moves already."

Holly, ever the performer when new people are around, jumps off of her stool and starts to twirl about, her little arms up and over her head, and I see her heading right for the corner of the countertop.

Erin must sense it, too, because she starts to move forward just as I do to avoid the knock on the head, but we're both too late. Holly collides with the corner, and her nose starts to bleed.

"It's okay," Erin says, completely cool, as she grabs a towel and holds it to Holly's nose. "Hey now, it's okay. I know that hurts. I'm sorry. We're going to stop the bleeding and make it feel better. Johnny, will you please grab me a couple of ice cubes from the freezer?"

I'm still poised to jump in, but I can see that Erin has this under control, so I hang back and watch how she handles it.

"Owie," Holly cries.

"I know, sweetie." Erin drags her hand down Holly's hair as she keeps the pressure on Holly's nose. Johnny fetches the ice and hurries over with a few cubes in his hands. Erin expertly wraps it in the towel and presses it against Holly's nose once more. "It's already stopped bleeding. Now, this ice is going to help it feel better."

Holly's not crying anymore and is watching Erin with big, wet brown eyes.

"How'd you know how to do that?" Johnny asks.

"Well, I have a really big family, and someone was always getting smacked in the face and getting a bloody nose when we were growing up. That's what happens when you toss footballs and baseballs and all kinds of things around when you're not supposed to. It hurts like crazy, but this helps."

"I can hold it," Holly says as she takes the towel in her little hands. "Like this?"

"Yep, just like that. Good job." Erin nods and steps back, still smiling at the kids.

"She isn't always a spaz," Johnny says. "She was just showing off."

"Huh." Erin frowns and looks around the room. "I don't see any spazzes here. I just see a little girl who loves to dance. My aunt is a professional ballerina. She has a dance school in Seattle. I think you'd love to learn to dance, Holly."

That brings a huge smile to my daughter's face, and I know without a doubt that Erin would be a great addition to my kids' lives. I may have a hard time keeping my hands to myself because she's fucking gorgeous and does things to me that I haven't felt in a very long time.

Hell, maybe ever.

But for my kids, I can suffer through it.

Even Johnny is grinning as Erin reaches over and ruffles his hair.

"Well, guys, I'd better head out because I have to work this afternoon, but I might see you again soon, okay?"

"Okay," they reply in unison, and I escort Erin to the door to gather her things and then out to her car, which I eye warily.

"Is this your car?"

Erin sighs. "No, it's a loaner. My car is in the shop, and I don't know when I'll get it back. Brooks is trying to come up with some answers for me. In the meantime, Peter was nice enough to loan me this one."

"I don't want my kids riding in that pile of rust."

Erin frowns. "It runs just fine."

"That may be, but when you're driving my kids around, I want them in a vehicle that I know is in perfect shape. You'll take my Suburban."

Her eyes fly to my big SUV and then to me. "But that's *your* car. I can't just take your car away from you."

"I also have the Jeep, so it's no big deal."

"This is ridiculous. The car is *fine*."

"Not for my kids," I counter, shaking my head. "I'll drop the SUV off to you tomorrow. That's if you're taking the job."

"I like your kids a lot," she admits with a smile. "They're cute, and they're not little monsters. Their dad has some alpha vibes going on, but I can deal with that."

I like her smart mouth. I want to bite it. But for now, I shove my hands into my pockets.

"The kids get out of school at 3:00. You'll want to get in the pickup line by about 2:30."

"Got it." She nods and walks to the driver's door. "I'll be there to get them Monday afternoon. Have a good weekend."

She waves and takes off, the car making all kinds of noises as she drives down the driveway. I absolutely do *not* want my kids to ride in that thing. Hell, I don't even like Erin riding in it.

Brady will follow me into town tomorrow to drop off the Suburban and bring me back to the ranch.

"REM HIRED A NANNY," Millie announces to the family at dinner later that night. We're all seated around my big dining room table, finishing up a dinner of fried chicken with all the fixings that my mom made from scratch. "My friend, Erin. She's the *best*, and she already told me that she absolutely loved meeting the kids."

"Erin?" Chase's head comes up at that. "I like her a lot. She's happy and nice. And she's *hot*."

"Why don't I take the kids outside to play with their new drones," Dad suggests, standing from the table. "Let's go find some cows and see if we can spot other animals, too."

"Yay!"

Both kids run after my dad through the back door to the yard.

"Those drones were a cool gift," Millie says to Ryan, who's sitting right across from me. "They're in heaven. It'll be fun to fly them around the ranch."

"I had to bring them something fun," Ryan says with a shrug.

"Tell me more about the pretty Erin," Brady says, waggling his eyebrows.

"No," I reply curtly. "Keep your hands off my fucking nanny."

"Well, I see that Rem is his old charming self," Ryan says, earning a glare from me. "Last time I checked, it was still not against the law to date someone, even if they're a nanny."

"You're such a fucking smart-ass," I reply. "And how do you know if I'm charming or not? You haven't been home in *two fucking years*. So, why now?"

"Just because I choose to have a job that isn't here in Bitterroot Valley doesn't mean that I don't want to come see my family, you know."

"Seems that way to me." I'm just so fucking *pissed off*. I want to punch him in the face. "So what the fuck are you doing here?"

Ryan just stares at me, his face sober, and wipes his mouth with his napkin. "You know what? I think I'll head home."

"No." Millie raps her fist on the table, getting all of our attention. "No. You'll stay because, as Rem just pointed out in a *really* shitty way, we haven't seen you in a long time, and we miss you. Rem, you need to chill the hell out."

"My kids don't even know you," I say, my voice even now. "And they *want* to. They ask about you. They may enjoy your expensive gifts in the moment, but that's not what they want from you, Ry. They just want *you*. So, the question stands. Why are you home now, and how long will it be before you leave, and I have to tell the kids that I don't know when they'll get to see you again?"

Ryan blows out a breath and digs his fingertips into his eyes. No one objects to the question this time, because I know that they're all wondering the same thing.

"We like having you here," Brady adds.

"I'm home indefinitely," Ryan finally says with a weary sigh. "I can work from anywhere, and I've decided this needs to be my home base for a while. Why? Shit, I don't know. It's just my gut telling me that this is where I need to be because I miss all of you, and I want to be here. Jesus, I want to get on a horse and brand some calves."

"That's coming up in a couple of weeks," Mom says, wiping a tear from her eye. "We could use your help."

I don't trust it. He won't be here long.

He never is.

"I want to play with the drones," Chase says, standing from the table. "Why should the kids have all the fun?"

"I'm with you," Brady adds and joins Chase. Mom and Millie go out, too, leaving me here with Ryan.

For a long minute, we just watch each other over the table. Yeah, it's good to see him. But I'm so mad at him that I want to kick his ass.

"I'll earn it," he says at last.

"What's that?"

"The trust." He blows out a breath and looks more emotional than I've seen him since we lost the state football championship my senior year. "I know it'll take time, but I'll earn it."

"It'll take time," I echo with a nod. "Fuck, let's go play with the drones."

Ryan grins. "I have a couple more for the rest of us."

"Break them out."

"I SHOULD HAVE JUST GONE to get them myself." I brace my foot on the bottom rung of a fence as Brady and I watch Ryan work with a mare in the ring. "It was a slower day today, and I could have gotten away to pick them up."

"Most days won't be this laid-back, you know that," Brady replies. "Let them all get used to each other. Erin has your car, and from what I hear, she's a competent girl. Stop worrying so much."

I smirk and check my phone. She should be in the pickup line by now.

"You obviously don't have kids. Life is all about worry, my friend."

"Stop looking at your phone. Jesus, did you put a location tracker on hers or something?"

"Wait, I can do that?"

Brady rolls his eyes. "No, stalker, you can't. It's an invasion of privacy."

"I'm just going to text her and ask her where she is."

Me: Did you make it to the pickup line?

"That's it, annoy the fuck out of her on the first day," Brady says as my phone pings with a reply.

It's a selfie of her in my car.

Erin: I'm here!

"Hey, she *is* hot," Brady says, looking over my shoulder. "Are her eyes...green?"

"Yeah." I clear my throat. "Green eyes, brown hair."

The sexiest damn lips I've ever seen in my life.

Not that I'll say that out loud.

After a few minutes, my phone pings with another text. This time, it's a selfie of Erin with the kids in the back seat.

Erin: Proof of life! All is well.

I smirk.

Me: Drive safe. Text me when you get to the house.

"You'd think he was on a horse yesterday," Brady says as we continue to watch Ryan, who's murmuring to the horse. "He always was a natural."

"We all are," I counter. "We grew up on horses."

"Yeah, but it's as if Ryan speaks their language. I was always jealous of that." Brady shrugs. "When *are* we doing the branding?"

"Next weekend. We have one more storm coming through the middle of the week, and then the weather clears up. We'll be good to go for the weekend."

"Cool. It'll be good to have the extra hands."

"I think I want to buy a few of my own horses," Ryan says as he joins us at the fence. "I have stables at my property that I've never used."

"You can always come out here and ride," I remind him. "You don't even have to let one of us know. Just come ride."

"I know, and I appreciate that," Ryan replies. "But there's something to be said for being able to walk out your back door to your own stable, saddle up a horse, and just go. I miss it."

"There are always horses for sale in the area," Brady says. "You won't have a problem finding a couple."

"That's what I figured," Ryan agrees. "I might need to hire someone to come out now and then to help me, especially if I have to travel."

"You can find that easy enough, too," Brady says. "I know some guys who would appreciate the work and are trustworthy."

"Appreciate it," Ryan says with a nod and then turns to me. "You're doing a good job out here, Rem. The ranch is thriving, and that's thanks to you."

I nod, looking around at our family's legacy. "I had a good foundation to work from. I'm just building on what was given to me."

"It wasn't given," Ryan replies. "It was earned."

"Damn right," Brady says.

"Yeah, well." The phone in my hand rings, and my heart stutters when I see it's Erin. She shouldn't be here yet. "What is it? What's wrong?"

"Jesus, nothing's wrong, nervous Nellie. I brought the kids to the coffee shop to see Millie and to get them a treat, and I'm wondering if you want something. They have the huckleberry muffins again."

Ryan and Brady are laughing at the nervous Nellie comment, which makes me regret the speakerphone, but my heart has settled down now that I know they're safe.

"Yeah, I'll take one. Hell, buy whatever they have left, and I'll pay you back."

"Okay, will do. See you soon."

She hangs up, and I turn to my brothers. "Shut up."

"We didn't say anything," Ryan says with a laugh.

"I'm gonna start calling you Nellie," Brady says. "It just fits you so well."

"Fuck you." But I can't help but laugh. "You're a couple of jerks."

"Ah, come on, Nellie. Let's go meet her at the house for some muffins."

CHAPTER SEVEN
ERIN

T hat first sip of coffee just hits different when it's your day off.

Curled up on my couch, wrapped up in a red throw blanket that my mom sent me, I take a long, deep breath and then another sip.

I love quiet mornings, watching the mountains. Well, the tiny bit that I can see from my little apartment window anyway. I like watching the world wake up with me.

And for the first time in a week, I don't have to work at either job.

I can admit that I'm exhausted, but not in a bad way. My first week with Holly and Johnny was great, and I was able to keep up at the coffee shop, as well, which is exactly what I was hoping for. So far, everyone seems happy, and I was able to give Brooks the go-ahead to get started on the car repairs.

Yeah, I'm going to be tired from working two jobs for a while, but that's okay. I don't mind.

With half of my cup consumed, I reach for my phone and open the 'gram so I can see what all my cousins are up to. It looks like a few of them went out on the town last night, so I *heart* the posts and comment on a few.

I'm glad that Zoey and Millie talked me into being on the app, even if I'm incognito, so I can keep up with everyone. Speaking of Millie, I search her name and immediately give her a follow, and then notice that she posted a photo an hour ago from out at the ranch.

The caption reads, *Sunrises at the ranch FTW!*

Holy shit, the photo of the mountains is just incredible, with the first rays of sunshine touching the peaks almost lovingly. The mountains in this area always take my breath away, but I haven't seen the ones in this photo out at the ranch. And the trees! They're so green and beautiful.

I never thought I'd be the girl who has a thing for trees, but here we are.

Closing out the app, I bring up Millie's number and shoot her a text.

Me: You're up early! I didn't know you were spending the weekend at the ranch. How big is it, anyway? I haven't even seen those mountains, and I spent all week there!

I sip my coffee as I see the three dots start to dance on the screen, indicating that Millie is typing out a response.

Millie: I bunked with Brady last night! Girl, you should come out here today! Come now. It's a big day on the ranch that you shouldn't miss. I can show you around, including where I took that pic. Wear clothes that can get super jacked up and come on!

I'd planned to get some chores done today. Groceries, cleaning, all the things that I haven't had a chance to do since I've been working two jobs. I haven't even seen Roger all week, and I should look in on him.

But I really do love the ranch, and I'm curious to see more of it. I *really* want to see where she took that photo.

When I don't answer right away, Millie sends another message.

Millie: Get your ass out here, Montgomery.

That makes me laugh, so I stand and wiggle out of the blanket as I reply.

Me: I'll be there in an hour.

It takes less than that for me to dress in old jeans and old sneakers, along with a *Nash* concert T-shirt, and drive Remington's Suburban out to the ranch.

At first, I hated this huge SUV. It's *ginormous*. Parking it is a bitch, even with all the cameras and sensors on it.

But there was a day during the week when another storm blew through, making the roads icy, and I felt completely safe in the big vehicle with the kids. Much safer than I would have felt in either the loaner or even *my* car.

I hate to admit that Grumpy was right, but he was. This is the safer choice if I'm going to be driving his children around, and I won't argue about it again.

Even though I like arguing with Remington. It's just so...*easy*. And, if I'm being honest with myself, it's sexy.

Remington Wild is maybe the sexiest man I've ever met, and I guess that means that I like broody men because I can count on one hand the number of times I've seen him smile. Of course, he always aims them at the kids. I don't know what I'd do if he ever smiled directly at *me*. Probably strip naked and beg, which isn't exactly normal for me.

He makes me feel things that are purely unprofessional.

Millie's waiting for me when I pull up in front of the main farmhouse, and she grins when I get out of the car.

"I'm so glad you're here," she says as she wraps her arms around me and gives me a hug. "You can watch us brand and castrate the calves."

"I'm not branding or castrating *anything*," I stress. "I'm not a cowboy. You can't make me do it. Maybe I'll just go back home."

"Don't worry, city girl," she says with a laugh. "You don't have to. I want to show you around the ranch a little, and you can just watch what we do when everyone else gets here. All the families from the neighboring ranches come to help each other out."

"Even the Lexington family?"

That makes her stop in her tracks, and she narrows her eyes at me. "No. They're not included. Don't say that name on this ranch. I'm pretty easygoing about it, but if my dad or brothers hear it, they might become homicidal."

"Wow, that's some rivalry y'all have going there."

"You have no idea. Anyway, everyone's already out

getting set up for later. Neighbors will start arriving within the hour. If you'd like, you're welcome to hang out with my mom and some of the other women in the food tent."

"That's not sexist at all."

That makes Millie laugh again. "I know, right? But people have to eat, and there's always some good food that's prepared in that tent. However, if you want to watch the branding, you're welcome to do that, too."

"Let's see how it goes," I reply. "I don't know if I want to watch baby animals be tortured."

"It's not torture." Millie's voice is calm and patient as she leads me to the Jeep, and we hop in. "They need to be branded so we know who's who in case a fence fails. They need vaccinations so they don't get sick, and the boys have to be castrated. It just is what it is, and they'll be fine."

"Says the girl who grew up on a cattle ranch."

Millie grins and drives right on the fields, no roads, as she takes me on a tour of the place.

"We won't be able to cover everything in an hour," she says. "There's a lot of land here. But I'll show you my favorite spot, where I took that picture this morning. By the way, I love your T-shirt. Nash is my favorite band. Were you lucky enough to see them in concert?"

"I—" I sigh and then just nod. "Yeah, I have."

"That's *awesome*."

It only takes about ten minutes before Millie stops and cuts the engine of the Jeep. My stomach is a little jittery from all the bumps and being jostled around, but when I see the mountains, I feel my jaw drop.

"Holy shit, Mill."

"I know." Her voice is hushed as we simply stand here and take it all in.

The mountains seem to be layered, one behind the next, reaching up into the sky with jagged peaks that still have plenty of snow on them.

"Does the snow ever melt all the way up there?" I wonder.

"By July, most of the snow will be gone," she replies. "And then in September, it'll be back."

"Wow." In front of the mountains is a valley that cradles thousands of evergreen trees of all shapes and sizes. They're so majestic, so *beautiful*, that all I can do is stare in complete wonder.

"I've always come here," Millie says and crosses her arms over her chest. "Most of us do, actually, because it's not far from home, yet it's probably the most beautiful view in Montana. When we need some time away, this is where you'll find most of us. I think we should add a bench here so we can sit for a while, but so far, I've been outvoted."

"You can just sit on the ground."

And so, I do, just sit on the ground and lean back on my hands so I can look up at those incredible mountains.

"How could you stand moving away from this?" I ask. "You left this for town."

"I wanted to be closer to work," Millie says as she sits next to me. "And I needed something of my own. This is my *home*—it's in my blood—but it's Remington's now. And I'm not a kid anymore, so it was time to do something else. But I love coming out to the ranch sometimes to just be. It's my happy place. Oh, look!"

Millie points to the trees, and right before us, a doe walks out of the brush, with two tiny spotted fawns following behind her. They're *so small*.

"Those are early babies," Millie whispers. "And so sweet."

The mom's ears twitch, and she sees us watching her. She doesn't run away; she simply continues to walk, with her babies following close behind.

"I get it," I whisper when the deer wander out of sight. "I totally get it."

<hr>

"Erin!" Johnny comes running from the temporary fence where he is watching the men set up for the upcoming work. He comes to an abrupt stop right in front of me and smiles up, showing off his teeth, and the gap where he obviously just lost one. "You're here!"

"I am." I sense Remington walk up to us, but I keep my eyes on the boy and ignore the goose bumps that just rolled over my body. "Something's different about you. Hmm."

Johnny's so excited, he's practically vibrating.

"Don't tell me," I murmur, rubbing my chin as if I'm thinking really hard. "Did you get a haircut?"

"No!"

"New boots?"

"These are *really* old." He widens his lips and pushes his tongue through the hole in his teeth.

"Well, look at that. You finally lost that stubborn tooth."

"This morning," he says with a nod. "Tonight, the tooth fairy will come. I hope I get a million dollars."

"Wow, that's one rich tooth fairy." I turn to Remington now and wink at him. "I hope it's okay that Millie invited me to come out and watch."

"I don't mind," Rem says simply. If I'm not mistaken, his eyes warm when he looks at me, as if he's actually happy to see me. "Do you want to come help?"

I eye the pen where a whole bunch of black calves are gathered, and I wince.

"Can I just watch for now?"

"Sure, Doc," he says and pats my shoulder. "You can watch."

Rem strides over to the pen, and Johnny runs after him, ready to jump in to help.

"That's the food tent," Millie says, pointing to the left.

"That's more than a *tent*."

It's a white event tent, the kind you rent for weddings, with screened-in walls to keep the bugs out. There are about a dozen tables set up with chairs for workers to sit and eat, and on one end is a huge makeshift kitchen area, complete with a generator for powering everything.

"This wasn't here on Friday."

"We got everything ready to go yesterday," Millie says as she walks with me to the tent. "About forty people come to help, and no one leaves hungry, let me tell you. Tonight, once all the work is done, we'll have chili and cornbread and then s'mores around the bonfire. You have to stay for that."

For a brief moment, I think of all the things I should be doing at home today and then cast those thoughts aside.

I *want* to be here. This is absolutely fascinating, and the air already vibrates with energy.

"I'll stay," I agree with a nod, and then smile back at Joy when she waves for me to come inside the tent.

"I'll see you a little later. I'm in charge of vaccinations," Millie says as she hurries over to the cows.

"Erin, welcome," Joy says as she holds the screen aside for me. "If we didn't have the screens, we'd be overrun with flies and bees. Now, you have a choice. You can help cook."

I raise an eyebrow. "Or?"

"Or you can help cook."

I laugh and follow Joy to the kitchen area. "As luck would have it, I'm pretty decent in the kitchen. I'm especially good with a knife. What can I do?"

Joy starts to give orders, and the day flies by.

There's so much commotion with all the kids and people bustling about. They come into the tent to grab a snack and a drink, and then they're off again to do whatever it is that they're doing in that temporary pen.

The calves cry and make noise, and it makes me

cringe, but Joy is awesome about patting my shoulder and telling me that everything is going as it should.

By the end of the day, we're a sweaty, tired bunch of people, but I think I had one of the best days of my life.

I *love* the sense of community out on the ranch. It kind of reminds me of my big, loud family back home in Seattle, and that makes me a tiny bit homesick.

Before I know it, everyone has finished with the calves, as they're being led out of the pen and off to the pasture to be reunited with their mamas, and all the hard-working people make their way to the tent to load up on hearty chili and cornbread.

As tired as everyone obviously is, there's so much laughter and camaraderie that it makes me smile. I even know some of the people here from the coffee shop, and that makes me feel like I'm part of something.

Like I belong to this community. And I have to blink to keep tears from sneaking into my eyes.

"Let me get this straight," a man named Leonard says after sampling his chili. "You make a damn good coffee *and* you cook? Where have you been all my life?"

"She's too young for you, Leonard," Rem's dad, John, says as he joins us and fills a bowl with chili as the other man laughs and walks away. "What did you think of all the commotion today, Erin?"

"I think that what you have out here is incredibly special, Mr. Wild."

John's face softens, and he nods. "I do, too. You're welcome here anytime, whether you're working or not."

"Thank you."

I don't know why that makes me a little emotional. Maybe because John reminds me of *my* dad a little. I mean, they look nothing alike, but they both have such an incredible work ethic, and they obviously love and protect their families. I can't help but think of my father and the other men in my family.

"Let's go sit by the bonfire," Millie says as she joins us. She gives her dad a hug before leading me over to where the fire is already burning as the sun sets behind the mountains. There's a big s'mores station set up with all the fixings and sticks to use to roast the marshmallows.

I see Holly struggling to get a marshmallow on her stick, so I step in to help her.

"Hey there, beautiful girl. I haven't seen you hardly at all today."

"I was working hard," she informs me as she watches me wiggle the puffy marshmallow onto a stick for her. "I'm extra hungry."

"I bet you are. Did you get some chili?"

"Yeah, but now I want this."

"I get it, trust me. Come on, I'll help you if you want."

"Yeah!" Holly bounces on her toes. "Let's do it!"

"Hey, can I come?" Millie asks, laughing as she tags along. We find a spot on some logs-turned-stools near the fire and sit down. I immediately help Holly put her marshmallow into the fire.

"It's really warm," she says. I have my arms around her, helping her hold on to the stick.

"Yeah, you need to be mindful of the fire, okay? We

can always get more marshmallows, but we can't get any more Hollys."

The little girl giggles and then gasps when her marshmallow catches on fire. I help her blow it out, and then we build her treat.

"I'm gonna go eat with Johnny," she announces and hurries off. "Thank you!"

"You're welcome." I grin after her and then get to work on my own s'more. I look around for Millie and discover she's wandered off to talk to a couple of guys on the other side of the fire, so I sit on my stool and layer my chocolate and graham crackers, along with the burned-to-a-crisp marshmallow.

"So, you're one of those kinds of people, huh?"

I turn as Remington sits on the stool next to mine. "What kind is that?"

"The kind that burns the fuck out of their marshmallow."

"It's delicious." I take a bite and moan in happiness, not oblivious to the way Remington sets his jaw in reaction. "See? Delicious."

His eyes have dropped to my lips, and before I know it, he's reached up and is wiping some chocolate from the corner of my mouth.

And there's that tingle again, the one that seems to pop up whenever I'm close to this man. He's just so...*fuckinghellhot.*

"What did you think of today?" he asks. He doesn't take his eyes off me, and I love the way the fire is reflected in those hazel eyes, lighting up the gold flecks that live in there.

"It was fun. Interesting. Hard work."

His lips tip up on one side. "It's all of that. I'm sorry that you gave up your day off to be here."

"I'm not sorry." I take another bite and close my eyes when all that gooey, melty sugar hits my system. "I liked being in the kitchen with your mom. She's a hoot, and she's *so* proud of you and your family. I got to meet all of your brothers and your dad, too. And I got to see some of the actual work that goes into this place. It's so beautiful here, Remington. I didn't know that a place could be so gorgeous, and that's kind of saying a lot because I've been to a lot of beautiful places."

"Where was your favorite place to visit?"

"Before I came here? Iceland. But now it's here. I could be here in Bitterroot Valley for the rest of my days and never get tired of it. I *knew* the second I landed here that this was where I was supposed to be."

"How did you know?" He asks as he makes his own s'more.

I lick my lips, thinking it over. "It was deep down, in my gut. In my *heart*. It was like the universe was welcoming me home, and for the first time in my life, I felt like I belonged. Does that sound silly?"

"No." He shakes his head and looks into the fire. "It doesn't sound silly at all. When you're home, you're home."

CHAPTER EIGHT
REMINGTON

L eave it to me to hire the hottest goddamn nanny on the planet. Her skin is luminous in the firelight, and those green eyes of hers... well, I don't think I've ever seen anything like them. She's fucking gorgeous, and my kids *love* her.

If she was shitty at the job I needed her to do, I could dislike her, fire her, and send her packing. But no, Erin Montgomery has a rock-solid work ethic, legs that go on for days, and an expressive face that never fails to show me exactly what she's thinking.

And right now, she wants me to kiss her.

She's fighting it. That unscrupulous work ethic has her arguing with herself, but she's been watching my lips since I sat down next to her. She thinks she's being inconspicuous about it, but she's not.

And that's just one of the things that I find attractive about her. There's no guesswork. What you see is what you get with Erin, and that's fucking sexy as hell.

"Thanks for not making me feel silly," she says as she licks the last of the marshmallow from her thumb.

Jesus Christ, I can think of other things I'd rather that mouth was sucking.

"Sometimes," she continues, as if she hasn't just made me hard, "the long-time locals here in Bitterroot Valley get angry that an outsider like me would feel like this is home."

"I'm not an asshole," I reply and watch as she pulls a peppermint candy out of her pocket and pops it into her mouth. "I mean, I *can* be, but not about that. Not everyone is born in a place that feels like they belong. Sometimes, you have to find it."

Her whole face lights up at that, and I feel like I just won the lottery.

"Yeah, that's it exactly. It's not that I don't like Seattle, or even love my family there. I do love them. But I don't want to live there."

"Makes sense."

"Do you have any aunts and uncles, cousins?" she asks.

"I have one aunt. My dad's sister, Melissa. She's married to my uncle Brian, and they live in Spokane. They only come over for holidays or special events."

Erin nods thoughtfully. "Do they have kids?"

"Two. Their oldest, Spencer, is in the military. Last I heard, he was stationed in Germany. Shelly is a real estate agent in Portland."

"And you don't see them often?" she asks, as if that's a foreign concept for her.

"About once a year."

I glance over to see that my dad has Holly on his lap, and her eyes are drooping shut. Johnny sits next to my mom, his head leaning on her arm. No one has left yet, and that's fine by me. I *like* having my neighbors here, the way we've done for generations, coming together to help one another and then celebrating a hard day's work afterward.

"You love this," Erin murmurs, and I glance down to see her watching me with those gorgeous green eyes. "Having these people here."

"Yeah, I do." I nod thoughtfully as I stretch my legs out in front of me. "We've done it this way for a hundred years or more. Times change, with technology and such, but this stays the same. I guess there's something to be said for that."

Surprised that I've said so much to her, I glance over and see that she's smiling at me.

"What?"

"You're not always grumpy after all."

I can't help the surprised laughter that slips out at that, and when I smile up at her, Erin's eyes dilate and fall to my mouth.

Yeah, she wants me to kiss her.

"I'm going to take my kids to bed," I say as I stand, needing to put some distance between myself and this woman before I do something stupid like kiss her silly in front of my entire family and all our friends.

My brothers would never let me live it down.

I walk over and smile as Johnny looks up at me through heavy-lidded eyes.

"I think I'm tired, Dad."

"Looks that way to me," I agree and share a smile with my parents. "Why don't I take you and your sister up to bed?"

"But the party isn't over," Holly says without even opening her eyes. "I have to stay. I'm the hostess."

"With the mostest," I agree as I pick up my daughter out of my dad's arms and kiss her on the cheek. "Everyone will understand. Come on, buddy."

Johnny takes my hand without a fight, which tells me that my kids are both exhausted. This was the first year that Holly was old enough to really pay attention to everything going on, and she soaked it up with excited brown eyes.

She's a Montana girl, through and through.

"You did so great today," I say to both of my kids. "I'm really proud of you. Thank you for listening and helping out so much."

"It's our job," Johnny says. "This is gonna be our ranch someday."

"It's your ranch now, but yeah, I understand what you mean. Are you guys happy here?"

Johnny opens the front door ahead of me and closes it behind me as I lead them up to their bedrooms.

"Where else would we go?" Holly asks with a yawn.

"Well, nowhere, but I want to know if you like the ranch."

"I don't," Johnny says with a sleepy, toothless grin. "I *love* it. It's really badass."

"And you've been hanging out with cowboys too much. Don't say that word at school." I kiss the top of his head. "I'm glad you took showers before dinner. Go brush your teeth before bed."

I set Holly on the ground, and they both trudge into their bathroom to follow my orders. They definitely don't follow the brush-for-two-minutes rule because they're back in about twenty seconds flat, but I don't want to argue the point tonight.

We're all too tired for that.

"'Night, Dad," Johnny says as he walks to his bedroom.

"I'll be right there," I tell him and lead Holly to bed. She jumps in, and I tuck the covers around her before leaning in to kiss her forehead. "I love you, beautiful baby girl."

"Love you, Daddy."

"You did so good today."

"I know."

I grin, pleased that my girl has such healthy confidence, and turn off her light before closing the door behind me and walking down the hall to Johnny's room, which happens to be my old room when I was a kid.

The light is already off when I walk inside, and he's under the covers, breathing evenly.

"Love you, big boy," I whisper in his ear.

"Mm," is all he says as he rolls over the other way.

My kid is a sound sleeper, so I feel confident reaching

under his pillow and finding his tooth, replacing it with a five-dollar bill.

With the tooth tucked into my pocket, I leave his room and close the door behind me.

I need to get back out to the bonfire to make sure I'm there to thank everyone for coming to help today as they leave. But when I walk out the front door, I see that Erin is walking by herself to the Suburban, obviously ready to head home for the night.

"Oh, hey," she says with a small smile. "How are they?"

She nods to the second floor of the house, obviously meaning the kids, and I shove my hands into my pockets.

"Already dreaming. But they had fun today."

"I know that I told you this the other day, but they're really great kids, Rem. I like them a lot."

"Good, because Holly asked if she could keep you after you left on Friday."

That makes Erin laugh. "I'm glad it runs both ways. Also, just to let you know, my car is officially being fixed, so I shouldn't need your SUV for too much longer."

"I don't care about the car. Use it."

"But it's *your* car. If you're still uncomfortable with my ride after it's fixed, we'll discuss it."

I rock back on my heels. "Are you *always* this argumentative?"

"I'm not arguing."

"Yes, you are. I don't give a rat's ass about the car. The kids are comfortable in it."

"Yeah, but the weather is only going to get better as

we head into summer, so my car will be fine." She puffs out a breath when I simply stare at her. "I'm trying to do the right thing here. You shouldn't just hand your vehicle over to me."

"Why not? It's mine. If I want Mickey Mouse to drive it, I'll hand it over to him."

"I mean, that seems silly. He's a mouse."

I lick my lips, wanting to push her up against my car and kiss her until neither of us can fucking breathe. But I don't want her to quit on me because my kids love her, and it's been nice having her help this past week.

Just as I'm about to back away, her eyes fall to my mouth, and she presses her lips together, then *licks them.*

And just like that, my self-control evaporates into the cool spring air, and I rush to her, cup her face in my hands as her back flattens against the door of the SUV, and I take a ragged breath as I stare down at her. At her amazing green eyes and the way the firelight dances in them. At her kissable lips. A war wages inside of me. This is *wrong.* I shouldn't kiss this woman.

Erin bites her lower lip, and that's it. My control snaps.

"Fucking hell, those lips," I growl before lowering my mouth to hers and sinking into her. She moans and shoves her hands into my hair, holding on as I plunder her, exploring every bit of her sweet mouth as I block out the laughter and voices around the crackle of the bonfire, and just lose myself in this woman.

She's soft and smooth and smells like woodsmoke and peppermint.

And when I finally lift my head to look down into her eyes, she's breathing raggedly, her eyes wide, and swallows hard.

"I shouldn't have done that." I nuzzle her nose with mine. "But damn it, you'd tempt a saint, and I'm not a saint. You're so fucking beautiful."

"I—" She swallows again and drags her hand down my cheek. "Same goes. The fucking beautiful part."

I grin down at her, but we hear voices walking toward us, and she frowns and shakes her head, so I step back, already feeling the absence of her against me and wanting nothing more than to yank her inside and take her to my bed.

"I apologize if I overstepped."

Erin scowls before looking down at her hands and then looks back up at me. "You didn't. I know that I could have pushed you away, and I didn't want to. I'll see you tomorrow, after school."

She hurries into the Suburban, starts the engine, and without a single glance at me, drives off toward the highway into town.

"Shit." I shake my head and stare down at my dirty boots. "That was a fucking mistake, Wild. You're an idiot."

Calling myself every name in the book, I head back to the fire and my friends.

It's time I had a goddamn beer.

"You're almost...chipper this week." Brady narrows his eyes at me. "What's wrong with you?"

"Nothing." I shake my head and hang my saddle over the saddle rack, then turn to take the blanket off the back of my horse before grabbing a brush to brush him down. "It's just been a decent week. The kids are good, no animals have been killed, and the weather's finally not being an asshole. It's as smooth as it gets around here, and it puts me in a decent mood."

"Ryan's coming over to ride this evening," he says and then laughs when my smile turns into a scowl. "Whoa, there went the good mood. He's been here for a couple of weeks now. Haven't you kissed and made up yet?"

"I'm not mad. It's fine. You guys have fun riding."

"Oh, I'm not riding with him."

"He's going alone?" I turn and frown at my brother. "Not that it matters. He's a grown-ass man and can ride alone if he wants to."

"No, I think he's bringing a date."

I laugh and shake my head. "Of course, he is. Typical Ryan. Who's he dating?"

"How the hell should I know? I'm not a gossip." Brady tries to look offended, but it just makes me laugh harder. "I hear he picked up a tourist at the bar the other night and told her he could show her a good time on a horse."

I pat my own horse down and walk him to his stall. "Don't let him anywhere *near* this one."

"He knows which horses are available. He's not stupid, you know."

I snort and roll my shoulders. I want a hot shower and some time with my kids. "I'm headed in."

"Me, too. See you tomorrow."

I wave at Brady as he heads toward the cabin, and I set off for the house. Since the weather has been better, I've been walking to the barn every day. And when I reach the house, I see the Suburban is parked out front, and the lights are on inside.

It's been almost a week since the bonfire and the kiss right here in the driveway, and so far, things haven't been at all weird between Erin and me. Neither of us has mentioned the kiss, and I've been careful to maintain a friendly but professional distance.

In return, Erin has been funny, calling me Grumpy in front of the kids and making them laugh, efficient, and her usual sexy-as-fuck self.

"You've gotta get over the sexy factor," I whisper to myself as I climb the stairs to the back door and find all three of them in the kitchen, huddled around the island. "Hey, gang."

"Dad!" Johnny's eyes are bright and full of excitement as he pops his head up to greet me. "You have to come see this."

"We *all* helped," Holly is sure to assure me as I walk toward them. I crane my neck to see what's on the counter and find...a cake.

"You baked a cake?"

"The best cake ever!" Holly holds her arms out to

me, so I pick her up. "It's blue and purple inside, and Erin let us decorate it ourselves, without any help from her."

"That explains the blue icing on your neck." I lean in and make a fuss about licking the frosting. "Mmm, delicious!"

Holly giggles and wiggles out of my arms, and I turn to Erin, who's smiling at us all.

"They wanted to help," she says simply.

"What's the occasion?" I ask her.

"For what?"

"The cake." I eye the tall, round cake on the counter. "Usually, it's someone's birthday or something."

"Dad," Johnny says, "it's *Erin's* birthday."

My eyes fly to hers, and I watch with fascination as she blushes.

"Really?"

"Yeah. I let it slip because my sister called to sing to me earlier, and the kids heard, so they insisted that I have a cake. So, together, we baked me one. Oh, I have a casserole in the oven, if that's okay. Your mom actually made it and brought it over."

"We *love* casserole," Holly informs her. "Come on, let's cut our cake!"

"Not until after dinner," I reply, without looking away from Erin. "You'll stay and eat with us. I know there's plenty, and the kids will want to help you celebrate your birthday."

Erin smiles and nods. "That sounds like fun, thanks. We can eat any time."

"If you don't mind getting things ready here, I'll go clean up."

"You got it," she says and turns to the kids. "Who's going to help me set the table?"

"Me!" both of my children volunteer in unison as I head for the stairs and up to my room to clean up. I don't even want to think about the fact that when I ask the kids to help with dinner, they both whine and complain, as if I'm asking them to dig ditches rather than simply set the table.

They like her, and I'm happy about that. She spends a good amount of time with them, and if I can talk her into working full time through the summer, she'll be spending even more time with them. So, it's good that they want to help her and don't give her a hard time about things.

Fifteen minutes later, I walk into the dining room and find that everyone has food on their plates, along with some salad and a piece of bread, and the other three are waiting for me to join them.

"This is fancy." I sit at the head of the table and take it all in. Not only did I not have to do this myself, but it looks nice, and no one is yelling or arguing over anything.

"Erin said the polite thing to do is to wait to eat until our whole party has arrived," Johnny says. "That means you."

I chuckle and look at the woman at the other end of the table. She's grinning and looks...*happy*.

"Well, I'm here, so let's dig in."

"Good, because I'm *hungry*," Holly says as she takes a bite of her bread. Holly always goes for the bread first. She's my carb girl.

"Johnny, you should tell your dad about what happened at school today."

I blink at my son. "Did something bad happen?"

"No, it was *good*," he says. "I got an A in math."

I blink again and then reach over to give him a fist bump. "That's my boy. Good job, buddy. That's another reason for some cake."

Dinner is actually fun, full of chatter about school and my day at work, and Erin even shares some fun stories about her customers that make us all laugh.

Finally, it's time for cake.

"We tried to make the colors the same as the Seattle football team," Johnny informs me. "But we got this one too purple."

"I think it's pretty," Holly adds.

"Why the Seattle team?" I ask Erin, who just shrugs.

"I like them," is all she says before taking a bite. "Oh, my goodness, this is *delicious*. You guys did the best job ever. I've never had a cake this good."

Both kids preen under Erin's praise, and it isn't long before we've cleaned up from dinner, and the kids are ready to head up for showers. I'm relieved to have a few minutes alone with Erin.

"Thanks for dinner," Erin says as she walks toward the door with her purse and jacket. "I'll see you on Monday."

"Don't you want to take this cake with you? It's yours."

"I can't eat a whole cake," she says with a laugh. "You guys eat it. Share it with your parents or something."

"If you're sure. Hey, Erin—"

I'm interrupted by Johnny yelling out, "Daaaaaaaad!"

Erin laughs. "You go. I'll see you next week."

I don't want her to leave yet. I want to *talk* to her, the way we did by the fire last week. Jesus, I want to kiss her again more than I want my next breath. She should be living here, on the ranch. She's here most of the time anyway.

But when Johnny yells for me again, I blow out a breath, resigned to discussing the living arrangements with her another time. "Yeah, I'll see you next week. Drive safe."

Erin waves, and then she's gone, and I hurry up the stairs to the bathroom.

"What's up?"

"I lost another tooth!" Johnny holds the small tooth in his fingers triumphantly. "Maybe I'll get another fiver."

I can't help but laugh at that. My kids come up with the funniest things sometimes.

"I bet you do," I reply and get the shower started for him. "Now, let's get you clean."

When both kids are clean and in their pajamas, we're settled downstairs to watch some TV before bedtime. This has always been one of my favorite times of the day.

I know that a day will come when my kids won't want to snuggle up with me on the couch, so I'm enjoying this quiet time with them.

Suddenly, my phone rings, and Erin's name lights up the screen. Did she forget something?

"Hello?"

"Rem?" I can hear the panic in her voice, and it has me scooting to the edge of the couch. "I'm sorry, but I'm in the ditch. I can't get out. I need help."

Her words come out all at once, and I glance over to see that both of my kids have heard her. Their eyes are round with worry.

"Are you hurt?" I ask immediately as I stand.

"No." She pauses. "No, I don't think so. But the Suburban—"

"How far toward town did you get?" I ask, interrupting her.

"About halfway, maybe."

"I'm on my way. Stay where you are."

"I can't really go anywhere," she says with a forced laugh. "Please hurry."

"I'm on my way," I say once more, gentling my tone. "I'll be right there."

I hang up and turn to the kids, who are also standing in the middle of the room.

"We have to save her," Holly announces.

"I'll go get her, but you two are going to Grandma and Grandpa's house. It's safest."

They don't argue and move faster than I've ever seen them move before, grabbing their jackets and pushing their feet into shoes before rushing out to the Jeep.

When we pull up to the small house my parents live in now, Mom answers the door, worry on her pretty face.

"What's going on?"

"I need a favor."

CHAPTER NINE
ERIN

"Holy shit." I drop my phone in my lap, relieved that Remington's on his way, and take a deep breath. "Holy shit."

Feeling perilously close to hyperventilating, I lean forward and press my forehead to the steering wheel.

I can*not* believe that I put Remington's Suburban in the ditch. I don't even know if it's okay. I haven't tried to get out. Well, I didn't try all *that* hard.

I just called him as soon as it happened. I was on the verge of tears and a panic attack, but hearing his voice calmed me right down.

I could have called Millie or Brooks, but Rem was the first person who popped into my head. He's *not* grumpy all the time, he's just...serious. He has the weight of the world on his shoulders. His kids adore him, and I can admit that I feel an intense attraction to him.

It isn't Millie or Brooks that I want to come help me.

It's Remington.

I've just managed to slow my breathing and get my heart rate in check when I see the Jeep pull up behind me. Remington, wearing a frown on that handsome face, hurries over to the driver's side and opens the door.

"Are you okay?" he asks immediately, cupping my cheek in his hand as he stares into my eyes intently.

"Yeah." I swallow hard and nod. "Just shook up. I'm not hurt."

I unclip the seat belt and turn to him, embarrassed to find that my lower lip wants to quiver.

"I don't know why I want to cry."

"Adrenaline," he says and simply pulls me into his arms, holding me tightly against him. "Scared the fuck out of me. What happened?"

"There was a deer." I can't help it; I break down into tears. My adrenaline is through the roof.

"Fucking deer," he mutters as he tightens his arms and comforts me. "Come on, let's get you into the Jeep, and I'll see what's up with the Suburban."

I nod and let him lead me to the passenger side of the Jeep. Once he gets me all settled in the seat, he drags his fingertips down my cheek, as if he just can't keep himself from touching me.

"I'll be right back."

I nod and offer him a brave smile as he shuts my door and walks back to the Suburban. He takes a quick look around the entire car, then hurries back to the Jeep and gets inside.

"It doesn't look like there's much damage. I'll have a couple of the ranch hands come get it in the morning."

"Will it be okay out here all night?"

He glances over at me and grins. "It's not going anywhere. Come on, let's go home."

"Uh, Rem?"

"Yeah?"

"I live in town."

"I'm taking you to *my* home." Without any further discussion, he flips the Jeep around to head back to the ranch. "I don't want you alone tonight."

"I'm sorry," I begin, shaking my head. "I should have called Brooks or Millie. I shouldn't have bothered you because you were probably in the middle of putting the kids to bed, but you were the first person that came to mind when it happened."

"You absolutely *should* have called me," he disagrees, his hands white on the steering wheel where he grips it.

"I don't have anything at your place. Clothes or toiletries."

"I'm sure I have everything you'll need for one night." He glances my way. "You're obviously still upset, Doc. You're shaky and as pale as the snow on a January morning. I don't want you to go home alone. Besides, I need to make sure that you're not hurt."

"I'm *not*." I clear my throat. "But I guess you're right. I don't want to be alone right now. What a way to end my birthday, huh?"

"It's not over yet," is all he says as he turns into his driveway. We're quiet as he parks and leads me back inside the house. I can still smell the cake I helped the kids bake. The TV is on in the family room.

"Where are the kids?"

"With my parents," he replies and leads me to the kitchen. "Let's boost you up onto the counter."

Before I can object, Rem grips my hips and lifts me onto the countertop, and I raise an eyebrow.

"Why am I up here?"

"So I can check you over," he replies, looking into my eyes. "Did you hit your head?"

"No. Seriously, it didn't hit hard. I just went into the *ditch*. To avoid a deer. And yes, I know that you're not supposed to do that, but I couldn't live with myself if I hit and killed a poor, defenseless deer."

"Hmm," is all he says as he goes to work, checking me over. I admit, I *like* having his hands on me, even if he is just making sure that I'm not injured.

"Rem?" He pats down my legs, and I want to wrap them around his waist. "I'm *fine*."

With a sigh, he rests his forehead against mine, and for the first time since I met him, he seems...vulnerable.

And that's just as sexy as his firm muscles and handsome face.

Unable to hold back, I frame his face in my hands. "Thank you for coming to my rescue."

"You should move out here, to the ranch."

I blink, then scoot back so I can look at him better. "What?"

"You heard me. You're here most of the time anyway."

"I can't just move here, Remington." I scoot off the

counter and walk away from him. "I have an apartment. I have another job."

"You can quit the other job."

"Whoa." I hold up my hand, stopping him. "No. I *need* that job. Besides, I like it there."

Rem pulls his hand down his face in agitation. "Obviously, I'm fucking this all up. I'm not trying to be a controlling prick. I'm being logical."

"Logical." I laugh at that and pace away from him. "It's not at all logical for me to quit the job that I need."

"Listen, I was going to ask you to work full time through the summer anyway," he says. "I'll need the help, and my mom enjoys having more free time. We'll renegotiate your salary for that, and I'll more than make up for what you'd lose by quitting the coffee shop."

"I'm not quitting." Yes, I sound stubborn, and I don't care. "But maybe I could go down to one day a week."

"Why would you do that?"

"Because they're like family to me," I reply, my voice raising. "They gave me a chance when I moved here, and I love it there. I want to stay."

"Fine." He sighs and shoves his hands into his pockets, which I've discovered he does when he's agitated.

"And I don't want to move out of my apartment." My voice has quieted, but I feel just as strongly about this. "I rent from Roger Sherman. Do you know him?"

"Sure."

"He's alone. I like him, and I want to stay living nearby, in case he needs me."

"I'm not saying you can't have any ties to town. If

you want to go visit Roger every single day, I say do it. I just don't want you driving back and forth so late or early in the day that it's dangerous. If you're here more and more, it only makes sense that you would live here."

"As your nanny."

Now his eyes narrow, and his jaw tightens.

"Listen, I'm going to just be brutally honest here because that's how I was raised, and I like spelling things out. I feel the chemistry between us. The attraction. Do you think I don't want you to kiss me again? Because I totally do."

He takes his hands out of his pockets and balls them into fists.

"But I'm not moving in here, and into your bed, when you have two little kids here who—"

"Jesus, that's not what I'm asking," he says, shaking his head. "I'm fucking this up. Come here."

He reaches for my hand and leads me through the house to a doorway at the end of the house that's always been closed. When he opens it, my jaw drops.

There's a pretty queen-sized brass bed dressed with white linens. A wooden dresser is on one wall with a big mirror over it, and there's a chair by the window that looks perfect for curling up with a book or gazing out to the mountains and pasture.

"There's an en suite bathroom," he says, gesturing to the door. "*This* would be your room. I'm not going to confuse my kids, Erin. And I'm not asking you to do anything that you're uncomfortable with. The room is part of your salary, so you'd be saving money on rent anyway."

Well, when he puts it like that, it would help me out a lot.

"Yeah," he continues, "there's chemistry here. Attraction. Fucking hell, I want to toss you onto that bed and kiss every inch of your body so bad that I ache with it, but I'm not an asshole. There's a line."

"There's a line that we both seem to want to cross," I toss back at him and watch as those eyes narrow on me once more. "Like I said, I'm being honest. But I do work for you. I need the job, and if that means that we keep this strictly professional, then that's what we'll do."

"Do you think I can't do both? Be professional *and* have a personal relationship with you?"

"Maybe you can. Maybe it's me who can't."

His sigh is loud and deep as he watches me from across the room. "Why didn't you tell me that it's your birthday?"

I blink in surprise at the change in subject. "We may have chemistry, but it's not like we talk a lot, Rem. It would have been weird if, in the middle of you telling me what to make for dinner, I interrupted with, *'By the way, it's my birthday tomorrow.'*"

"Here's what we're going to do," he says quietly as he shoves his hands back into his pockets. "We're going to *talk.* I want to get to know you better. And I'd like for you to move in here."

"I'll talk with Roger tomorrow."

He lifts an eyebrow. "That was easy."

"I'm *not* easy. But I'm also not stupid. I've had safety drilled into me my entire life, so I won't argue that it's safer to stay out here. And, yeah, I want to get to know you better, too."

He rocks back on his heels, watching me carefully before walking to me. I don't back away because I know what he's going to do, and I've been wanting it since that night at the bonfire.

As soon as he reaches me, my hands dive into his thick, dark hair, and I hold on tight as he kisses the ever-loving hell out of me. It's hot and full of need and makes me feel so desired in a way I never have before.

This time, he lifts me, and I wrap my legs around him, clinging to him as he kisses me like he's drowning and I'm his lifeline.

"So fucking sweet," he murmurs against my lips. "Jesus, you're so damn sweet."

I moan and press myself even harder against him just as someone's phone starts to ring.

"Damn it," he mutters. "It's my mom."

I grin. "I haven't heard that line since high school."

Remington laughs and sets me on my feet before pulling out his phone. After one last lust-filled look at me, he answers.

"Hey, Mom. Yeah, she's fine. I brought her here to the ranch because she was a little shook up. Yeah, I'll come get the kids here in just a minute. I'm sure they're tired and ready for bed. No, you don't have to do it. I'll be there soon. Thanks, Mom. Bye."

"Is it going to freak out the kids if I'm here?"

"No. They'll be happy to see that you're safe. They were worried about you, too. I'm going to go get them really quick. Make yourself at home here."

"I don't have anything with me to make myself at home with," I remind him with a rueful smile. "But thanks. It's a really nice room."

"I'll get you some things once I get back. Or, if you want to, go on up to my room and grab a T-shirt to sleep in and whatever you want out of my bathroom."

I raise an eyebrow in surprise. "It's okay. I can wait."

"Your call," he says with a shrug. "I'll be right back."

He turns to leave, but then rushes back and kisses me, more gently than before, but no less passionately.

"That's gonna have to tide me over for a bit," he murmurs. "Be right back, Doc."

He winks, and then he's gone, and I can't help but touch my tingling lips.

"What a weird birthday," I murmur.

"WELL, DAMN." Roger sighs and looks so sad it makes me want to break down into tears. "I'll sure be sad to see you go."

"I'm not going very far," I assure him. "And I'll still be able to come visit. You haven't seen the last of me, Roger."

He smiles, but it doesn't reach his eyes. "It's okay, honey. I know you have the best of intentions. But people move on. As they should. I'm glad that you're enjoying your time at the ranch. I always liked John Wild a lot. He's a good man. Has good kids, too."

"They're all very nice people," I agree with a nod. "I'm not kidding when I say that I'll still come by. It may not be quite as often, but what would I do without you?"

That brings the smile to his eyes as I reach out and pat his hand.

"I'm sorry if I'm leaving you in a lurch with the apartment."

"Oh, you're not. I'll rent it out quick enough. Rentals are hard to find around here."

"That's true. Would you like me to leave the furniture? I won't have a need for it, and it fits the apartment so well."

"I'll buy it from you," he says sternly, and from the look on his face, I know that he won't let me argue the point. "And I appreciate the offer."

I can't help myself. I walk right into Roger's arms for a long hug. "Thank you for everything, Roger. I am so grateful for everything you've done for me."

"It wasn't much." He tightens his hold and then releases me. "And you have done a lot for me, too. It's just what friends do, right?"

"Yeah." I smile at that and nod. "That's what friends do. I'll have the place all clean and ready for you by the end of the week."

"I appreciate it," he says. "And if you ever need a place, this one is waiting for you."

"That's wonderful to know." I kiss Roger's cheek and then head for the door. "Thanks, Roger."

"You betcha."

I was dreading that conversation. I don't like letting people down, and I know that Roger is lonely. But I'll find a way to visit with him at least once a week. Maybe more. Maybe the kids will enjoy a trip into town to bring Roger some soup or cookies.

I'll make it fun for all of us.

"Now I have to pack," I mutter to myself as I stare at everything in my apartment. Thankfully, I don't have a ton of stuff. Since Roger will keep the furniture, I just have to pack up my clothes and a few personal things, along with the stuff in the kitchen.

It shouldn't be too bad.

But rather than dig in, I flop onto the couch and open up social media so I can see what my cousins have been up to.

It looks like Hudson bought a new motorcycle. He looks so proud of the new Harley, so I give it a heart and comment under the photo, *Born to be wild,* with a wink emoji.

It seems that everyone has been busy and has no problem documenting it on socials, so it takes me a little while to comb through and comment here and there. Before I close out of the app, I see that I have a message.

It looks like it's from a spammer, so I don't open it before deleting and closing the app.

With a gusty sigh, I look around again.

"I really do have to pack." Remington and the kids will be back in a couple of hours to pick me up, and I'd like to have most of my things ready to go by then. They dropped me off so I could get some stuff done while Rem ran errands. He offered to help me, but I'd rather dive in and take care of it myself. It won't take long.

Thankfully, the Suburban was just fine after my incident. There wasn't even a scratch on the bumper. I really lucked out there. It's not good to wreck your boss's vehicle.

Or the hot guy you've been kissing and lusting after.

Especially when those people are one and the same.

"Okay, let's not overthink this," I mutter as I stand and walk into the bedroom, open the closet, and pull out my suitcases. "Just pack."

I have more than I originally thought, but I guess that happens when you live somewhere for any length of time. You accumulate things.

Luckily, Roger has a few empty boxes in his garage, and I'm able to finish gathering everything that I'll move out to the ranch with me. I'm just packing the last few things when there's a knock at my door.

When I pull it open, Remington stands on the other side, leaning on the doorjamb.

"You know," I say, and then have to pause so I can swallow hard. "You read about how hot it is when a guy leans on the doorjamb, but I had *no idea*."

A slow smile spreads over his lips as he looks me up and down. "Happy to oblige. Is that your stuff?"

He gestures to the two suitcases and three boxes in the living room.

"Yep."

"Where's the rest of it?"

"That's it."

His eyes turn to mine. "That's *all* of your stuff?"

"Yeah, I don't have much. Roger's keeping the furniture."

"Okay," Rem says as he walks in and lifts two boxes, one stacked on the other.

"Those are heavy, you know."

His eyes narrow. "I don't need to take insults from you."

With a laugh, I grab a suitcase and follow him down to the waiting Suburban. With one more trip each, we have everything piled into the vehicle, and Holly and Johnny are practically bouncing in their seats as I get in next to Rem.

"You get to sleep over at our house," Holly announces. "We put special stuff in your room."

"Shut up," Johnny says. "It's a surprise."

"I'm not going to tell her what it is," Holly says in her own defense and then grins at me. "It's flowers, and I put my favorite teddy on your bed so you're not scared, since it's a strange place and all."

"Holly!" Johnny exclaims, but I laugh and look over at Rem as he puts the vehicle in gear.

"Come on," he says as he pulls away from the curb. "Let's go home before Holly spills any more secrets."

CHAPTER TEN
REMINGTON

"Hey, Mom." I smile at her as she holds her front door open for me, inviting me inside. Do I have time for a chat with my mom today? Not really, but she requested that I come see her, and I learned *very* early in life to stay on my mother's good side. "What's up?"

"Does something have to be up for me to see my son?" she asks as she leads me to her kitchen, where she's already poured me a mug of black coffee and has a fresh huckleberry muffin waiting for me.

"Usually," I reply with a nod and sip the coffee, watching as she smiles over at me. "You look nervous. Whose ass do I have to kick?"

"You're so much like your father," she says with a sigh. "It's one of the things I love about you. Rem, I quit."

I feel my eyebrows climb in surprise. "I'm sorry?"

"I quit," she repeats, and then sighs again, louder this time. "I know that we've tried to find a new bookkeeper several times and that no one has worked out, but I'm serious when I tell you that you have thirty days to find someone and get them trained. This is business. Sure, it's a *family* business, but it's business all the same. I'm done working. I've done this job for almost forty years, and I am burned out. I want to enjoy my grandchildren, take trips with my husband, and maybe watch some Netflix without worrying about the financial side of this ranch."

"I know, Mom." I let out a sigh of my own and sip more coffee. "And you deserve to do all of that. I'll make it happen. There are offices in town that I can hire to take it over. Thanks for being patient."

"I love you, and I can see that you're already overburdened. More so than what your dad and I had to deal with, now that the ranch has expanded and is more profitable than ever, and on one hand, I'm sorry for that."

"Sorry that we're successful?"

"Sorry that it's not as simple as it used to be. That you're pulled away from your kids more and more. However, I will say that I really like Erin. She's smart and funny, and the kids adore her. She's been a lovely addition to the ranch."

I nod and can't help but smile a little at the thought of my beautiful nanny. "They do love her. Things are going smoothly there, especially over the past couple of weeks since she moved in. She's a huge help."

"And she's beautiful."

I narrow my eyes, watching my mother. "Are you trying to play matchmaker?"

"I don't have to," she replies with a big laugh. "Honey, I can see how you look at her."

"And how is that?"

"Like you've waited for her all your life. And that's something else that I love about her. She's awoken something in you that's been sleeping for a very long time."

"I think it's weird to be sitting in your kitchen, discussing whether or not I'm hot for my kids' nanny."

"Oh, please. I may be your mom, but I'm not dead when it comes to these things. I see it, and I like it very much. Erin's good for you."

I frown over at her. "How is that?"

"You've smiled more in the past month than you have since Holly was born. That tells me everything I need to know."

"Mom—"

"All right, I'll stop." She holds both hands up in surrender as my phone rings.

I frown down at my dad's name.

"Are you and Dad in cahoots? Now he's calling me."

"I have no idea what he's calling for," she assures me as I accept the call.

"Hello?"

"Hey, son, there's a vehicle I don't recognize on the property, making its way to your house. Thought I'd let you know."

"Thanks, I'll head there right now." I click off and turn back to my mom. "I have to go check something out. I'll look for that bookkeeper right away."

"Thanks, honey." She boosts herself up and kisses my cheek before I head back out to the Jeep and to the farmhouse.

Sure enough, there's a rental SUV sitting in front of the house and a man walking up to my front door.

"Can I help you?" I step out of the Jeep and toward the porch, and the man turns to me, pinning me with sharp blue eyes.

I know that face.

"I'm looking for Erin Montgomery," he says, his voice all business. "I'm told she moved out here."

"That's right." *Where do I know this guy from?* "Can I tell her who's calling?"

"Her father," he replies easily and offers me a hand to shake. "Will."

"Will *Montgomery*," I reply slowly as I shake his hand and realize exactly who he is. "Erin didn't mention that her father is a football legend."

"Yeah, well, that doesn't surprise me. Is she here?"

"I believe so." I open the door, gesture for Will to follow me, and call out, "Erin? Are you here?"

The house stays quiet, and I can tell that no one is here.

"She took the kids to school this morning, but she usually comes back out to the ranch afterward." I frown and turn back to Will. "I'll call her."

"Please do. She won't answer me." His voice is full of frustration.

Erin answers on the third ring. "Hello?"

"Hey, where are you? Are you at the ranch?"

"Yeah, I'm out at the barn. Do you need me?"

"I'll come to you," I reply and end the call as I turn back to Will. "I'll take you out to the barn."

"What exactly does my daughter do here, and why is she living with you?"

I stop at the sharpness in his voice and narrow my eyes at the older man. Sure, I'm starstruck, but he's on my property. "Erin took a live-in position as a nanny for my two young children. I can show you her room if you'd like."

"Yeah, I want to see it."

I lead him to the back of the house and open her door. "I won't go in there because it's an invasion of privacy, but this is her room."

Will sighs and steps just inside the door, looks around, then comes back out again. "Okay, let's go to the barn."

With a curt nod, I lead him back through the house.

"We'll take the Jeep," I say simply and wait for him to get in with me before setting off to the barn. "I want to make it clear that I'm not holding her captive here or anything. My kids love her."

"Of course, they do. She's the best there is," he says before rubbing his eyes. "She hasn't been returning my calls, and I decided to come out here to make sure she's safe."

"As a dad, I get that. I promise you, she's safe. You'll see for yourself."

I can't blame him for being worried. If Holly stopped taking my calls, I'd do the same thing.

As soon as we reach the barn, Will hops out of the Jeep, and we walk into the barn, where we find Erin mucking out a stall.

"You have my daughter shoveling shit?" Will demands, and Erin's head whips up, her eyes huge as she stares at her father.

"Dad? What are you doing here?" she demands as she leans her shovel against the wall.

"I have the same question," Will replies.

I hang back, cross my arms over my chest, and watch the show unfold.

"I work out here," Erin says with a scowl. "I mean, not *here*, in the barn. I was bored and came out to ask if there was anything I could do to help. But I work at the house as the nanny for Holly and Johnny. I already told Mom all of this."

"But you haven't told *me*," Will replies with frustration. "And you won't return my goddamn calls."

Erin bites her lower lip and winces.

"So, I chartered the jet and came out here, only to find that you're shacked up with *him*," he points his thumb at me, "and are out in a barn, shoveling shit. What in the actual hell, Erin?"

"First of all," Erin retorts, anger rising in her cheeks, "I'm a grown woman. If I want to shovel shit for a living, I will. Besides, I'm mucking out a stall, not simply *shoveling shit*. Second of all, I *like* it out here. I'm grateful that Remington gave me the job because I needed it."

That makes her shut up, and her eyes widen as if she didn't mean to say that.

"What do you mean, *you need it*?" Will asks, his voice suddenly very quiet.

"My car broke down." She tries to keep her voice

nonchalant, but it only aggravates Will more. "It's no big deal. I just needed a little extra income to pay for the repairs, that's all."

Without any regard for the fact that I'm standing here, along with Lucky and Bruiser across the barn, Will steps closer to his daughter and shoves his hands into his pockets.

"You have a trust fund with millions of dollars in it that's available to you with the click of a fucking button," he says, anger radiating through him. "You've made it clear how you feel about my money, but I will not have my daughter driving an unsafe car in a town where we have *zero* contacts, all because of your goddamn pride. Buy a new car, Erin."

Her chin lifts in defiance. "Remington lent me his vehicle until mine is fixed. I figured it out, Dad. Everything's fine."

"Everything's fine," he echoes and backs away from her. I can see the hurt in his eyes, and Erin must see it, too, because she rushes to him and wraps her arms tightly around him. He does the same, holding on to his little girl. "It's not fine, baby. You don't have to shovel shit to make ends meet."

"I'm not," she assures him, not letting go. "I'm honestly not. I really did come out here because I was bored. The kids are at school, and the house is too quiet. I really love the ranch, Dad. Let me show you around a little. I'm so happy to see you. I've missed you like crazy."

"Missed me so much that you won't talk to me?"

Erin offers her dad a watery smile. "I knew you'd

react this way, and I didn't want to have the argument. I didn't expect you to just show up. Wait, where's Mom? Are you guys staying at London and Drew's condo?"

Who are London and Drew? The family has a condo in Bitterroot Valley? Obviously, I don't know *anything* about this woman, and that unnerves me. Will may have questions, but I have a shitload of my own, and I intend to get them answered *today*.

"No, I came alone, and I'm headed back before dinner."

"You didn't even *tell* Mom you were coming, did you?" Erin gasps. "Dad, you'll be in so much trouble."

"No, I won't." He shakes his head, sweeps her hair off her cheek, and takes another deep breath. "Let's go outside and talk."

"Okay." As they walk past me, Erin mouths, *I'm sorry.*

When they're out of earshot, Lucky joins me. "Is that Will Montgomery? The greatest quarterback Seattle ever had? The Hall of Famer?"

"Looks like it."

"Did you know he was Erin's daddy?"

"Nope."

Lucky nods thoughtfully. "Okay, then."

He wanders away to get back to work, and I see Will and Erin walking slowly toward the house, in deep conversation. Deciding to stay out of their way, I get back into the Jeep and drive home, giving them a wide berth. Once inside, I go directly to my office.

So, Erin doesn't really *need* the job. Mine or the one at

the coffee shop. She's, what, out here playing the part of the broke girl?

I don't like games, especially when it comes to people who have access to my kids. Particularly when it's women that I want in my bed.

I feel like a fool.

An hour later, the front door opens, and I hear Erin call out, "Rem? Do you have a minute?"

I walk out and take her in. She looks...contrite.

"What do you need?" I ask.

"My dad would like a minute."

I nod and walk past her, not touching her, and join her father on the porch. I lean against the railing.

"What can I do for you?"

Will shakes his head and looks out over my pasture, to the mountains beyond. "What kind of security do you have out here? It doesn't look like there's much."

I raise an eyebrow. "I don't know if you noticed, but we're in the middle of nowhere. What kind of security would you like me to have?"

"Cameras, alarms, a gate to start."

"I have cameras," I reply. "I don't need a gate. We don't have the kind of crime you're used to in the city."

"You have children," Will says, turning to me. "You understand what it is to worry about their safety."

"Of course, I do. And I know that they're safe here. They're safe in town. I'm not ever going to put anyone or anything that I love at risk. The most dangerous thing out here is the wildlife, not the people."

"She was once almost taken," he says quietly, his

blue eyes full of regret as he levels them at me. "Because of me. Because of who I am."

"Are you saying that *my* children aren't safe because she's here with them?" My stomach clenches at the thought.

"No." He shakes his head. "Not at all. I'm saying that I worry, and I'll always worry. She's twenty-five now, and I'll worry when she's sixty-five."

"Why are you telling me all of this?"

"Because she lives out here, and because I see the way you look at my daughter. I don't exactly love it, but" —he shrugs—"not much I can do about that."

And that's twice today that someone has mentioned to me that I look at Erin in a certain way. Jesus, do I have *lovesick* written across my forehead?

"She's safe here," I say firmly. "I give you my word, Mr. Montgomery. I have questions for her because I didn't realize that *you* are her dad, but she's safe here."

"You didn't know," he says as realization dawns. "About her family, about her money."

"No." The answer is curt because hell, my feelings are a little bruised. "I didn't. Look, I don't give a rat's ass about money, but I do care about honesty."

He nods at that. "I'm headed back to Seattle. I'm going to leave my number with you." He sets a card on the railing. "If you or Erin ever need *anything*, all you have to do is call."

"Mr. Montgomery—"

"My daughter lives in your house," he interrupts. "You can call me Will."

"Will. I don't *need* anything. This ranch is successful beyond my father's wildest dreams. If anything, my parents might have wondered if Erin was here because of *our* money, not the other way around."

That makes him laugh. "Well, that's something, I guess. It's frustrating when your kids no longer want or need your help. When they pull away. I love her."

"I know you do. You wouldn't be here otherwise."

He pats me on the shoulder. "I think you do understand. I have to get back to Seattle before my wife divorces me."

"You said you wouldn't be in trouble."

"Oh, that was a bald-faced lie. Megan's been champing at the bit to get out here to visit Erin. But it was a spur-of-the-moment decision when Erin sent me to voicemail again this morning."

"Bring your wife out here anytime. I hear there's a condo you can use."

"And you didn't know about that either," he says with a laugh and pats me on the shoulder again. "Good luck with that one. She'll keep you on your toes. But fuck with her, and they'll never find your body."

And with that, he walks down the steps to his rental. Erin walks out and joins me at the railing as her father waves at us and pulls away.

"I have so many questions," I murmur as Erin and I watch Will drive down the driveway and around the bend, disappearing from sight.

"I know," she says with a sigh. "First of all, I never meant to keep who my family is a secret."

"Didn't you?" I turn to her, wanting to see her face. God, I want to touch her so badly that my fingers ache, but I can't. I need answers first.

"No. I didn't. They just didn't come up."

"That's not true. You made that cake in Seattle colors, and when I asked why, you simply said because you like that team."

"I *do* like the team."

"But you had the perfect opportunity to tell me *why* you like the team. You didn't do that. You never expand on your cousins or your immediate family. Who are London and Drew, and why do they own a condo here?"

"Drew is my cousin, and London is his fiancée. Drew is the quarterback coach for Seattle, and London owns the team."

"London *Ambrose*," I repeat with a slow nod, putting the puzzle together. "One of the wealthiest women in the country. Your cousin is engaged to a billionaire."

"Yes. He is. And you don't have to sound so fucking judgmental about it."

"I'm not judging—"

"Yes, you are. And I've had to deal with shit like this my *entire* life. I have *very* famous people in my family, but to me, they're just people I love. I *love* them, Remington. I get tired of meeting new people, and when they find out who my family is, all they want to talk about is the celebrity piece of it. They don't care about who they are as *individuals*. Do you know that the last person I dated didn't really give a flying fuck about me? He just kept asking when he could meet my dad."

"He was an asshole."

"Yeah. He was. That happens more often than not. So no, I'm not embarrassed or ashamed of where I came from, but for just once in my life, who they are wasn't a factor for me. No one knew or cared here. I was just Erin, the new girl, living a pretty normal life that I really liked. And now, here we are. You're asking questions and looking at me like I'm a fucking science experiment."

"Stop that shit."

CHAPTER ELEVEN
ERIN

His eyes are hot, the gold flecks practically shooting fire as he rounds on me, still not touching me.

"You're not a goddamn science experiment. You're a woman living *in my home*, taking care of my kids. For fuck's sake, Erin, it's more than that, and we both know it. I *want* you. I've wanted you since the first time I saw you in that coffee shop. You said yourself that the feeling's mutual, yet I've been thrown for one hell of a loop."

"Why? Because my father's famous? Because I have a trust fund at the ready that I could use to make my life easier?"

"Yes."

Well, at least he didn't lie about it. Sure, it stings, but he didn't lie.

"I didn't figure you for a gold digger." I regret the words as soon as they're out of my mouth, and I clamp my hands over my lips as Rem's eyes narrow into pissed-off slits.

"Do you think," his voice is quiet and way too calm. Anger radiates from him, his muscles bunching in agitation. "That I give one shit about your motherfucking money?"

"No." I shake my head. Jesus, I want to reach for him, hug him, and soothe him. "No, I don't, and that was so completely out of line."

"But you do think it because otherwise, you wouldn't have said it. You threw me for a loop because I see a man walking up to my front door, and it's Will fucking Montgomery, who happens to be looking for his *daughter*. That threw me for a loop. Hell, it would have thrown anyone, but don't ever think that I give a shit about your money."

"I *don't* think it." I drop my head into my hands now, so embarrassed that tears threaten. "How can we know absolutely *nothing* about each other, after all of these weeks, and you still want to kiss me?"

Wait, did I just say that last part out loud?

Fuck me.

"Let's sit." Rem gestures to the chairs on the porch, and I drop down into one and pull my legs up to my chest because I need to hold on to something. "We have a few hours before the kids come home, so let's take some time to actually get to know each other."

"I'm sure you have other things to do."

He shakes his head. "Nothing more important than this. Obviously, you have some frustration surrounding your dad and the money he made. Talk to me about that."

I lick my lips, trying to pull my jumbled thoughts together. "It was *wonderful* to see him. I haven't been home in a few months, and I have been missing them. I love my dad, and we get along well 99 percent of the time. He's fun. Will Montgomery is the class clown of the family, you know? He's funny, and everyone wants to be near him. Even me."

I stretch my legs out now and cross them at the ankles, looking out at the pasture.

"The biggest bone of contention between us is money. I have a trust fund, like you heard. It's not simply a couple million, Rem. It's more like fifty million. It's an uncomfortable amount of money."

"For some," he agrees, and I smile.

"Yeah, for some. Obviously, I didn't grow up poor. The opposite, actually. I never wanted for anything, and I'm grateful for that. Luck of the draw, birth-wise, you know?"

He nods, listening.

"And it's not just my dad that's done well. We have actors, other pro sports players, financial gurus, freaking *rock stars*. Leo Nash is my uncle. Did you know that?"

Rem blinks rapidly in surprise. "No, I didn't."

"Yeah. So, there are a lot of celebrities in our family. A *lot* of money. Influence. And I'm going to be honest with you right now, Grumpy."

His lips twitch. "Please do."

"It makes me so fucking uncomfortable." I cover my face with my hands again.

"Look at me."

I shake my head. "I feel so ungrateful. What's wrong with me that I'm the only one in my entire huge, loud, crazy family to feel like I had to flee? I've known for a while now that I wanted a quieter life. A simple one. The big city isn't for me, even though Seattle is where everyone I love lives. I hate the noise, the traffic, the crime. I was just itching to move away. And then all my cousins—I'm super close to all of my cousins and their spouses—decided to take a ski trip to Montana late last year. I'd already told my cousin Drew that I was thinking about leaving Seattle, and I'm glad I did because he was on that trip, and I was able to bounce things off of him. Do you have someone like that?"

"Yeah." He nods, and I love that he's watching me, *listening* to me. "I do."

"Good, because we all need that. Anyway, we got here, and as soon as we landed, I thought to myself, *This is home.* I actually skipped out on the skiing and most of the touristy things with my cousins because I wanted to absorb Bitterroot Valley. I wandered through town, ate at restaurants, and talked to people. I applied for the job at the coffee shop before the others even left town."

"And you didn't leave with them."

"No." I shake my head. "I didn't leave with them. They were worried, of course, but they also knew me, and they trusted me. The hardest part was telling my parents because, although I've been out of the house for a while now, I know they always assumed that I'd stay in Seattle. I don't like disappointing them."

"I have a question."

I sit back and nod. "Go ahead."

"I understand wanting to leave the city, but why not use the trust fund when you need it?"

"It's not my money." I shrug and then laugh. "And I've been told often to stop being so stubborn, but it's *not* my money. It's my parents' money."

"That they set aside for *you*."

I lick my lips again. "It's nice to know it's there for a true emergency, but I wanted to make my own way. It's always been important to me to be self-sufficient and independent. My family doesn't understand. They think it's stubbornness, but it's just how I want my life to be."

"Your car going tits-up isn't a true emergency? Jesus, Doc, what do you want, to be homeless before you use it?"

"Yes. I know it sounds so weird, but I'm doing fine on my own. Sure, I've had a few bumps here and there, but I'm fine. I'm not hungry or cold. My bills are paid. I enjoy my jobs. I don't have any reason to complain. If I hadn't found the position with you, I probably would have broken down and used the trust for a new car because we're in the boonies in Montana, and it's not like I can ride the bus or something. But it worked out."

"It worked out," he repeats and then lets out a gusty laugh.

"Okay, it's my turn to ask personal questions because I want to change the subject."

Rem nods. "Fair enough. Ask away."

"What happened to the kids' mom?"

That seems to surprise him because he frowns and leans forward onto his knees, staring down at his hands.

"She died," he says before rubbing his hand over his face and sitting back once more. "She died in childbirth with Holly."

"Oh, shit." I want to reach out to him, but I don't. Instead, I scratch my fingers through my hair. "I'm sorry, Rem. I wasn't expecting that."

"Neither was I. We didn't know that anything was wrong. Jessica went into labor, and the labor progressed normally, but right after she delivered Holly, she collapsed. Everything happened so fast. I was pushed out of the room, and the next thing I knew, a doctor was telling me that my wife had died."

He turns to me now and sighs.

"She had what they called an amniotic fluid embolism, and it killed her within minutes."

"My God. I'm so sorry, Remington. Truly."

"I'm sorry, too." He rubs his hand over his face again. "And because we're being honest here, I'll go on to say that I *am* very sorry that Johnny and Holly will never know her. She was a good woman, and she loved her babies."

"But?"

"It's not a *but*. It's more of an *and*. Jessica and I got married because she was pregnant with Johnny. I know that sounds old-fashioned and stupid, but it's true. She was a good friend to me, she got pregnant, and we decided to try to make a go of the relationship. It wasn't bad. It was...*fine*. She was a good mom and a great friend. We built a good life together, but..."

He trails off.

"But there wasn't passion."

"No. There wasn't passion. I never would have wanted what happened to happen to her, and I would have done anything to stop it if I could have."

"Of course, you would have. Just because you weren't head over heels for her doesn't mean that you didn't care about her. It was tragic for all of you. I'm very sorry that happened."

"I was a mess for a while," he says with a slight smile. "I thought I'd be able to figure it out because I'd had one kid before, and I remembered the sleepless nights and diapers and all the things. But it's so different when you have to do it by yourself."

"I can't even imagine."

"Thank God for my parents and the rest of my family. It was a group effort for a long time. Hell, it still is. But it also made me bond with them in ways I may not have if Jessica was here. I don't know... I get all philosophical about it when I start to think about it."

"I don't mind philosophy," I reply with a smile. "They're very well-adjusted, happy, confident kids, Rem. If you ever start to wonder if you're doing a good job, just look at them. You are."

He blinks and blows out a breath.

"Are you still mad at me?" I ask.

"No."

"Good."

He takes a deep breath. "Come here, Doc."

I cross to him and sit in his lap, loop my arms around him, and hug him close. His arms immediately circle my back and clench tightly as he buries his face in my neck and takes a long breath.

"No more *avoiding* topics," I promise him. "Even if it's uncomfortable."

"Deal. And if there's a question, we answer truthfully."

"I did—" I sniff when he raises an eyebrow. "Okay."

"Your uncle is really Leo Nash?"

I narrow my eyes. "Yes."

"Nash is my favorite band."

I can't help but laugh as I get off his lap. "Same. He's great in concert. Now, I should head for town because I'm going to get the kids a snack from the coffee shop before I pick them up."

I wish I had more alone time with him. I want to ask more questions about his family and the ranch. I want him to kiss me again.

"Hey, Doc."

I turn back to him. "Yeah?"

In reply, he frames my face and neck in his hands and lowers his mouth to mine, kissing me gently. Hypnotically. Jesus, the man makes my knees turn to jelly, and his hands drift down to my waist so he can hold me up as he devours my mouth.

When he pulls back, his mouth just an inch from

mine, his gorgeous hazel eyes are intent on me as we both fight to catch our breath.

"That's some spicy shit," I whisper, and that seems to break the moment, making him laugh.

"Spicy shit," he echoes. "Tonight, after the kids go to bed, let's talk some more."

I raise an eyebrow. "Just talk?"

"We'll start there."

"Sounds like a plan."

"I SAVED SOME GOODIES FOR YOU," Millie informs me as I walk up to the counter at the coffee shop. "I know the kids love the cookies, and I grabbed you the last orange-cranberry muffin."

"You're the best," I reply with a grin as I accept the bag of sugared treats from her. "I'm also going to need an iced latte."

"Sure. You never drink coffee this late in the day." Millie frowns at me as she gets the espresso ready. "What's up?"

"My dad showed up at the ranch today."

Her eyebrows climb. "Like, from Seattle?"

"Yeah, and he had words with Remington, and I'm not sure what those words were because it was private. But that's not the worst of it, and I need you to *not* get mad at me right now, okay?"

"I'm super confused," she admits as she shakes my

iced latte and sets it on the counter for me. "Why would I get mad that your dad showed up at the ranch?"

"Because my dad is Will Montgomery, the football player."

Millie frowns. "I don't watch football."

That makes me laugh, and for some reason, it puts me at ease. "He's famous. A lot of my family is famous."

"Okay."

"And you don't care."

"Not really, no. Wait, did Rem give you shit?"

"Well, yeah, and I get it. I mean, I'm around his kids a lot, and—"

"And that has nothing to do with whether or not your dad is famous. Jesus, I'm gonna have to tell Rem to get a fucking life."

"No, it was fine. Really. Because, um—"

"Okay, just say it."

"Fine, but I'm going to need you to hold your ick factor here. I want to jump his bones."

"Remington's?"

"Of *course*, Remington's."

"Why?" She scowls as if she's totally unaware that her oldest brother is fucking hot as hell.

"Well, he's hot, Millie. And there's chemistry between us that is *smoking*. Like, I'm surprised that the smoke alarms don't go off just from the way he looks at me."

"Ew. But okay. Just, maybe not when the kids are awake, you know?"

"Gross. Of *course* not, Millie. In fact, I've been holding

back a lot because of the kids. They live there, and they're young, and it's not appropriate—"

"It's not like you're the nanny, and he's having an *affair* with you while his wife is asleep upstairs. That's way different. Sure, be discreet around the kids, but I say do what makes you both happy. Rem hasn't been *happy* in a long damn time. If you're what does that for him, great. But maybe I'll see if the kids want to stay at my place tonight."

"Really?"

"Sure, we haven't had a sleepover in a while. We can watch movies and pop some popcorn. I'll text Rem and tell him that I'm grabbing them from school."

"You don't have to do that."

"I know that I don't have to." Millie grins at me. "But I see the look in your eyes. This way, you don't have to worry about anyone waking up or asking questions. Have fun, babe."

"You're the best friend a girl could have."

"I know. You'd do the same for me." She opens the bag of treats and passes me my muffin. "Go get ready for your night of sexy fun. Just saying that does make me want to gag, though. I don't want any of the details."

I laugh as I head for the door, and once there, I turn back to her. "Hey, Millie?"

"Yeah?"

"You might not know who my dad is, but Leo Nash is my uncle."

Millie's eyes go wide, her jaw drops, and I laugh with joy.

"See you!"

I DECIDE ON PIZZA.

Sure, I could make a big dinner and try to impress Remington with my kitchen prowess, but at the end of the day, I go with the easy way out because I have to take a shower and shave my legs.

I *desperately* need to shave my legs.

But before I can head to the bedroom, I notice that I have a notification from social media, which is weird because that *never* happens.

Opening the app, I see that it's another message from what looks like spam, so with a shake of my head, I delete it and double-check that the oven isn't on too hot —I don't want to burn the already-made pizza—and shift my attention back to the task at hand.

I hurry to my suite of rooms and immediately strip down to take a shower and get ready for Rem to come in from whatever he's doing on the ranch this afternoon.

He said earlier that he wants to talk more, and that's perfectly fine with me. We got off to a good start today in getting to know each other better, but there's still so much to learn about him. Besides, who doesn't like to talk over pizza?

I've just finished shaving both legs, along with all the other must-shave places, and am thinking about getting out of the shower when I hear two taps on the bathroom door just before I hear it open. The walls of this glass shower are completely steamed up, thank goodness.

"Doc?"

"That's me." I grin, hoping he can see an outline of me in here, giving him just a little tease.

"Is it true that Millie has the kids for the night?"

"I don't think that's something she would lie about. I'll be out of here in just a sec."

He's quiet, and I turn to the faucet and shut off the water. When I open the door, a *very* sexy Remington Wild is waiting for me, a towel in his hands.

He steps forward and wraps me in it, and I'm surprised to find that it's warm.

"Did you put this in the dryer?"

"No one likes a cold towel." His eyes, usually so stern and intense, are soft as he gently pats me dry with the towel. His gaze roams over me, and I don't even have time to feel at all self-conscious because the sheer joy in what he sees is written all over his face. "Jesus, you're beautiful."

"And you're overdressed."

He doesn't reply to that, simply continues to study me, touch me, and arouse me until I shiver and feel myself get wet.

"Are we going to do this right here in the bathroom?"

"No," he murmurs before kissing me gently on the forehead. "I just wanted to look at you. I hope that's okay."

"Are you kidding? Having someone else dry me off is damn hot. Who knew?"

He chuckles, kisses my cheek, and then tosses the towel aside.

"Holy shit," is all I can get out before I'm scooped up and carried to the bedroom, and Remington is kissing the fuck out of me. Talk about a shift from lazy and slow to hot and urgent.

His hands are firm on my ass, his fingertips *almost* close enough to touch my pussy, but just too far away, and I wrap my legs around him and hold on for my life as all coherent thought flees my mind.

"Jesus Christ, I've thought of this a thousand times," he says as he nibbles his way down my neck as he carries me. "You, wet and naked in my shower."

"Why are you so sexy?" I demand and frame his face in my hands, wanting him more than I've ever wanted anything else in my life. "You're just *so* fucking hot that I don't know what to do with myself."

With a groan, his lips return to mine, as if he just wants to *consume* me. He lays me down on the bed and journeys down my body, licking away the last of the water from the shower, stopping to nibble on a nipple and to brush his nose over my navel.

I'm a squirming mass of pure sensation as I reach for him, running my fingers gently down his stubbly face. "You need to get naked *now*."

He grins and shimmies out of his clothes, then joins me once more, but he doesn't lie next to me.

No, he parts my legs and lowers his face, right there in the end zone, feasting as if he's starving.

"Holy shit," I moan, reaching down to clutch his hair in my hands. "Fucking hell, Rem."

His mouth is *insane*. In mere seconds, I'm tossed into the stratosphere, coming apart at the seams, calling out for him as my body comes undone.

And then suddenly, I hear the rustle of protection, and he's braced over me, panting, watching me with hot eyes.

"You're so fucking beautiful." His voice is firm as he slowly pushes inside of me, the stretch feeling so good until he can't get any further, and his forehead rests on mine. "So sweet."

"Hard and fast," I instruct him, my core still quivering from the last orgasm and already feeling on the precipice of the next. "Fuck me hard and *fast*."

With his mouth on mine again, he starts to move, and I groan in frustration when it's *not* hard and fast.

It's hard.

But there's no fast.

"Rem."

"I've been waiting a long damn time for this," he says in my ear. "If you think I'm here for a quickie, you're dead wrong."

My back arches when he plants himself all the way inside of me and grinds against my pubis, against my *clit*.

I gasp, and his hand glides up my side, over my breast, and covers my throat. He doesn't squeeze, doesn't block my airway at all.

And it might be the sexiest thing anyone has ever done in my life.

With his eyes pinned to mine, he moves again, a little faster this time. His thumb rubs up and down over my jawline where he's gripped me.

He couldn't have turned me on more if his mouth was on my clit again.

"Remington," I whisper and close my eyes, *so close* to orgasm, but I feel him lower his face to my ear.

"Open your pretty eyes and watch me when you fucking come."

My eyes snap open, and with our gazes locked, I fall over into the most delicious orgasm ever, swamping me with emotion and sensation like I've never felt.

Rem's jaw clenches, but he doesn't close his eyes as he follows me over. When he takes his hand off my throat, the cool air makes me long for it to be there again.

"I liked that," I manage to get out, and he raises an eyebrow.

"Which part?"

"Well, all of it, but particularly the throat thing. Sexy."

His lips tip up into a soft smile, and he glides the backs of his fingers over my skin, up to my throat. But he doesn't grip; he doesn't *claim*.

"It didn't hurt you?"

"No," I whisper and kiss his shoulder.

"Good." He dips down to kiss me, rubs his nose against mine, and then rolls off of me and pulls me with him, still in his arms.

CHAPTER TWELVE
REMINGTON

"I thought about making you a big dinner," she says as she lays snuggled up in my arms. "But then I was running out of time, so I snagged us some pizza from Old Town."

Right now, I'd eat just about anything. I'm *starving*. But I don't love the idea of leaving this bed. Of leaving this *moment*.

Erin kisses my chin, then disentangles herself from me and walks back into the bathroom.

Everything about her is amazing. She has curves in all the right places, and she fits against me perfectly.

I hear the water running and decide to leave her room and head up to my own to clean up and put on some clothes.

When I walk into the kitchen, Erin's already there, with two pizzas on the island. She's in black leggings and a University of Washington sweatshirt that's full of holes, the neck is cut off, and it hangs over one shoulder.

And just like that, I'm hard again.

"Millie told me that you like sausage and onions and peppers, so that's what I got you."

"And what do *you* like?"

"Just plain ol' pepperoni. When I was a kid, I claimed that I was allergic to onions, but it turns out that I just hate them." She slides pieces of the pie onto plates, and we each open a bottle of beer and make our way into the family room, where we can sit on the couch.

I love that Erin feels comfortable enough to pull her feet up and wrap up in a blanket. "I'm glad that you feel comfortable here and have made it your home."

"It's a comfortable house," she says and takes a bite, then covers her mouth with her hand so she can speak more. "Everything here is cozy and comfy. Warm, you know?"

"Yeah, I get it."

"Did Jessica do that? Decorate and make it homey?"

I frown down into my pizza, and Erin reaches out for me and rests her hand on my shoulder.

"I'm sorry. It was just a curious question, but if you don't want to talk about that, it's totally okay."

"No, we agreed to talk more tonight, and this is part of that, right?" I take a bite and then reach out to take Erin's foot and pull it into my lap, massaging the arch of her foot. "We didn't live in this house when Jess was alive. My parents still lived here, and we lived in a house on the other side of the property, not too far from the barn. I've since turned that into a new bunkhouse for the ranch hands. Anyway, when my dad decided to retire and build a smaller house for him and Mom to live in, I packed up the old house and brought the kids here. I ended up buying new furniture because the old stuff didn't really fit in here. And it was time for a fresh start."

Erin takes a sip of her beer. "That makes sense. You have good taste in furniture."

I grin at her and then frown when I remember the conversation I had with my mom the other day.

"What's wrong?" Erin asks.

"Oh, I just remembered that I have to try to hire a new bookkeeper for the ranch. My mom's done the job since she married my dad, but she wants to truly retire so she can do other things, and that's understandable. But every time we've tried to hire someone, it didn't go well."

"I might apply for it," Erin says nonchalantly and grabs another slice. "Maybe I could do that while the kids are in school."

I feel my eyes narrow, and my heart picks up the pace. "Are you qualified?"

"Absolutely. I went to college for business management and minored in accounting. I did the books for the last job I had in Seattle. I'm sure that I could learn what you need, if Joy's willing to train me."

Chewing my own food, I think it over. This almost sounds too good to be true. "I'd have to have you speak with Mom because she's the one who knows exactly what we need."

"Of course." Erin shrugs, drawing my attention to her smooth, bare shoulder as she licks some sauce off her thumb. "Happy to do that."

"You don't even know what I'd pay you or how many hours it would be."

"Grumpy," she says, "I was shoveling horse poop the other day in the barn because I was *bored,* and you won't let me clean the house."

"I have a housekeeper that comes once a week."

"And she does a great job, but I'm saying if I get bored enough to muck out stalls, then I most certainly have time to work on the bookkeeping. I mean, I understand that it would mean that I'm privy to the financial side of things, and if you'd rather I didn't have that information, I totally get it. I would, of course, sign any NDA or contract that you'd want me to sign."

Shit, I hadn't even thought of that, but it would likely be the smart thing to do. "I can have something drawn up if it ends up being something we want to pursue."

"Great." She grins and takes a sip of beer. "So, now that we have that figured out, I have questions."

"Shoot."

"I want to know about this rivalry with the Lexington family."

I set my empty plate aside and stretch my feet out, resting them on the coffee table. "Who told you about that?"

"Your sister." She looks like she wants to say more, but she shakes her head and continues. "She said that your two families hate each other."

"Hate's a strong word, but yeah. We don't get along."

"Why?"

"It's always been that way."

Erin laughs and sets *her* plate aside, then pulls a peppermint out of the tiny pocket on the side of her leggings and pops it into her mouth. "Wait, you're telling me that you have it out for a whole family just because it's *always been that way*? That seems...stupid."

I can't help but laugh with her. "Well, when you put it like that, yes. It's stupid. But we've owned land that borders each other for more than a hundred years."

"Yeah, Millie mentioned that part. Your two families basically settled the town back in the day."

I nod and switch to her other foot. "We did. There were always fights about property lines. *Way* back in the day, they would shoot at each other for it."

"The wild, wild west," she says, her eyes shining with interest. "Cool."

"Yeah, cool until someone got killed. We're not as violent these days, but it's not unusual for lawsuits to happen."

"For fuck's sake, Remington, it's been more than a hundred years, and you guys can't figure your shit out? If the women were in charge, it would have been settled a century ago."

"That might be true." I shrug, then lift her foot and kiss her big toe. "For the most part, we don't like each other. Don't trust each other, really. I don't give a rat's ass what they do on their property as long as it doesn't make its way onto mine. As long as what they do doesn't interfere with my beef or my people. But inevitably, I find fence taken down here and there."

"It's so weird to me," she murmurs, but she settles

back with her eyes closed as I continue to knead her foot. "You're *really* good with your hands."

"I'm glad you think so. Do you have a favorite flower?"

"Daffodils," she says, her eyes still closed. "They're happy, and they're the first to pop up in the spring, as if they're too excited to be here and can't wait another minute."

Most women would say roses or something common. But not this girl.

"They should be popping up soon," I reply. "It's getting warmer."

"Is it possible we might have more snow this spring?" she asks.

"Probably not, but it's never impossible. I've seen it snow in July."

Her eyes pop open at that, and she frowns over at me. "*July*?"

"Yeah, when I was a kid. It was a freak storm that blew through. I think that's a once-in-a-thousand-year event, though, if that's even a thing. We're probably done with snow now until October. We might even get lucky and it'll hold off until November."

"But maybe earlier up in the mountains."

"Definitely earlier, higher up. Did you go to the University of Washington?"

She frowns over at me, and I gesture to her sweatshirt.

"Oh," she chuckles as she looks down. "No, I stole

this from a boyfriend a long time ago. Like, a *long* time ago. It's comfy and warm."

I don't like that. No, I don't like that at *all*.

Without a word, I pull Erin up from where she's reclining on the couch and guide her over to me. She straddles my lap, and I run my hands up her thighs, over her ass, and under the sweatshirt.

I keep moving until I pull it completely over her head and toss it aside.

"You didn't like that answer," she guesses.

"No. I didn't like that. When you're with me, you won't wear things that remind you of other men."

"It was a *really* long time ago."

"I don't care." I lean in and brush my nose across one tight nipple, then pull it into my mouth and suck. Her hands tighten in my hair, and she moans as I pull back and blow on the wet nub.

"I'll throw it away," she whispers, then moans again when I pay the same attention to the other nipple. "Holy shit, you're good at that, too."

"How much do you love these leggings?"

"Don't care about them right now."

I grin against her skin and then rip the leggings at her crotch, giving me access to her. She's not wearing panties, and my fingers slide through her already slick center.

She moves her hips, urging me to touch her more, to push my fingers inside of her, and so, I do. Just one at first, and then another, watching her gorgeous face as I work her up to orgasm. Her muscles clench around my fingers, and her cheeks darken. Her pretty plump lips part, and I press the pad of my thumb against her clit to send her over the edge.

"Fuck!" she cries as she shivers, and I lay her back on the couch and tug my jeans past my hips, pulling the condom out of the back pocket in the process. To my surprise, she plucks the condom out of my hand, rips it open, and rolls it down my shaft herself, watching me with green eyes filled with pure, unadulterated lust.

I brace myself over her, push one of her legs up, my hand in the crook of her knee, and then bury myself inside her.

She gasps.

I groan.

I can't take my eyes off where we're joined, watching as I push in and out, my cock slick from her, her pussy red and just a little swollen. She reaches for me, and I lean in to kiss her, completely lost in her. She tastes like peppermint and makes the sexiest little noises as I move, and before long, we're both losing ourselves, falling over into oblivion.

"You're not nearly as pissy as you were a couple of weeks ago."

I glance over at my brother as we ride our horses through the pasture, headed toward the higher elevations, to see if it's dry enough to move the cattle up next week.

"Is that a compliment?"

"Hell yeah, it is," Brady says with a laugh. "You're almost jovial. I think you cracked a joke back there at the barn with Lucky."

"I do have a sense of humor."

"Not for a while, you haven't." I ignore that, and he continues. "I'm happy to see it. Maybe you had some seasonal depression or something through the winter. The weather's been better lately."

"I'm hoping it's dry enough up here for us to move the cattle next week."

"It should be. Like I said, it's warming up. We haven't had any rain to speak of for a little while now. Might be a hot summer."

"What, are you a weatherman now?"

"I'm just making conversation. So, talk to me. What's been going on to lighten you up?"

Just a couple of days ago, Erin asked me if I have someone in my life that I can really talk to, someone who gets me. Brady is that person for me, so I let out a sigh and tell him everything he needs to know about Erin.

"I like her," he says when I've finished. "And you can tell that the kids just love her. I think it's great."

"She's more than a decade younger than me."

"But she's not a kid," he reminds me. "Is that the only thing that worries you?"

"It's the biggest thing. If it was Holly, I'd kick my ass."

"If it was Holly, we'd all kick your ass," he says. "But it's not Holly. She likes it out here, on the ranch."

"What does that have to do with anything?" I scowl over at him, but Brady just smiles back at me.

"Not everyone can deal with ranch life, man. You and I both know that. It's hard."

"I would like to take this opportunity to remind you that I've been sleeping with her for about six minutes, not preparing to take her as a bride."

Brady snorts and then laughs outright. "Yeah, well, it's good to know that she could hack it. Because you'll never live anywhere else."

No. I'll never live anywhere else. The ranch is my home, and it's my responsibility. One I knew that I'd take on from the time I was Johnny's age. It's an honor to me.

So, while I won't admit out loud that Brady's right, I wouldn't have anything to do with a woman who couldn't handle living at the ranch, I'm also not willing to admit that I've thought of anything long-term with Erin.

Even if I *have* thought of it. Because it's too soon.

"I like her," he says again.

"I do, too."

"I like that she seems to lift your whole vibe. That's saying something."

I glance his way, and Brady just grins. He's the most laid-back guy I know.

"Whoa," Brady says, looking at something on the ground. "I thought you said that no one's been out this way since late last fall."

"They haven't."

"Then why are there fresh footprints in that mud? Man footprints."

I tell my horse to stop, and I dismount, walk over to the prints, and squat. Brady joins me.

"The mud is half dry," I say grimly. "But yeah, the prints are fresh. I haven't sent any of our guys up here since last year. It was too wet to get here safely with the horses."

"We're not anywhere near the Lexingtons'," he says, looking around. "Hiker?"

"Maybe, but we have no trespassing signs posted, and they had to jump a fence."

"It's happened before."

I stand back up and prop my hands on my hips. "I don't like it. Let's set up some game cameras out here to keep an eye out. It might have been a hiker, but it doesn't sit well."

"Agreed. I'll make sure we get the cameras set up by tomorrow."

I nod and walk back to my horse and snag my phone from the saddle bag.

"I'm going to snap some pictures. Keep a record."

We spend fifteen minutes taking pictures and measuring and logging the footprints before we're on our way again.

"I think we should add some patrols to the guys' duties," Brady says. "It's time we pay closer attention to the more remote parts of the property, especially now that we have more people in the area. I'm not saying that they all mean any malice, but we don't want someone wandering out here and getting hurt."

"Not a bad idea."

It's just past dinnertime when I return home, and I hope that there's something left over for me because I'm fucking starving, thanks to the trip across the ranch taking longer than we anticipated.

I kick off my dirty boots at the back door and walk into the kitchen. Both of the kids are sitting at the island, eating what looks like meatloaf, and Erin is loading the dishwasher.

"Hi, Dad," Johnny says. "Erin made meatloaf."

Erin turns and grins at me. "It's still hot. Want some?"

"More than anything in the world."

"Dad's always hungry after work," Holly says and shoves some mashed potatoes into her mouth.

"I would be, too," Erin replies with a smile.

She's wearing jeans that hug her ass perfectly and a pink sweater that falls over one shoulder. This time, she's wearing a pink lacy thing under it that makes my fingers itch to touch her.

Instead, I brush my fingers against hers when she hands me the plate from the cabinet and watch with satisfaction as her lips turn up in a little secret smile.

Jesus Christ, I just had her this morning after she

returned from taking the kids to school, but I want her again.

"Smells good," I murmur, meaning her, not the meatloaf.

"It *is* good," Holly says. "Come sit by me, Daddy."

"I would *love* to sit by my best girl." I kiss my daughter's cheek before I take the stool next to hers and dig in. Holly's right, it's good.

I enjoy watching Erin laughing and engaging with the kids. They have an easy camaraderie with each other that's way more relaxed than I ever hoped for when the whole nanny idea came to be. And I know, without a shadow of a doubt, that Erin isn't simply nice to my kids because she's sleeping with me.

In fact, I suspect that it's probably the opposite.

"What did you do today, Dad?" Johnny asks.

"I was on the horse all day. Had to do some scouting for next week. What did you guys do in school?"

I listen to stories of an escaped class hamster, a fight during recess, and someone who fell asleep during reading time.

"Sounds like a busy day," I say with a grin and turn to Erin. "How about you?"

"I spent most of the day in town. Did some shopping and checked on my car. Brooks says it'll be done by the end of the week." She smiles and leans on the other side of the island as she chats with us. "I also made an appointment to chat with your mom on Monday."

"Good," I reply with a nod.

"I think I'm going to join Millie in town tonight for a floral arrangement class."

"You want to learn to arrange flowers?"

"Not really," she replies with a laugh. "But I miss Millie, and I think it sounds fun. I'm heading out in about fifteen minutes, unless you need something."

"Nope, I think we're good to go. How about you two?"

Johnny nods, clearly not at all concerned with Erin leaving for a few hours, but Holly frowns.

"Maybe *I* want to arrange flowers."

"Another time," I tell her. "Erin should go enjoy some time with her friends."

"But Millie is *my* aunt," Holly insists.

"Yes, she is," I agree. "And she's Erin's friend. You don't always have to be included in everything, sweet girl."

"Is it because I'm too little?" she asks.

"They will probably have adult drinks there," Erin chimes in. "Plus, it ends way past your bedtime. But, if you want to visit the flower shop after school one day, we totally can."

"Okay." That placates Holly, and I smile over at Erin.

"Have fun tonight."

"I plan on it." Erin hangs a dish towel over the side of the sink and then leaves the kitchen. I follow, catching up to her in her room. She turns and lifts a brow. "You can come in."

I've been careful not to just assume that I can waltz into her private space any time I want, but at her consent, I step in and close the door, then pull her to me and kiss her. She makes that little noise, low in her throat, and pushes her fingers into my hair.

When I pull back, I smooth my finger down her nose.

"Have fun tonight, Doc."

I pull the door open and walk out but hear her reply, "Thanks, Grumpy."

CHAPTER THIRTEEN
ERIN

Tonight was just what I needed. I've missed the hell out of Millie, so when she invited me to the flower class, I knew I wouldn't say no. We laughed, had a glass of wine, and made a pretty decent arrangement of flowers, if I do say so myself.

Driving out to the ranch in the dark isn't my favorite thing, especially since I had the deer incident a few weeks ago, but it's an uneventful drive, and soon, I'm turning down the driveway, headed toward the farmhouse.

I'm a little surprised by how much I love living on the ranch. I knew that I wanted to get out of the big city, and the small town of Bitterroot Valley is perfect for that, but I actually prefer being out at the ranch. It's quiet and peaceful, not to mention absolutely gorgeous. When this job ends and it's time for me to move back to town, I'll be sad to say goodbye to it.

"I'm not thinking about sad things," I mutter to

myself as I bring the Suburban to a stop and grab my purse and the bouquet of flowers before heading inside. The house is quiet, and I assume everyone is sleeping, so I tiptoe to my room and close the door before setting my flowers on the dresser and hanging my purse on the hook behind the door.

When I turn around, I see a sweatshirt folded on the end of the bed.

It's a Montana State University sweatshirt, in blue and gold, and when I pick it up and smell it, it smells like Remington.

"He gave me his shirt," I mutter before burying my nose in it once more. It's definitely seen better days, so it's obviously something that he once wore often.

I absolutely *love* it.

After a quick shower, I tug the sweatshirt over my head and hug my arms around me before I slip into bed. With the sweatshirt wrapped around me, it's almost as if I'm lying with Remington, and that feels damn good.

Yeah, I love it here. My life is awesome right now.

IT'S SUNDAY MORNING, and it's my day to work at the coffee shop. I have the early shift, so I'm up and out before anyone else is even awake yet. It's the one day that Rem sleeps in, so I'm sure to be quiet as I walk out the door, lock it behind me, and get into the Suburban to head into town.

I came home in the dark last night, but the sun is

already starting to rise now. I love that the days are lengthening. Soon, it'll be light out until late into the evening, and I'm looking forward to quiet nights out on the deck, watching the world fall asleep.

The drive into town is easy, and soon, I'm parked in my space behind the shop and unlocking the back door. I'll be by myself for the first hour or so, getting things ready, but Millie will be in to help with the church rush, and then she'll close after my shift ends.

Happy to see that everything is clean and ready to go for today, I get to work refilling napkins and cups, making sure fresh beans are in the grinder, and humming to myself as I work.

Early Sunday mornings are quiet, but when Millie comes in at eight, things start to pick up.

"Hi, Brooks," I say with a smile when the man walks up to the counter. He's tall like Remington, with dark hair and hazel eyes. "How's it going?"

"Can't complain," he replies. "Your car's ready. I thought I'd come in and tell you in person, and grab some coffee, of course."

"You're kidding." I grin at him. "That's *awesome*."

"Thanks for waiting so long. It's been a busy month in the shop."

"There was no hurry, but it'll be nice to have it back. I can come get it tomorrow, if that works."

"Whenever you're ready for it," he assures me and places his order for black coffee.

"Hey, Brooks," Millie says with a wave as she steams some milk.

Brooks moves down to chat with Millie as I take the next customer. He's a man I haven't seen before, just a little taller than me with black hair and brown eyes and a little scruff on his face. There's nothing particularly striking about him.

"Hey there," I say with a smile. "Where are you visiting from?"

"Oh, I'm not." There's a southern accent in his voice. "I just moved to town a few weeks ago."

"Welcome to town. You'll like it here. I'm fairly new, too. What can I get for you?"

He places his order and gives me the name Clay to write on his cup, and then I move on to the next customer.

Millie and I work well and efficiently together, and before I know it, it's almost noon when we finally have a lull.

"Busy morning," Millie says as she wipes down the counter. "Makes the time go by fast."

"Super speed," I agree and glance at the door when the bell dings.

Summer Quinn, the owner of the floral shop, comes in, carrying a huge bouquet of blood-red roses.

"Hi, Erin. Delivery for you." Summer grins and passes me the note. The envelope has the logo for *Paula's Posies* on it. Summer bought the shop from Paula years ago but never changed the name of the business.

"I didn't think you delivered on Sundays," Millie says.

"Just half of the day through the summer," Summer replies. "Open the card, Erin. It's super sweet."

You look beautiful today.

That's it.

It can't be from Remington because he hasn't seen me today.

"I guess my brother *can* be sweet when he wants to be," Millie says.

"Hmm," is my only reply to that. "Hey, Mill, do you mind covering things for a sec? I want to make a call."

"No phone sex while you're at work," Millie replies with a wink as Summer snorts with laughter. "Sure, no problem."

"Thanks."

With blood rushing in my ears, I hurry back to the break room and quickly dial my dad's number. Of course, he's likely off doing something fun on a Sunday and doesn't answer.

So, I call again.

This time, he picks up and sounds annoyed. "Hey, baby, can I call you back in about an hour?"

"No." I swallow back the panic and fight to sound calm. "I need to speak with you right now."

"Okay, no problem." He pulls the phone away from his mouth. "Gentlemen, I need to take this. I'll be right back."

I hear rustling, and then he's back.

"What's wrong?"

"Maybe nothing." I pace the room as I break out in a cold sweat. "I need to know if you've been notified by the court that the asshole who stalked me years ago has been released."

"I haven't been, no. I can reach out to your uncle Matt and see what he can find out. Why do you ask, Erin?" His voice has taken on a hard edge, and I know the alpha is firmly in place.

"It might be nothing at all. I mean, odds are that I'm just overreacting."

"You don't usually overreact. What happened?"

"I just got flowers at work, and the card is very much like what he used to send me. Word for word."

"Maybe you have a secret admirer, and it's a coincidence." I can picture my dad pacing, pushing his hand through his hair.

"It could be," I agree and make myself take a deep breath. Having a panic attack isn't going to help anything here. Hell, for all I know, I might be sounding an alarm for no reason at all. "But my gut doesn't think so, and I need to know if he's out of prison, Dad."

"I'm on it," he assures me. "I'll call you back when I know anything, but it's Sunday, so there probably won't be news until tomorrow."

"Damn weekends," I mutter. "Okay, thank you so much. I'll have my phone on me all day tomorrow."

"Good. And watch your back. Don't go out by yourself. I know you can take care of yourself, but let's not take any chances, okay?"

"You don't have to worry about that. I'll be careful."

"Love you. Talk soon."

He hangs up, and I have to sit in a chair because I'm so light-headed. Finally, when I've calmed down, I walk back out to Millie and find that Summer has gone.

Without a word, I grab the roses and take them directly over to the trash and throw them away.

"Uh, are you and Rem fighting or something?" Millie asks.

"No. They weren't from Remington." I'm embarrassed that tears want to push their way out of my eyes, and Millie's smile turns to a concerned frown.

"Whoa, what's up?"

Thankfully, there's no one in the coffee shop right now, so I lean on the counter and cross my arms over my chest.

"Do you remember when I told you that I'd once had a stalker, and that's why I wasn't on social media?"

"Yeah." Her eyes go round. "Oh, shit."

"I don't know for sure that those are from him, but he always, *always* sent me blood-red roses with a card that creeped me out. Remington hasn't seen me today, Millie. He wouldn't know how I look. But that's the kind of shit *he* would say."

"Yikes," she whispers. "What do we do?"

"I just called my dad to find out if the asshole's been released from jail. They were supposed to notify us. Dad hadn't heard anything, but he's going to look into it. My uncle Matt is a cop, pretty high up in Seattle, so he'll have people he can reach out to, but they likely won't be able to find anything out until tomorrow, since it's Sunday."

"So, we have to keep your brain occupied on other things for today. I can do that. Your shift is about over, but if you hang out and wait for me, I'll take you out shopping and for a late lunch. Anything you want."

"I'll take you up on that. But rather than wait, I might just run over to check on Roger. I haven't been over to visit as often as I thought I would."

"Oh, that's perfect," she says. "But I'm going to walk you out to your car."

"My dad's going to really like you," I inform her. "He doesn't want me doing anything by myself."

"It's just common sense," she replies and follows me out the back door. She waits while I get into the car, start it up, and pull away.

Millie really is the best friend I've ever had.

I love seeing all the spring flowers that have sprung up in town as I drive through the neighborhood to Roger's house. I notice that someone is parked in the spot reserved for the garage apartment, and I'm relieved that he was able to find someone else to live there so quickly.

Roger answers the door, and his face lights up when he sees that it's me.

"Erin, you don't have to knock."

"I figured I would. Didn't want to startle you." I immediately walk into his arms for a big hug and then frown when I look around the living room. It's definitely more disheveled than usual. "How have you been?"

"Oh, I'm just fine." He turns to walk away, and I notice that he's limping.

"What happened to your leg?"

"I stumbled off the steps in the backyard." He shakes his head. "I just get clumsier and clumsier."

"Did you have it checked out?"

"It's just a little sprain."

"Is it your ankle?"

"The knee."

Still frowning, I prop my hands on my hips. "Do you mind if I look at it?"

Roger pauses, but then shakes his head. "I don't mind. It's a little bruised up."

But when I push his pants up around his knee, I see that it's more than a *little* bruised up. It's all black and blue and a little swollen.

"Roger, we need to ice this. It's swollen. You sit right there, and I'll fix you up."

"You really don't have to fuss." But he doesn't object too hard when I start making an ice pack in a towel and then lay it over the knee. "Thank you."

"I'm sorry. I should check in with you more often."

"It's not your job to take care of me, you know."

"It's not a job at all; it's out of love and you know it." I lean in to kiss his cheek. "Now, while that does its job, tell me about your new tenant."

"I don't know much," he says while he watches me bustle around his kitchen, making us each a cup of tea. "He's new to town. Single guy. Does computer work from home, and he said the apartment worked because it's furnished."

"Oh, I'm glad that worked out." I remember the customer from earlier today. "Is his name Clay?"

"You've met him?"

"I just waited on him at the coffee shop. He was kind of shy."

"Definitely quiet, but that's fine by me."

"I'm making you a few ice packs, and I'm putting them in the freezer so you can just grab one and then sit and put it on the knee. Put it back in the freezer when you're done, and it'll be ready for next time."

I glance over at him and find him smiling at me. "I've missed you, kiddo."

"I've missed you, too."

"I can't believe I found so many new things at Polly's," I say as I nibble on a baby back rib. Millie took me to Rocky Mountain Smokehouse, the best BBQ place I've ever been to, after spending about an hour and a couple hundred dollars at A Pocket Full of Polly, my favorite dress shop in town. "I mean, I guess I need to get some things for summer, right?"

"Totally. And that sundress? The green one? Holy shit, you looked hot in that."

I grin and nibble my rib. "Thanks. It was a good find. I have to say, between hanging out with Roger for a while, and then time with you, I haven't had time to think about the scary things."

"Good, and we're still not thinking about that. So, are you having a lot of sex with my brother?"

I choke on my water and cover my mouth with a napkin as I cough and sputter, making Millie grin.

"Jesus, that was an abrupt change in subject."

"Go on, answer the question."

"We make time for it," I reply. "Usually when I get back from taking the kids to school."

"That's handy. I think my parents are planning to offer to take the kids for the weekend next week. They want to go to Spokane for a few days, do some shopping, and visit with my aunt Melissa."

"Oh, nice. The kids will love that. How far away is Spokane?"

"It's about a six-hour drive is all," she replies. "Pretty easy. The kids always love staying in hotels with a pool."

"Of course, they do. Do people not have pools here? I grew up with one in the backyard."

Millie watches me for a minute and then laughs. "No. We only get about three months of good weather. Four if we're lucky. It's a waste of time and money to put in a pool."

"That makes sense. Well, they'll have fun."

"And you'll have a whole sexy weekend to yourselves." Millie wiggles her eyebrows. "Score."

That makes me laugh, and then I sit back and pat my stomach. "I'm *full.*"

"Too full for cheesecake?"

I bite my lower lip. "Are we sharing?"

"Fuck no, we aren't sharing."

"Yeah, I want cheesecake."

IT'S LATE when I get back to the ranch. Millie and I ended up staying at the restaurant for a while, just chatting away the hours.

I haven't done that in a long time, and it was fun.

I did text Remington to let him know not to expect me for quite a while, and he just told me to have fun.

He's not suffocating, which I really appreciate. He doesn't even bat an eyelash when I say I want to spend time with my friends. Not that he *should*, but some would.

I'm glad he's not a jerk.

When I walk into the house, it suddenly hits me that I'm so, so tired. What an emotional rollercoaster of a day, between getting the flowers, discovering that Roger had fallen and was hurt, and then the fun few hours with Millie.

It was all over the place.

I want a hot shower and comfortable clothes, so I head for my bedroom first and make a beeline for the shower.

Thirty minutes later, bundled up in sweats and Rem's sweatshirt, I make my way to the kitchen for a glass of wine. I've just taken a glass out of the cabinet when Remington walks in and smiles at me from across the room.

Holy shit, that smile is devastating.

"How is it that you can make my heart go pitter-patter with just a smile?" I pull the cork out of the bottle and pour half of a glass. "Would you like some?"

"No thanks." He's in a simple white T-shirt and red flannel pajama pants, and he pads on bare feet over to me. "You like the sweatshirt."

"I sleep in it." I sip the wine. "It smells like you, and it's comforting."

He cups my cheek and rubs his thumb over my skin. "Something's bothering you. Didn't you have fun with my sister?"

"Yeah, we had fun. We shopped and ate; what's not to like?" I set the glass down and then step into his embrace, enjoying the way his arms come around me as he holds me close. My head rests on his chest, and I can hear his heartbeat. I'm all talked out when it comes to the potential stalker, and I don't really have anything to tell him anyway, so I decide to wait to fill him in until I hear from my dad tomorrow. "It was kind of an all-over-the-place kind of day. How about yours? How are the kids?"

"They're passed out." He kisses the top of my head. "We took the horses out today and then helped my mom plant some flowers."

"Nice."

"My parents are taking the kids next weekend."

"Millie mentioned that. They'll have fun."

Rem tips my chin up so I'm looking up into his face. "So will we." His eyes narrow. "Are you sure you're okay?"

"Just tired. It was a late night last night and an early morning today. All I need is a good night's sleep."

"Want to watch a show for a little bit?"

"Absolutely." I grab my wine and follow him into the family room and get settled on the couch while he finds us something to watch. We end up on a blind dating show, where at the end of the season, the couple has to decide if they're getting married. "I love stuff like this."

"Reality TV?"

"Yeah. It's like crack to me."

Curled up beside Remington, with my head on his arm and my hand in his, we watch TV until I fall asleep before the end of the first episode.

CHAPTER FOURTEEN
REMINGTON

The credits roll, and I back out of the app before turning off the TV and glancing down at Erin. She's breathing deeply, obviously asleep. I'd like to stay here like this, in the dark, for a little while. I've grown to crave time with this woman. The more I get, the more I want. I'm *greedy* for it.

For her.

My family isn't wrong when they say there's been a change in me since Erin came into my life. I feel lighter, happier. More at ease. My responsibilities haven't changed, but Erin makes my life so much easier with her help with the kids, and more than that, just being near her quells the stress I always seem to carry.

I'm grateful to her for that.

Rather than wake her to go to bed, I lift her into my arms and carry her through the house to her bedroom. The room is filled with the scent of her now, along with peppermints, thanks to the bowl of them on her dresser.

I lower her to the bed and cover her with blankets, tucking her in.

She stirs and opens her heavy eyes and smiles up at me. "Thanks."

"My pleasure, Doc."

I can't resist leaning in to kiss her soft lips. I want to stay here, or better yet, take her up to *my* bed and get lost in her before we both fall asleep, tangled up together.

But that can't happen with the kids in the house.

"Sleep well, beautiful," I whisper as she burrows down into the covers and falls back to sleep.

The more time that Erin spends out here on the ranch, with not just me but also my kids, the more I'm convinced that she belongs here. I know that it's fast, but I don't know what life would be like without her.

I do know that it would be fucking miserable.

After my parents come back with the kids next weekend, I'll sit down with Johnny and Holly for a serious conversation. I'm not sure yet what I'll say, but I need to know how they feel and how they'd react to Erin integrating more into our family, not just as the nanny.

The thought makes me nervous and excited all at once, but I'm past ready to have Erin with me, in my bedroom, every night.

I'M NOT QUITE FULLY awake when I make it downstairs to the coffee maker, and I'm surprised to find Erin already there, brewing herself a mug.

"You're up early." I move in, kiss her forehead, and wrap my arms around her. She leans in, hugging me back.

"I woke up about an hour ago and couldn't fall back to sleep." She yawns and steps back when her coffee is finished brewing, then grabs the flavored creamer she loves. "I might as well get started with the day. Do you have a lot going on today?"

"Just the usual amount." I set to work getting my own coffee ready. "What time are you meeting with my mom?"

"Around noon. She's going to text me when she gets back from her Tai Chi class." Erin grins over the rim of her steaming mug. "I love how active your mom is."

"She rarely stops moving," I agree. "I think she was so used to being busy, chasing around so many kids for all those years, that it's become a habit, and she just keeps going. And I'm glad for it. Dad's the same. He may be retired, but there's hardly a day that he doesn't come out to the barn to oversee something."

"Well, I think it's great. I'm going to do some morning yoga and some meditation, and then I'll get the kids off to school."

Knowing that the kids are still in bed, I pull Erin against me and kiss her long and slow. I'm satisfied when I pull back and she's just a bit breathless, those sleepy eyes wide awake and firing at me now.

"If I can manage it, I'll swing by later," I promise her.

"Sounds good to me." Erin winks at me. "I'll be here all morning."

THANKS TO A HAY order that went horribly wrong, and a busy morning of interviewing for summer ranch hands, the day slipped away from me, and there was no time to go to the house for some time with Erin.

"How many head do we have going to auction this fall?" I ask Lucky from across my desk.

"Eight hundred," he replies. "Wait, that's eight hundred and two."

"That's up a little from last year," I murmur, taking notes. "Okay, and who do you think we should hire from today's interviews?"

"If I'm being honest? None of them."

I don't disagree. I wasn't particularly impressed with any of them.

"I have to hire someone, Lucky. Brady will be out on the circuit soon, and summer's busy."

"You're preaching to the choir, son. I get it. I'm just saying that if I'm being truthful, not one of those four boys are cowboys."

I toss the pen down and rub my eyes, take my hat off, and scratch my head.

"Shit, I guess it's back to the drawing board. I'll put out another ad. I'd like to have two more hands hired before June."

"We'd all like that," Lucky says with a chuckle. "But those boys today wouldn't have fit in, and none of them had the build to do the work. They'd just be exhausted, and likely hurt, every day. That's not what we need."

"You're right about that. We don't need it. Hell, three of them admitted that they applied for the job because their dads made them."

Lucky winces. "I'll ask around again to see if anyone I know is looking for work."

"I appreciate it. I'm going to go see how it's going with my mom and Erin. Erin applied for the bookkeeping position."

"We like her," Lucky says as I stand. "Now, *she's* someone who fits in."

"Yeah." I grin and settle the hat on my head once more. "She does. I'll come back out here in a bit."

Lucky nods and walks away as I climb into the Jeep and set off for my folks' house. Erin and Mom are walking out of the house as I pull in, both of them smiling and happy.

That's a good sign.

"Oh, hey, Rem," Mom says as I walk toward them. "Erin and I were just finishing up here."

"How did it go?" I push my hands into my back pockets so I don't just immediately grab for Erin and kiss the hell out of her.

"It went well," Mom replies, looking over at Erin happily. "I even gave her a little quiz, and she passed with flying colors."

"It wasn't an easy quiz, either," Erin says with a laugh. "I might have started to break out into a sweat."

"You did great," Mom reaffirms and wraps an arm around Erin's shoulders. "She's accepted the position, and we'd like to dive into training on Wednesday."

"Wow, that's great. I'm glad that you had a good meeting."

"Oh, Joy," Erin begins, "would you mind giving me a ride into town? My car is done, and I'd like to pick it up and bring it out to the ranch before I have to pick the kids up from school."

"I can do that," I offer before Mom can reply.

"Oh, I know you're busy," Erin begins.

"I can take an hour and help you with this. I think it's the least I can do."

"That's perfect because I have to get ready for my book club. I'm hosting tonight," Mom explains. "It's my turn. I'll see you Wednesday morning, Erin."

"I'm excited," Erin replies and then follows me over to the Jeep. "Seriously, your mom is the absolute *best*. She's so dang smart. I didn't realize that she's continued to further her education every couple of years because things change so fast in the world of finance, and she's totally on top of it. I liked her a lot before, but now I think she's the shit."

I snort at that as I pull onto the highway.

"My mom is totally the shit. So, you still plan to use the Suburban when you have the kids, right?"

Erin immediately nods. "Oh, yeah. I know that you're the most comfortable with that, and honestly, I like driving it. It's so big. It feels very safe, and that makes me feel better, too."

"Good." I reach over and take her hand, lifting it to my lips. "I want to keep all three of you as safe as possible."

She grins over at me. "I get that. I'll drive the big car. But I definitely have to get my vehicle and pay Brooks."

From the number of cars in the parking lot at Brooks's garage, I'd say the man isn't hurting for business.

"Hey, Erin," Brooks says as he wipes his hands on a rag. "Remington."

"Brooks," I reply with a nod.

"Wow, this is a little more than we thought," Erin says as she looks at the invoice. "Cars are expensive to fix."

"They're ridiculous," Brooks agrees. "But she's in top shape now and should last you for many years. I've warrantied all my work for a year. If *anything* happens between now and then, you just call me, and we'll fix it."

"That's pretty great," Erin says with a nod before passing Brooks her credit card. "I'm just glad it didn't happen when I was on the freeway between here and Seattle. That would have *sucked.*"

"Big time," Brooks agrees with a smile as he runs her card.

When the bill is settled, all three of us walk out to where Erin's car is waiting. It's actually a small SUV and doesn't look all that old.

"This isn't a beater," I say with surprise.

"No, I don't drive a *beater*," Erin replies.

"I admit, I had the same reaction," Brooks says with a laugh. "No, it's a good car. Sucks that you were just outside of the warranty, though."

"You should have just bought a new one," I tell her.

"A new one would have been a lot more than what I just paid for the repairs. Besides, it won't get driven as much now, since I use the Suburban so often with the kids."

If I have my way, she'll be in the Suburban most of the time.

Hell, *every* time if I can talk her into it.

"Thanks for the ride," she says with a smile and opens the door. "I'll see you later."

She gets in and turns the engine, smiling even wider when it roars to life. After a quick happy dance in the front seat, she pulls out of the parking lot.

Brooks and I watch her go, and he slides his hands into his pockets. "She's a great girl."

"Yeah." I nod slowly. "She is."

"There something going on between the two of you?"

"Yeah." I turn to him now and level my gaze with his. "There is."

"Figures." Brooks lets out a humorless laugh. "The good ones are always taken. Well, good luck there, man."

I've always liked Brooks. He's about a year older than me and moved to town when we were in middle school. He's always been a nice guy.

"Thanks. And thanks for fixing her up."

"It was kind of a shit show," he admits. "But it's solid now."

"Good to know."

"I BOUGHT SOME HORSES," Ryan says as I walk into the barn after returning to the ranch.

"How many is *some*?" I counter.

"Six," Brady replies with a grin. "Our brother doesn't do anything halfway."

"That's a lot of horses for one person."

Ryan shrugs. "They were all together at this farm, and I couldn't break them up."

"Aww"—Brady ruffles Ryan's hair—"you're just a big softie."

"Where are they?" I ask.

"At my place, but I'd like it if you and Brady would come out and take a look at them. They were neglected for a while, and they're a little skinny. I got a clean bill of health from the vet, so none of them have disease, but they need some work."

"You have time for six rescue horses?" My eyebrows climb in surprise. My brother is a workaholic. He barely takes time to *eat*.

"Yeah, I do. I told you, I'm here for the long haul."

"Let's go see them, then. Hey, Lucky!" The older man turns when I call over to him. "Want to go see some horses?"

"I'll never turn that down," he says with a grin.

The four of us ride in Ryan's brand-new truck over to his ranch. It's about a ten-minute drive. The first thing that comes into view is the house.

It's fucking massive.

Ryan had the old house that once stood here torn down, and, to his credit, it needed to be. It had been abandoned for a long time, so the house was crumbling and not safe, even for restoration.

The new dwelling has a wall of windows that gives him a view of the mountains, and now the six horses grazing in his pasture.

The new barn is also nice, with ten stalls and a tack room that most cowboys would drool over.

Which Lucky does when we walk inside.

"We have a tack room at the ranch, you know," I remind him with a laugh.

"Not this fancy," he replies. "Of course, once it starts getting some use, it'll get dirtied up."

"I hope so," Ryan says. "It's just been sitting here, and it's time there was some life in this barn. Come on, I want to show you the horses."

As we walk out to the pasture and get a better look at the horses, I see what Ryan was talking about. Their manes and tails haven't been brushed out in a long time, so they're full of burrs and are tangled.

Three of them are way too skinny. One has a broken hoof.

"This is going to be a lot of work," I murmur as one of the mares nudges my shoulder. I turn and rub my hand down her neck, and she sighs. "God, they're just a bunch of lovers."

"They're all like that," Ryan agrees. "They're docile and sweet, and someone really failed them. None can be ridden as is, but I'll get them healthy again, and then they'll be great for riding."

"You said you had them all tested for disease?" Lucky asks.

"Yeah, and they were all negative. They've been treated for worms and given vaccines. The corral they were in was just mud. They were all caked in it, and I washed them all. You could tell they felt so much better after a bath."

"I bet they did," Brady murmurs, nuzzling one of the horses. "I'll help in any way I can."

"We all will," Lucky puts in, making Ryan grin.

"Thanks. I'll need some help."

My phone rings, and when I glance down, I see that it's Will Montgomery.

"This is Erin's dad," I say as I accept the call. "This is Rem."

"Hi Rem, it's Will. I just left a message for Erin but wanted to reach out to you. It turns out that the man who was in prison for stalking Erin has been released. She asked me about it yesterday, but it was Sunday, and we had to wait for someone to be in the office. I saw your security setup when I was there, but how do you feel about beefing it up?"

"Hold on." I pinch the bridge of my nose. "Erin had a *stalker*?"

That grabs everyone's attention. They walk closer, listening.

"I'm sorry. I thought she would have told you. Yeah, about five years ago. He's been in prison, but she had something happen at work yesterday that scared her, so she reached out to me. He's been released. Now, he can't *legally* leave Washington, and in the restraining order, it says that he can't ever live within a hundred miles of Erin, but people don't always care about restraining orders."

My heart has plunged into my stomach. Why didn't she tell me about this last night?

We'd agreed on no more secrets. No more lies.

"Do you know where he is?"

"Well, he met with his probation officer last month, as usual. So, we don't think he's left the state."

"He's been out for more than a month, and no one told you?"

"I'm pissed, too, trust me."

"I'll beef up security," I assure him. "We'll get started right away."

"Thanks. Until we have eyes on this guy, I think it's smart."

"How bad was it? Five years ago?"

Will sighs in my ear. "It was as fucked-up as it gets. Talk to her about it."

"Oh, trust me, I will."

I hang up and turn to the other men, who are quiet.

"How much did you hear?"

"Most of it," Ryan replies.

"I want cameras *everywhere* on the ranch. We'll install a gate, as well."

"What about motion lights?" Brady asks. "Especially at all the access points to the ranch."

"That's a good idea. Let's do that. I'd like it all in

place by the end of the day tomorrow. This is the priority."

They nod in agreement.

"One more thing," I add. "Bruiser will be riding with Erin *everywhere*. He's now her own personal bodyguard."

"You got it," Lucky says.

CHAPTER FIFTEEN
ERIN

"Erin!"

"Well, hi there, sweet girl." I laugh as Holly runs out of the school, obviously excited to see me waiting for her in the pickup line. A few days ago, I decided to start getting out of the car and waiting on the curb, soaking up the sunshine, and I can tell the kids like it when they come hurrying out to join me. "Did you have a fabulous day at school?"

"Yeah. The hamster got loose again! We couldn't find him for about an hour."

"Where did you find him?" I ask.

"He was in Miles's backpack, eating his lunch."

I snort out a laugh, but Holly's face turns serious.

"It's not funny," she insists. "Miles didn't have a lunch after that, so we all pitched in and gave him some of ours."

"Well, that was very nice of you. What did you share with him?"

"My string cheese." Holly shrugs, as if it's no big deal.

"That's your favorite part."

"I know, but he lost his *whole* lunch." Holly dumps her backpack into the back seat of the Suburban and then joins me again on the curb. "I wonder what's taking Johnny so long."

"Maybe he's talking with his friends."

"Probably. He likes to talk. His teacher told Dad that sometimes he talks too much."

I grin and push Holly's hair off her cheek, tucking it behind her ear. "You know what? I had a teacher who told my parents the same thing, and my dad told her that maybe I had something important to say, and she shouldn't tell me to shut up."

"Johnny doesn't have anything important to say," Holly replies. "He just likes to talk."

That makes me laugh, and then I glance up when I hear Johnny yell out, "I'm coming!"

"No rush, buddy," I assure him as I open the back door for him. "Everything okay?"

"Yeah, I was just talking."

Holly and I share a smile as the kids get settled into the back seat, and then I walk around to the driver's side and open the door. Glancing down at my phone, I see that I missed a call from my dad.

And just like that, all the fear I'd managed to keep pushed down all day comes rushing up to the surface.

I don't want the kids to hear this conversation because I don't want to frighten them, so I wait before pulling away from the school and instead, call Dad back, *not* putting him on speaker.

"Guys, we'll leave in just a second, okay? I have to call someone."

"Do you have any snacks with you?" Johnny wants to know.

"Yes, actually, I do. Here are some cookies."

I pass the cookies back to them and then dial my dad's number.

"Hey," I say when he answers. "I just missed you. I was picking up the kids. What did you find out?"

"Well, he *is* out." My heart stutters. "But the last we know, he was still in Washington. So, if the flowers are from him, it's possible that he sent them from Washington."

"True." I nibble on my lower lip. "I thought he had five years left inside?"

"He did," Dad confirms. "And it's being looked into. All you can do is watch your back and be careful. If anything else weird happens, call your local authorities and then me."

"I actually have an in here with the cops. Remington's brother is on the force, so I'll let him know right away," I reply, nodding to myself. "Don't worry, I won't be careless."

"I know you won't. Stay in touch, you hear me?"

"I will. Love you. Talk to you later."

I hang up and absolutely *refuse* to have a panic attack right here in front of the kids. I have to hold it together and get them home safely, then I need to have a conversation with Remington.

"Are you okay, Erin?" Holly asks.

"Of course, honey. Why do you ask?"

"It looks like you're crying," she replies, and I swipe at my cheek, surprised to find tears there. "Are you sad?"

No, I'm terrified.

"No, I'm just worried. Sorry about that. Let's go home, yeah? I was thinking about making some homemade pizza for dinner."

"Can we choose our own toppings?" Johnny wants to know.

"Of *course,* you can."

When we pull up to the farmhouse, I see that Chase's truck is in the drive, and Joy's waiting out front.

She smiles when we pull in, but I see worry in her eyes.

What now? Did he somehow get out here and hurt someone?

Damn it, I should have talked to Rem last night, but I was just so tired.

"Hi, favorite grandkids," Joy says, hugging them both tight. "You're going to come home with me for a while."

"But Erin's making homemade pizza," Holly argues with a frown.

"And she still will," Joy promises. "We'll just have a snack in the meantime."

"They've had cookies," I inform her.

"You shouldn't have told her that," Johnny whispers loudly, making us both laugh.

"You and John should join us for dinner," I offer, and Joy nods.

"That sounds great. I'll have them back over in a little while."

With a kid on each side, the three of them walk away, and I head up to the house and push inside.

"Erin?" Remington calls out. "Come to my office, please."

He doesn't sound particularly happy that I'm home, and my already knotted-up stomach starts to do the salsa as I walk to the doorway of Rem's office.

He's sitting behind his desk. Chase stands at the window, Ryan and Brady sit in chairs, and John leans against the bookshelves. Even Millie watches me with red-rimmed eyes from across the room.

The whole family's here.

"Uh, hi."

"Have a seat," Brady offers, standing from the chair.

"If it's all the same to you, I think I'd rather stand." I lift my chin and walk into the room, my eyes on Rem's.

"I spoke with your father just a little while ago," Remington begins, and all of this suddenly makes sense.

"Is anyone hurt?" I blurt out. "Did he somehow get to the ranch and hurt someone?"

"No," John replies and reaches out to pat my shoulder. "You're not in trouble, Erin."

"Bullshit," Remington disagrees. "I want to know why I heard that there's a stalker who is out of prison and obsessed with you, from your *father*. Why didn't you tell me? You're with my kids. You live in my home. Jesus, you're...*you*. I can't protect anyone if I don't have the information, Erin."

"I didn't know," I reply as I round on him. "I just found out when I picked up the kids. I didn't know that he was out of prison."

Just saying the words makes me swallow hard and close my eyes, taking a deep breath.

"Okay," Millie says, rushing over to me to put her arm around me. "Now we know."

"You talked to Millie about it," Remington continues. "But you didn't tell *me*."

"You're right, I didn't tell you." I sigh, suddenly so fucking *tired*. "I'd spent all afternoon worried about it. No one could tell me if he was out of jail until today. Millie helped keep my mind off things all afternoon, and then I came home and was just exhausted. I didn't know anything for sure, and I didn't want to talk about it anymore."

"But he sent flowers to your job."

"I didn't know that they were from him yesterday. I *suspected*. I won't have you interrogate me like I'm the one who did anything wrong. I went through that once before, and I won't do it again. I'll pack my shit and get out."

"Whoa!" Brady says.

"No, wait." Chase holds up his hands.

"That's ridiculous." Ryan shakes his head.

All the men are on their feet, gesturing for me to stop. Even Remington has climbed to his feet, but his jaw is firmly set as he watches me through those hazel eyes, and I hate how frustrated he looks.

"Why don't you sit," Chase suggests, "and tell us what happened? I need to know so I can put out an APB in case this asshole has decided to come here. I've already spoken with your uncle Matt in Seattle, and he's given me some solid information. But it's always best to get it straight from the horse's mouth."

I have to talk about it all over again, is all I can think to myself as I lower into the chair, and someone passes me a glass of water. I pause, take a sip of the water, and play with a string on my dress as I think about where to begin. My gaze finds Remington's, and I wish that coldness in his eyes would go away.

"I was twenty," I begin. "In college. I started getting stupid messages on social media. Look, my dad is a famous football player and still works closely with the team. Not to mention, I have all kinds of famous people in my family, so it's not unusual to get some weird messages or comments from time to time. You learn to ignore it. One thing that's true is, people are really brave when they're behind their phone or a computer screen, you know?"

"Sure," Chase says with a nod. "Sounds reasonable."

"It evolved into getting flowers where I worked. Blood-red roses." I can't resist the shiver of disgust that rolls through me. "And the card always said something like, *You look beautiful today,* or *Wow, you smell great.*"

"Creepy as fuck," Millie whispers, and I nod over at her. "And that's why when the flowers came for you yesterday, and I said Rem is sweet, you ran out like you'd been stung by a bee."

"I knew they weren't from Remington," I whisper and close my eyes, completely mortified. "I'd told him I like daffodils, and he hadn't even seen me that day. He didn't know what I looked like."

"What does that have to do with it?" Ryan asks.

"This time, it was the *You look beautiful today* message," I reply. "We found out much later, after he was caught and was in questioning, that he liked to be nearby when I got the deliveries so he could watch my face when I read the card."

"Fuck," Brady mutters, shaking his head.

"He'd worked up this whole imaginary life in his head. He was convinced that I was his girlfriend and that Will Montgomery would be his father-in-law."

"So, he's a little obsessed with your dad, too," Remington adds, and I nod.

"For sure. But I'm the one he's convinced is *his*." I take a drink of water. "The way he watched me in court when I was giving my testimony was repulsive. He smiled and watched me with heart eyes, as if I were his soulmate."

"How did they catch him?" John asks.

"I got a text from what I thought was my sister's phone. She asked me if I could pick her up from a party because everyone else was drinking, and she didn't want Mom and Dad to freak. I knew she was going to that party, so I said, *Of course, no problem. Just shoot me the address*." I lick my lips and have to grip my hands together because they want to shake.

After all this time, I feel like I'm going to lose my shit.

"I put the address into the GPS and drove over there, and all the lights in the house were on. There was even loud music coming from inside."

"The fucker made it look like there was a party going on," Brady says.

"Yep. So I wouldn't question it. I texted her and said, *I'm here, come on out.* And she replied with, *Just come inside for a sec.*"

I have to take another drink of water.

"It's okay," Millie croons, rubbing my back. "Take your time. We're not in a hurry."

"It's best if I just get it all out." I sniff and puff out a breath. "So, that was weird to me, that message from Zoey. She never would have said that, and I suddenly got a weird feeling in my gut. It was almost as if someone was yelling in my head, screaming, 'This is not safe!', you know?"

"Yeah," Ryan says, nodding. "I know."

"I think we all know that voice," Millie says. "Especially women. Tell me you listened."

"I called Zoey. I didn't text her. I just called her, and she picked up. I said, '*I'm here, dude. Just come outside already.*' And she was confused. I knew. I *immediately* knew, and before I could put the car in gear to leave, he was standing in front of me, and he ran around to my door and opened it."

Rem's eyes narrow into slits. "He *opened* the door?"

"Yeah, but I threw it in gear, pushed on the gas, and lurched forward, which broke his arm and hit him in the head with the door. I didn't stop, either. I drove directly to my uncle Matt's house, and we made the report. He was arrested that night and went to prison."

"And now," John says, "he's out of prison."

"I don't know how or why. He was supposed to have another five years, and we were supposed to be alerted when he either came up for parole or was released. My dad wasn't notified. Dad said that my uncle is looking into how he got out early."

The room is quiet as everyone soaks in what I've just told them.

"If you need to fire me, I understand. I truly do." The thought fills me with so much sadness and so much regret that I want to crumple into sobs, but I firm my lip. "It would be nice if I could have twenty-four hours to find another place to live."

"You're not fired," Remington says, shaking his head. "A gate will be installed just off the highway first thing in the morning. We have men setting up cameras all over the property as we speak, as well as motion-detecting lights."

"They'll go off all the time, thanks to all the animals around," Ryan says with a laugh. "But it'll scare off any psychopaths, as well, so it's worth it."

"I have my men patrolling town," Chase continues, "with photos of the perp. As far as we're concerned, he's a wanted man. He's violated the conditions of his parole if he left Washington."

"Like I said, he could be trying to dick around with me *from* Washington."

"I hope that's the case," Chase agrees, "but we're going to treat this as if he's in town. We'll put up wanted posters all over town and talk with the business owners."

"What do *I* do?" I ask. "How can I help?"

"Bruiser will be riding with you when you take the kids to school or pick them up," Remington replies.

"Who's Bruiser?"

"One of my ranch hands. He's *huge*. I wouldn't fuck with him," Remington adds. "Of course, he's a fucking teddy bear at heart, but no one needs to know that."

"I'm fairly certain that I'm safe in the car—"

The look Rem shoots me could melt iron. "You'll have my *children*. And in case I haven't made myself clear to you up to this point, you mean something to me, too. If you think I won't do whatever it takes to keep the three of you safe, you don't know me as well as you think you do."

"Okay, *that* was sweet," Millie says to me, making me laugh for the first time. "Seriously, let these guys protect you. No one will be able to touch you with my family standing guard, I guarantee it."

"I do feel safer already," I admit with a small smile. "But I also feel immense guilt. You shouldn't have to go to this huge expense because of me."

"We should tighten up the security around here anyway," Brady says. "We have expensive horses and equipment."

"I'll also get in touch with the sheriff and the

highway patrol," Chase continues. "We'll have plenty of patrols out this way, too."

"Thank you." I shake my head. "That feels way too small for how grateful I am, but thank you. I'll let Bruiser ride with me. I'll agree to a curfew, and if you'd like a location app put on my phone, that's fine. I'm not too proud to admit that all or some of that might be needed. I won't put up a fight when it comes to safety for not just me, but for your entire family. I've come to love your family, and I would *never* want anyone to be harmed because of me."

"It's not because of you," Chase says. "It's because of a psychopath who shouldn't be out of prison. You haven't done anything wrong."

Those words are like a balm to my heart.

"I think we should go start overseeing some of the work," John says as he moves to the door. His gaze falls to me. "I told you before, you're always welcome here. That hasn't changed."

He winks, and then he's gone, and I have to swallow to control the emotion that wants to boil up and out of me.

"I love you," Millie says, hugging me. "We've got this, babe. I'll call you later."

"Thanks."

One by one, they offer words of encouragement before leaving, and then I'm left alone with Remington.

He watches me quietly for a moment, and then he stands, walks over, and closes the office door.

He doesn't return to his seat behind his desk. Instead, he scoops me up, sits down, and settles me in his lap.

"What would I do if something happened to you?" He buries his nose in my hair and kisses the side of my head.

"I thought you were mad at me."

"Oh, I was. I might still be a little, but damn it, I was *scared*. Not just for my kids, although that's in there. He won't touch my children."

"No, he won't." I have to pull in a breath as just the *thought* of either of those precious kids having even a hair on their head out of place fills me with absolute horror.

"And he won't fuck with you, either. I'll kill him first."

I pull back and stare up at him in surprise. "Rem—"

"I mean it. He doesn't know who he's fucking with."

CHAPTER SIXTEEN
ERIN

"Okay, I appreciate the protectiveness that this has brought to the surface, but really, maybe I should just move out for a while. I can easily commute back and forth to help with the kids, and that way I'm not putting anyone in danger all the time."

"No."

"But it would be the logical thing to do. You and I both know it. At least until we get everything figured out. I'm sure I could stay at my cousin Drew's condo. It's up on the ski hill, and the building has excellent security."

"No."

I blow out a breath and climb off his lap.

"You're being stubborn."

Remington simply lifts an eyebrow, as if he's saying, *"And?"*

"I get it," I say and start to pace because I'm full of nervous energy. "I know that you needed to bring your whole family in here because this could potentially be a problem for everyone, not just me. I mean, sure, it was a bit jarring to walk in and see the whole lot of you here, but I get it. It would go down the same way in my family. You stick together, and you work through things as a team."

I blow a stray piece of hair out of my eyes.

"The responsible thing for me to do is to move into town."

"No."

"Jesus, Grumpy." I turn, prop my hands on my hips, and frown at him. "Sure, I'll miss the sex, too, but it's just *sex*. We can live without it for a little while until this is resolved."

The room goes still as Rem's eyes narrow. Slowly, he lifts himself out of the chair and moves to stand just a couple of feet away from me.

"*Just* sex?" he repeats. "Do you think that what's been going on here is just...sex?"

"I mean, it *is* sex." I feel my pulse speed up.

His eyes drop to my neck. "The way your heartbeat quickens, thumping away there in your throat, and I haven't even touched you yet."

I swallow hard, unable to reply as he reaches out and drags his fingertip over my pulse. He leans in and brushes his nose over the apple of my cheek, then drifts lower to my ear.

"The way your breath catches when I touch you like this."

His hands push under my new dress, skimming up my thighs and my sides, and he lifts it up, over my head and arms, and lets it drop to the floor.

And he's right, my breath *does* catch.

"You have goose bumps," he continues, his voice still soft and crooning as he lets the backs of his knuckles trail up and down my stomach, up to my breasts, and around to unfasten my bra, dropping it to the floor, as well. "Your cheeks flush, but that's not all that turns a pretty pink."

"Rem—"

"Shh."

I reach for him, but he spins me around in a circle, boosts me up onto his desk, and spreads my legs so he can stand between them.

Once again, I reach for his pants, but he takes my hands in his, kisses them, and places them on his desk at my side.

"I don't get to touch you?"

"I'm not done making my point," he says and squats in front of me. With one finger, he nudges my panties to the side. "Put your feet on my shoulders."

As I do, he lowers his mouth to me, and I fall back on my elbows, already lost to him. Jesus, he eats me like he was *born* for it, and every single time, I see stars.

I cry out and move to grab onto his hair, but he quickly ducks out of the way.

"Elbow on the desk," he says, his hazel eyes on fire. "Now."

With my eyes on his, I follow his command, which makes him grin.

"Good girl."

You know, I always thought I'd deck the first guy to say *good girl* to me like that, but it turns out that it's hot as fuck.

He goes back to work, and once I've fallen apart, not just once, but *twice*, he kisses his way up my body and nibbles on my lips.

"The way I can make you fucking lose your mind is *not* just sex, Erin." He unfastens his jeans, and tugs them down past his hips, and then pushes inside of me, and I moan, delirious for more of him. "The way I fit inside of you, so goddamn snug and perfect, as if you were made for me."

He begins to move in long, easy thrusts and then picks up the pace, as if he just can't hold himself back any longer.

"The way I lose myself in you every time," he growls into my ear. "Don't you see that I'm falling in love with you? It fucking scares me, but it's true."

I have to wrap my arms around him now, and he lifts me, bracing me against the wall, and continues to pound me, as if he's punishing us both for ever having the audacity to think that this was ever just about sex.

"Rem," is all I can say as I hold on tight and succumb once more to the absolute bliss of an orgasm gifted to me by this man.

He follows me over, then leans his forehead on mine and works to catch his breath, watching me steadily.

"You'll stay," he says at last. "Because you leaving isn't a motherfucking option."

"No." I swallow hard, also fighting to catch my breath. "Leaving isn't an option for either of us."

"Why is Bruiser with us?" Holly asks from the back seat as I take them to school the next morning.

"He's just helping me out with something," I reply and offer Bruiser a smile.

"Does Dad know?" Johnny asks. "Because Bruiser's real important in the barn and stuff."

I can't help but laugh at that and look at Johnny in the rearview mirror. "Of course, your dad knows. He's the one who suggested it."

"I don't do much that your daddy doesn't know about," Bruiser assures Johnny. I pull through the drop-off line and say goodbye to the kids, then pull out again.

"I think it's silly that you had to take time out of your day just for this ride," I say to the man sitting next to me. "It's literally a drop-off."

"I do what I'm told," Bruiser replies.

"Is Bruiser your real name?"

"Nope."

"What *is* your real name?"

"Theodore."

I feel my eyes go wide, and I turn to him in surprise. "Bruiser suits you better."

"Yes, ma'am."

My phone rings, and I answer it with the tap of a finger on the display. "Hi, Millie."

"Erin?" My blood runs cold at the sound of her voice.

"What's wrong? Are you hurt?"

"I'm sick," she replies. "Stupid cold or something. I'm supposed to have the late shift at the coffee shop today, but I can't go like this. I'm disgusting, and I'll just get everyone sick. Can you cover for me?"

"I—" I glance at Bruiser, who nods. "Sure. I'll head that way now."

"You're the best *ever*," she says. "I'm sorry to do that to you. Is someone with you?"

"Bruiser's here. He'll stay with me today."

"You're the best, Bruiser. I owe you one. Now I'm gonna go die."

She hangs up, and I let out a gusty sigh. "I'm sorry. I know this takes a whole day away from you."

"I've been told to stick close to you. I'll just let the boss know where we'll be."

He places the call to Remington while I get us turned around and headed back to town and to the coffee shop. I'm not wearing my usual Bitterroot Valley Coffee Co. T-shirt, but I'm in jeans. Since I'm filling in, I'm sure it'll be okay.

"Thank God you're here," Marion says with a relieved sigh as I walk in. "Thank you *so much* for covering for Millie. That poor girl sounds awful."

"It's not a big deal at all. I just don't have the right shirt."

"I think you look great," she replies with a wide

smile. She glances over at Bruiser, who takes a seat in the corner of the café. "Is he bothering you?"

"No, definitely not. He'll be hanging out today as my own personal bodyguard. Marion, I don't know if Millie told you, but—"

"She filled me in on what I need to know, and Chase came in, as well, with a photo and pertinent information," Marion assures me. "I'm glad you have someone to protect you. I'm having all the locks changed here, and I'm installing some cameras."

I feel tears spring to my eyes. "Oh, you don't have to do that."

"I should have done it years ago," she says, shaking her head. "This was a reminder for me. You know that I just love you to pieces, and I'm going to do everything I can to keep you safe and comfortable here at work."

"How did I get so lucky to have such an awesome community of people around me?"

"You moved to Bitterroot Valley," she says with a wink. "We take care of our own here. Now, it was busy first thing, as it normally is, but it's calmed down a bit. If you can handle things out here, I'll go back and make some calls about those cameras and locks. I have to run payroll, as well."

"I can definitely handle it."

"Great. Holler if you need help. I'm just back in the office."

Before she turns to leave, Marion pulls me in for a quick hug, then hurries away.

"Marion isn't a hugger."

I jump and spin at the voice and then grin at Brooks. "You're right about that. It surprised me, but in a good way. How are you doing, Brooks?"

"I'm great." His eyes are serious as he watches me. "I'm also keeping my eyes and ears open. No one will get to you in this town, Erin. It's too small, and like Marion said, we take care of each other here."

"I'm learning that," I reply with a nod. "And I appreciate it more than you know. To be honest, it's embarrassing."

"Why?" Brooks frowns over at me. "You didn't do anything wrong."

"No, I didn't." I take a deep breath and let my tense shoulders drop. "You know what? You're right. I'm no longer allowing myself to be embarrassed about something I didn't do."

"Excellent. Now, I'll take a black coffee and some of that huckleberry-lemon bread."

"Oh, that sounds good, doesn't it?" I get to work pouring his coffee and then slide a slice of the bread into a little paper sleeve. "I think I'll have to snag a piece of this for myself. I had no idea what I was missing before I moved here, never having tried huckleberries."

"Montana gold," he says with a wink.

"Is it true that people have been shot over the huckleberries they've picked?"

"Unfortunately, yes. Many people carry protection when they go out to pick. The berries are worth so much money, and it takes so long to pick them, that sometimes the pickers are robbed."

"That's crazy to me," I murmur with a frown. "They're just *berries.*"

Brooks laughs. "Be careful who you say that to. Like I said, they're Montana gold."

"What makes them so special?"

"They don't grow just anywhere, so it's difficult to transplant the bushes. They only like higher elevations, over thirty-five hundred feet, and they're picky about humidity and sunshine."

"It's a wonder we have any of them at all," I reply with a laugh.

"Remington has lots of bushes out at his ranch," Brooks says. "You'll have to go picking this summer. Just watch for bears."

"Bears?" I stare at him, stunned.

"They like the berries more than we do, and that's saying a lot." Brooks winks and then turns to walk away. "I'd better get back to work. You have a good day."

"You, too!"

I glance over at Bruiser, who just gives me a nod. I walk over to him and smile.

"What kind of coffee can I make you?"

"Oh, I don't need anything."

"It's on the house, Bruiser. Seriously. Let me do something for you."

He nods slowly. "I'd take a caramel mocha and one of those slices of huck bread."

"You got it."

I glance up through the windows before turning away and feel my heart catch as I squint, trying to get a better look.

Could that be him?

There's a man across the street, looking this way. It *could* be, if he'd grown six inches in five years and dyed his hair red, but that's unlikely. A woman comes running up to him, and he kisses her, and off they go.

"What's wrong?" Bruiser asks, following my gaze.

"Nothing, I'm just being paranoid."

I wander back to the counter and make Bruiser's order, and once I've delivered it to him, I get to work with the mid-day cleanup of the machines and refilling supplies like napkins and cups. The creamer and half-and-half containers need to be refilled, as well.

Marion *did* have a busy morning.

Hearing the bell over the door, I turn to greet my next customer and find the new guy in town, Clay, frowning over at me.

"Erin?" he asks as he approaches. "I thought Millie worked today."

"She usually does," I reply. The kid has a crush on Millie. Not that I can blame him; she's beautiful and the sweetest there is. "But she wasn't feeling well, so I'm filling in. Are you settling into town well?"

"Yeah, I like it," he says, that southern twang heavy in his voice. "It's real nice."

"I hear you're renting from Roger."

His head comes up, and he narrows his eyes.

"I used to rent that apartment," I explain with a laugh. "And I still see Roger often. He's the nicest guy in the world. Do you like the apartment?"

"Uh, yeah." He clears his throat. "It's a good place. It was nice that it came furnished."

"Right? So convenient. Anyway, I'll stop talking your ear off. What'll it be today?"

Clay places his order and then moves down to the *pickup* area, his nose in his phone. A few more customers start to wander in, and the next couple of hours go by fast.

"You're a rockstar," Marion says with a smile as she joins me, ready to help. "I got so much accomplished back there. Thanks."

"It's no problem; the day is moving fast. Everything good with you?"

"Oh, yeah, everything's fine."

"I'm just going to run to the restroom really quick," I tell her and move to walk to the break room, but the hair on the back of my neck stands up, and I turn to the door.

In walks Summer with a bouquet of roses.

"Shit," I whisper and close my eyes. Like lightning, Bruiser is at the counter, taking the flowers from Summer.

He passes me the card.

"Sir, those are for Erin," Summer says, ready to knock Bruiser for a loop.

"He's with me," I tell her quickly. I open the card and feel my stomach sink.

I can't wait to marry you.

"Oh, Erin," Marion says as I crumple the card in my fist.

"I didn't think I should throw them away," Summer says. "I called Chase, like he asked me to do, and brought them over to you."

I close my eyes, ready to break down into sobs, but that won't solve anything.

"Don't throw that away," Marion advises, taking the card from me. "Come on now, and sit down."

"I can't do this," I whisper, shaking my head. I'm surrounded by the two women and Bruiser, and other customers are watching with interest. "I just can't do this, Marion."

"Oh, honey," Marion says, but I take her hand in mine, my eyes pleading with her to understand.

"I need to take some time off, Marion. I know this leaves you in a bind, and I'm so sorry, but I just can't deal with this every time I'm here."

"I understand," Marion replies, and I can tell by the tone of her voice that she means it. "Don't worry, I'll get your shifts covered. And this isn't you resigning, sweet girl. This is a sabbatical until all of this is resolved."

It feels like all I've done is cry over the past few days, but more tears well in my eyes.

"You know I'll want to come back," I say. "I love it here too much to stay away."

"Good." Marion smiles bravely, but I see the worry there, too. "Everything's going to work out, honey. You just wait and see."

"I know." I nod, wipe at the tears on my cheeks, and stand to get back to work. "I'll finish out today."

"Oh, I've got this now that my office work is done," Marion assures me. "You go on home, where you feel safe."

The sound of that is music to my ears. There's nothing I want more in the world right now than to be out at the ranch.

Bruiser's been on the phone this whole time, likely with Remington, and he's just hanging up when I turn to him.

"We'll have to come back in an hour to get the kids."

"Ms. Joy will pick up the kids today," Bruiser says. "Let's get on out to the ranch."

"Okay." I instinctively reach out and hug Marion. "Thank you. I'll keep you posted."

"You take care of *you*," she says sternly. "Drop in once in a while for a coffee."

"I'll do that." I hurry into the back and hang up my apron, grab my purse and keys, and walk back out to Bruiser. "Okay, let's go."

"You should know," Bruiser says when we're on the highway, heading toward the ranch, "Chase will be meeting us out at the ranch to talk to you."

"I figured."

"And Remington isn't too happy."

"He's frustrated," I reply. "And I don't blame him because *I'm* frustrated, too. Thanks for being there with me today. You really put me at ease."

"When you weren't busy worrying that the boogeyman was going to jump out and get you," he replies and shrugs when I glance over at him. "You don't have a poker face."

"Yeah, there is that."

CHAPTER SEVENTEEN
REMINGTON

"All of the cameras and gates are in place," I say to Chase. He just arrived out at the ranch after the news of the delivery to Erin at Bitterroot Valley Coffee Co. Erin and Bruiser should be pulling in at any time.

"Do you have cameras on the gates?" Chase asks.

"Several. Especially at the entrance that isn't used as much. Only the family and the guys who work here have the code to the lock pad."

"Good. I suggest you change the codes monthly."

"Yeah, I figured that, too. Any word from Washington?"

Chase shakes his head, then takes off his hat so he can rub his head. "No. It's always slow going to get information. All we know for sure is that he made it to his last parole meeting."

He looks at me for a minute. "You're hot for her."

"Yeah, so?"

His eyebrows climb at the admission. Hell, I'm not going to deny it at this point.

"You're screwing around with your *nanny*?"

"Don't make it sound like that. It's more, Chase. *She's* more. And we're going to do everything we possibly can to keep her safe from this asshole."

My brother just nods and rocks back on his heels. "I think it's good. We all like her, man. And Mom mentioned to me that she's going to train Erin to take over the bookkeeping for the ranch."

"That's right."

Chase just grins at me.

"Shut up."

The Suburban comes rolling up the driveway, and Chase and I both turn to greet them.

"Hey," Erin says to us with a tentative smile. "So, today was interesting."

"You." I point to Bruiser and narrow my eyes at him. "What did you see?"

"A lot of people drink coffee in this town," Bruiser replies. "And that's about it. There was nothing unusual, no red flags. Hell, between Erin and me, we recognized everyone who came into the shop."

"He's right," Erin agrees. "There was nothing out of the ordinary, aside from me being totally paranoid. I *hate* that feeling."

"Did you save the note from the flowers?" Chase asks.

"Yeah." She pulls a crumpled card out of her pocket

and passes it over to Chase. I read over his shoulder and feel my stomach twist.

I can't wait to marry you.

"Fuck that," I mutter and shake my head, pacing away.

"I admit, it rattled me," Erin continues. "Pretty bad, actually. I've taken a sabbatical from Bitterroot Valley Coffee Co. until this is all resolved."

Erin sighs, trudges up the stairs of the porch, and sits in a chair.

"I can't live like that," she goes on. "Always scared. I did it once before, and I refuse to do it again. I have enough to keep me busy out here, so that's what I'll do."

She must have been reading my mind because I was going to ask her, reasonably, to do that myself.

Now, I don't have to.

"Marion's awesome." Erin pulls her feet up under her, getting comfortable. "She assured me that I can come back anytime, so that's good. I just can't handle having to constantly look over my shoulder."

"You did the right thing," Chase assures her. "You have to be where you feel safe. Summer told me that the order for the flowers came through her website, so we're going to try to follow the IP address to find out where he's ordering from."

"Okay. Good." Erin nods, then buries her face in her knees. "This freaking sucks."

"I know." I reach out and brush my hand over her head. "I know it does. We'll figure it out."

"I guess the bright side is that I'll have lots of time

to train with Joy. I'll have it all under control soon, and she can start doing all the fun things that she's dying to do."

"You're not being held here," Chase reminds her. "You can go anywhere you want. We just ask that you let someone know where you'll be, and if at all possible, take someone with you."

"I'll do that." She sighs. "I'm not trying to make anyone worry or be a pain in the butt."

Her phone rings, so she pulls it out of her pocket and answers.

"Hey, Mom. What are you up to?"

Erin's eyes widen, but it's in happiness.

"You *are*? When? Holy shit, that's just a couple of days away! I'm *so excited*." She smiles up at us. "Okay, keep me posted. Love you, too."

She shoves her phone back into her pocket.

"My family's coming to visit. Well, just my parents and my sister, Zoey. They're going to stay up at Drew's condo."

"When do they arrive?" Chase asks.

"In just two days." The happy smile returns. "I can't *wait*. I think they know that this is just what I need right now. Plus, my mom probably threatened my dad with a divorce if he didn't bring her out here. She's been eager to come to Bitterroot Valley."

"Mom will want to do a family dinner," I say, glancing at Chase.

"Oh, for sure," Chase agrees. "Also, is it crazy that I'm excited to meet your dad?"

Erin smiles. "No, it's not crazy. He's pretty great. You'll love him."

We spend several minutes going over everything that happened at the coffee shop again for Chase's notes, and then it's just Erin and me, sitting on the porch.

"I'm exhausted," she whispers, closing her eyes and leaning her head back against the chair. "I don't even care that there might be spiders hiding on the back of this chair, and they could crawl in my hair."

"Wow, that's a lot of detail about a nonexistent spider."

Her lips twitch, but she doesn't open her eyes.

"I'm sorry that you were scared today."

"Mostly, I'm pissed off. I don't want to go through all of this again, and I shouldn't have to. Even if he's sending stuff from Washington, he's broken the restraining order. For that alone, he should go back to prison."

"That's what Chase said, too."

"I'm so embarrassed that I've brought this particular piece of baggage into your life. I don't want the kids to know about what's going on, Rem. I don't want them to be scared or worried that they could get hurt. Which they won't be, not just because they're so well protected, but because he's fixated on *me*."

"I don't plan to tell the kids," I reply. "Because I agree. I don't want them to worry."

"How are you going to explain that big-ass gate on the driveway?"

"I'll just tell them that we're adding new safety

measures to the ranch to make sure that the livestock and everything else is safe. Which isn't a lie."

"That's true." We both watch as a bald eagle circles the pasture, looking for a late lunch. "I'm grateful that your mom is picking up the kids, but I feel guilty because that's my *whole job.*"

"Cut yourself some slack," I reply. "You've had a shitty day. Mom doesn't mind helping out, especially in circumstances like this. But if it makes you feel some sort of way, you can cook dinner."

"Okay, I'll take that deal. I was thinking stuffed green peppers."

I wrinkle my nose.

"No? What part of that don't you like?"

"I'll eat it. I'll eat anything you make without an argument."

Erin smirks. "Sure, but I want to make things you *like.* How about I grill some steaks? You have a lot of Wild River Ranch beef in there."

"I'm down for that. I think you should take a hot shower and maybe a little nap first."

She cocks an eyebrow at me. "Do I stink?"

"No." I can't help but laugh at that. "It'll feel good and help you relax. Get comfortable and shake off what happened today. There's nothing else you can do about it."

"You're a good dad," she blurts out, and it makes my heart stumble. "I'm not implying that I think you're fathering *me* right now, because *no.* What I'm saying is, you're calm and reasonable, and despite your sometimes grumpy exterior, you're soothing. I've watched the kids seek you out when they're upset or sad, and that's because you're the one person in the world who can comfort them better than anyone else. You don't just have that effect on your kids."

I can't help but think about how grouchy I've been with my kids over the past few months, and through no fault of their own. It's all on me. I'm a *better* dad because of this amazing woman.

"Thank you."

"You're welcome." She stands and bends down to kiss my head. "I'm gonna go take that shower."

She walks inside, and I stay right where I am for a while, watching that eagle and looking out over my land.

Sometimes, I worry that I'm *not* the dad that my kids need me to be. I get so distracted, so busy while running this business. I don't want my children to look back on their childhood and wonder where their dad was.

I don't think Erin could have given me a better compliment.

"Dad!" Holly comes running out of her room, with Erin not far behind her. "Dad, look at my pretty braids! Erin did them. She says she can do them whenever I want."

Holly's long, dark hair is twisted and woven into some pretty impressive braids.

I definitely can't do that for her.

"You look absolutely gorgeous," I inform my sweet

girl and watch as her face lights up with happiness. "I was thinking about taking you and Johnny out for a ride on the horses. What do you think?"

"Yes. But can Erin come with us?"

"Erin has to go work with your grandma for a bit," Erin replies. "But you go have fun with your two guys, okay?"

"Okay! Johnny!" Holly races off to find her brother and share the good news.

"They love the horses," I say.

"I know. They talk about them often."

"Have you ever ridden?"

Erin shakes her head. "No. I'm not so great with heights, so I don't know that it's for me."

"It's not *that* high up," I disagree.

"I can't touch the ground with my feet, so it's high enough. I don't know, I might try it sometime. Do you need anything before I head over to your parents' place?"

"No, thanks. We probably won't be gone long. Holly doesn't have much stamina yet."

"She'll get there," Erin says. "Have fun."

Before she can walk away, I catch her hand in mine and tug her close. Her face lifts, ready for my lips, and I don't disappoint her. I kiss this woman every chance I get.

"Mm," she says when she pulls away. "That'll tide me over for a while."

Erin leaves just as the kids hurry out of Johnny's room.

"Can I wear my cowboy hat, Dad?" Johnny asks, the

brown hat already on his head. "If we're gonna be doing some cowboying, I need a hat."

"You can wear it," I reply.

"I need mine, too," Holly decides and hurries over to her bedroom. Seconds later, she returns with her purple hat on her head. "I can even wear it with my pretty braids."

"I see that. Okay, buckaroos, let's go saddle up some horses."

"SOMEDAY, I'll be able to saddle my own horse," Johnny mutters as we set out on the trail that leads us deep into our property.

"You pretty much did it all by yourself," I remind him.

"Not really. Lucky had to help."

"Well, saddles are heavy, and horses are tall. It's not easy, even for grown men sometimes. You'll get there, buddy."

"Yeah," Holly adds. "You're only eight. Cut yourself some slack."

I have to press my lips together so I don't laugh out loud.

"Are we going to the special place?" Holly asks.

"I thought we would, yeah. It's pretty this time of year."

And it's not a hard or long ride from the barn, making it easier on the kids. It's a gorgeous late spring day. The trees are all green now, and some wildflowers are starting to pop up here and there, spattering the property in pops of red and yellow.

Holly's already starting to fade on her horse by the time we reach our destination.

Our whole family has loved this particular spot for generations. The view of the mountains is mesmerizing, and sometimes you get lucky and spot a deer or a bear. I've even seen moose out here.

"It's so pretty," Holly whispers, looking up at the mountains. "Are those *our* mountains, Daddy?"

"Pieces of them. Mostly, we just use them to look at because they're too high up for anything else."

Johnny doesn't want my help to dismount the horse, so I walk over to Holly and help her down. She'll probably ride back with me, and I'll tow her horse back by the reins.

"Let's sit and have a snack," I suggest as nerves over the conversation I'm about to have with these kids start to rear their ugly heads. "I have some jerky and apples."

I spread out a blanket on the grass, and the three of us sit facing the mountains, and dig into the snacks.

"Didn't Millie think we should put a bench here?" Johnny asks. "I think I remember something about that."

"Yeah, but there's no need to. We can sit on the ground like this."

They nod and chew on their jerky, and I decide there's no better time than the present to talk to them.

"Hey, guys, I want to talk to you about something."

"Something bad?" Holly asks, chewing her jerky.

"No, not bad. In fact, I think it's really good."

"What's up, Dad?" Johnny asks, his face set in serious lines.

Jesus, there are times that he's so much like me it's like a kick in the stomach.

"How are things going with you two and Erin? Do you like having her here to help us out?"

"Yeah," Johnny says immediately, a bright smile on his face. "She's great. She taught me a fun way of figuring out double-digit addition. She made it really easy, and now I'm doing good at math."

"She braids my hair," Holly adds. "And sometimes, if she has to tuck us into bed because you're working late, she tells really good stories. She sings songs, too."

"She does?" That surprises me. I've never heard Erin sing. "What kinds of songs?"

"A lot of Taylor Swift," Johnny says. "And Nash. She likes them."

"A couple of weeks ago, when it was really cold outside," Holly begins, "I forgot my coat at home, and I was sad because I wouldn't be able to go outside for recess, so she went home and got it and brought it to the school for me."

I haven't heard any of these stories before. I knew Erin was great with my kids, but I had no idea that it was to this extent.

I glance down at Johnny's leg and frown. "Hey, off the subject, but how are your pants fitting you now? Just last week, we decided you'd outgrown them and needed new ones."

"Erin took me shopping after school," he replies, as if it's no big deal. "I got enough to last through the summer, since I mostly wear shorts in the summer anyway."

She took my kid shopping, paid for his clothes, and didn't ask me to reimburse her.

"That was nice of her," I murmur, and Johnny nods in agreement. "Well, guys, I want to be honest with you, always. I really like Erin myself. She's smart and funny, and I think she gets along with our family really well."

"She's pretty, too," Holly adds.

"She's definitely pretty," I agree. "I want Erin to be my girlfriend. I want her and me to be a couple."

Holly frowns. "Do I get to call her Mommy?"

"I think that's rushing things, sweetheart. Maybe, someday, if I were to marry Erin, that might happen."

"Are you asking us if it's okay if Erin is your girl-friend?" Johnny's face is still so serious, but there's curiosity in his eyes, too.

"That's what I'm asking you, but I'm doing a crappy job of it."

"That's a swear," Holly says.

"No, crap isn't a swear," Johnny replies. "You're thinking of shit."

"Oh, yeah."

I eye my son, who just smiles angelically.

"The thing is, I need to know if you're okay with that because there might be some times that I would want to hug Erin, or maybe kiss her, and I don't want you guys to be uncomfortable with it."

"It's kinda gross," Johnny says, wrinkling his nose. "But I guess grown-ups do gross stuff like that. Grandpa kisses Grandma all the time, and *ew*."

"Yeah, they do."

Holly and Johnny share a look and then nod.

"Yeah, we like the idea," Johnny says. "Erin is part of our family now anyway. She's the best."

Happy with the way that went, I reach for an apple.

He's right. Erin *is* the best.

CHAPTER EIGHTEEN
ERIN

"We're home!" Holly comes running into the kitchen through the mudroom, and I hold up my hand.

"Wait. Go take those boots off in the mudroom, please. All of you, take your boots off."

"They're not *that* dirty," Holly mutters as she walks back to the mudroom. When she's taken them off, she comes running back in her socks. "We said *yes*!"

"You said yes to what?" I ask as she throws her little arms around my waist and hugs me close.

"I didn't think they'd run right in and spill the beans," Rem says from the doorway. He's also sockless and has a pained look on his face.

"Yeah, Holly, you were supposed to keep your mouth shut so Dad could be romantic," Johnny says, shaking his head.

"It's too exciting," Holly replies. "Tell her, Dad."

"Someone tell me *something*."

Remington laughs and walks to us, then disentangles Holly from me, kisses her cheek, and sets her on a stool at the island.

"I asked the kids if they'd be okay with you and I...uh, you know...were *together*."

"He wants you to be his girlfriend," Holly announces with glee, which makes Remington cringe.

"Really?" I can't help but grin up at him and step just a little closer. "Is that true, Grumpy?"

The kids both snicker at the nickname, and Remington nods slowly, smiling down at me.

"Yeah, Doc. It's true. What do you think?"

"I think I'm in."

He cups my face and leans in to kiss me softly, almost chastely. Johnny makes a gagging noise, making us laugh.

"I know you have to do that, but *in front* of us? Really?"

Rem's eyes don't leave mine. "Get used to it, kiddo."

MY FAMILY ARRIVES TODAY, and I have zero chill.

After I took the kids to school, I kept myself busy by doing some laundry and cleaning the kitchen. Then I sorted through my bathroom stuff and purged all the creams and salves and fancy potions that I don't use and set them aside to donate.

I'm just about to go out of my mind with anticipation when my phone finally rings.

"Hey, baby doll," Mom says. "We're here!"

"Oh, my God, I'm so happy. Where, exactly, are you?"

"At the condo, getting settled in. This town is *adorable*. I can definitely see why you love it so much."

"You guys stay there," I reply as I sling my crossbody handbag over my head and grab the keys to my car out of the bowl on my dresser, along with a few peppermints. "I'll be there in twenty minutes."

"We're not going anywhere," she promises me. "I can't wait for you to get here."

"On my way."

I hurry out to my car and start it, then pause. Depending on how long I'll be, I might not have time to come out to the ranch and switch cars to get the kids, so I turn off the engine and hurry over to the Suburban.

Before I pull out, I shoot Remington a quick text.

Me: I'm going to the condo to see my family. They just got here! Don't worry, I'll still get the kids from school.

I send off that message and then pull through the gate and onto the highway.

I went to Seattle a few months ago for Drew and London's engagement party, but other than that quick trip, I haven't seen my family since late last year. I saw my dad for a couple of hours recently, but that doesn't really count.

I drive through Bitterroot Valley and make my way to the ski village, where the condo is. There's a code there to get through the gate, and then I park in visitor parking.

When I knock on the door, it's opened wide, and my mom immediately tackle hugs me.

"My baby," she says, holding on tight. God, she smells good. Do all moms smell like home? Because that's what she smells like. She kisses my cheek and then pulls back to look at me. "You look...*great*."

"Thanks."

Zoey and Dad both take turns hugging me, as well, and we end up in the kitchen, as usual, where it looks like someone already delivered some groceries.

"Your father was hungry when we landed," Mom explains as she sets out crackers, cheese, and fruit.

"Of course, he was," I reply and smile at my dad. "He's *always* hungry. But I'm a little hungry, too. I need to take you to the BBQ place in town. In fact, that's where we should have dinner tonight."

"That sounds good," Mom says, and once everything is spread out on the counter for us to pick at, she sighs and stares out the floor-to-ceiling windows to the mountain beyond. "It's just flat-out gorgeous here. I can picture it in my head, what it'll look like all snowy and pretty."

"It's seriously great in the winter," I agree. "But it's cold. Like, *cold.*"

"We'll have to come in the winter," Mom decides. "And this *condo*! London told me it was fancy and more than comfortable, and she was right. This place looks like it should be in a magazine."

I've always loved how my mom gets excited about beautiful things, as if she and my dad couldn't buy one of these for themselves.

It probably stems from where she came from. Mom

was a foster kid and was dirt poor. She definitely doesn't take anything about her life with Dad for granted.

"I'm gonna try out that huge tub in my bathroom tonight," Zoey announces as she reaches for a grape. "It's *insane*."

"Tomorrow, I'll show you all of Bitterroot Valley, and, if you're up for it, Remington's mom would like to have you all out at the ranch for dinner. The whole family will be there. I think you'll like them."

"I totally want to see your ranch," Zoey replies. "And maybe a cute cowboy. It's a yes for me."

"Same," Mom echoes, just as there's a knock at the door. "Minus the cute cowboys, of course. I can't wait to see the ranch."

Dad saunters over and opens the door, and there's... Remington. Standing tall and hot in the doorway.

And he doesn't look happy.

"Hey, what's wrong? And how did you know where the condo is?"

"He called me before you got here," Dad says. "I told him where to find us."

"You drove off *by yourself*," Remington says. "You're supposed to take Bruiser with you, or me."

"I was just coming to see my family," I reply with a frown. "I made no stops; I just came here."

"We have an understanding," Remington insists, and I notice my mom's face go all gooey and starry-eyed.

"I like you. Bring it in." Mom walks around the island to hug Remington. "I see why she calls you Grumpy, but I like you. Thanks for looking out for our girl."

"Rem." I take a deep breath, trying to keep my temper down. "I appreciate the caution, but it's my family. I knew I was going to be here until I had to get the kids, and Bruiser doesn't want to just hang here while we talk and joke around. That's a waste of his time."

"I'm Bruiser's boss, and *I* decide what's a waste of his time," Remington counters, and my dad smiles.

Smiles.

"I see that you're enjoying this."

"Hey, I'm on his side. The most important thing is keeping you safe."

"I'm *safe*," I mutter and grab a cracker. "I was excited to get here and see them, and it didn't occur to me that it wouldn't be okay to do that."

"Under literally *any* other circumstances, it's perfectly okay to do that," Remington says.

"He's kind of hot," Zoey whispers, loud enough for all of us to hear, and Remington's mouth tips up in a smile. "Just saying."

"I'm sorry for making you worry," I say. "I didn't mean to do that."

Mom smiles up at Rem. "Your town is beautiful."

"Yeah," he says with a nod. "It is. Did Erin mention that my mom would like to invite you all out to the ranch for dinner tomorrow?"

"She did, and we would love to accept that thoughtful invitation," Mom replies.

"My brothers might make fools of themselves," Remington warns them. "They're fans."

"I'm not worried. There'll be plenty to talk about,

then," Dad replies with a shrug. "Does that mean that you're *not* a fan?"

"No, I am. I just don't make a fool of myself." Remington shrugs and smiles at my dad, and that makes everyone laugh, putting us all at ease. "You stay with your family," Rem tells me. "I'll get the kids from school. Let me know when you're on your way home, please. Since you'll be riding alone, I want to make sure you arrive safely."

"Ten-four, good buddy." I offer him a salute, and I'm pleased when that makes him grin. "I'm sorry you worried. I'll walk you out."

"See you tomorrow," Dad says with a wave as Remington and I walk out the door and down to his Jeep.

"Thanks for grabbing the kids," I say when we reach the Jeep. "I appreciate it."

"It's no problem. I want you to have a blast with your family while they're here. Take tomorrow off, too."

"Oh, you don't have to—"

"I can handle it," he interrupts and cups my cheek in his palm. "Don't worry about us. You've more than earned some time with your family."

His eyes, those gorgeous hazel eyes, are soft and kind and not grumpy at all, and it makes me swoon *hard*.

"Thank you." I boost myself up on my toes and give him a quick peck on the lips. "You're the best boss ever."

He smirks. "Do you always kiss your bosses?"

"You know, I think you're the first one, actually."

His smile spreads. "That's good to know. Now I'm going to kiss *you*, but not as your boss."

I raise my brow. "No?"

"No." He lowers his lips, and I'm immediately swept away by him, absorbed in how he can make my knees weak and my breath catch, with just the touch of his lips. "Have fun. Keep me posted."

"Will do." I lick my lips, still tasting him there. "What time should we come to the ranch tomorrow?"

"Whenever you want. We can give them a tour before dinner."

"Oooh, I want a tour, too. I still haven't seen as much as I'd like."

Remington frowns down at me. "You haven't?"

"No."

"We'll fix that." He winks and climbs into the Jeep. "See you later."

Remington watches me, obviously waiting for me to go back inside before he takes off, so I turn and head back to the condo. Now that I have time to spare today, I can show off my new town earlier than planned.

I'm *so* happy that my family is here.

"THAT'S A LOT OF CATTLE," Dad says when we're driving back toward the farmhouse. "I don't think I've ever seen that many cows in one place."

"We're a mid-sized ranch," Rem says. "Some have a *lot* more than that. But we're one of the biggest in Montana."

There's a lot of pride in his voice. And there should

be. The Wild River Ranch is not just beautiful, it's profitable.

From what I've learned from Joy, not all ranchers can say the same.

"I'm officially starving," Zoey says from the back seat.

"Good, because I'm quite sure that my mom made enough food for an army."

When we arrive at the farmhouse, I'm not surprised to see that everyone has already arrived for dinner. And when we go inside, we're welcomed like old friends who haven't seen each other in a long, long time.

"Wow, it's really nice to meet you," Chase says as he shakes my dad's hand. "I've been a fan of yours forever."

"We all have," Ryan puts in.

"Especially Ryan," Brady adds. "He bid on, and won, your Super Bowl jersey."

Dad's eyebrows climb into his hairline in surprise. "*You're* the idiot that paid a million dollars for that?"

"What?" Joy gasps, and if she were wearing pearls, she'd be clutching them at her son's admission.

"I'm that idiot," Ryan confirms with a rueful smile. "It's framed in my office."

The Wild men are not only sexy, they're funny as hell.

"Okay, you can stop fawning over the poor man," Joy says, shaking her head. "Dinner's ready, and you all look hungry after spending the afternoon in the spring air."

"You have a gorgeous ranch," Mom says. "How do you ever get anything done? I'd spend all day, every day, staring at those mountains."

"Well, the good thing about mountains is, they're

still there when I've finished whatever it is that I need to do." Joy smiles and loops her arm through my mom's as they set off toward the dining room. "Now, Meg, I want to know everything there is to know about life in Seattle."

I smile over at Remington, but he doesn't smile back.

In fact, he's not even looking my way.

I follow his gaze and blink in surprise because Brady is totally hitting on my baby sister.

"Oh, that's not true," Zoey says with a giggle and lays her hand on Brady's biceps.

I glance over at my dad, whose eyes have just narrowed.

"Come on." I gesture for everyone to follow me. "We'd better get in there before all the food's gone."

I hang back and wait for Zoey.

"Do *not* tell me that you're going to start something with Brady while you're here."

"Nah," she says. "He's cute and nice, but mostly, I just like watching the vein in Dad's temple throb at the sight of me flirting with him."

I can't help the bark of laughter that comes at that. Leave it to Zoey to try to give our overprotective father a heart attack.

"I like the security measures you've added to the ranch," Dad says once we're all seated and have dug into our plates. "You've gone above and beyond, and I appreciate it."

"We take the safety of those we care about seriously," John replies and then smiles over at me. "And we care about Erin. Besides, it was time to beef up security around here."

"We have a pretty new gate," Holly announces with a sweet smile. "To keep the bad guys away and our cows safe."

"That's right," I reply and wink at her. "It *is* a pretty gate, isn't it?"

"I like it," she says with a nod and then nibbles on some fried chicken.

"Your kids are adorable," Mom says to Remington. "Johnny, how can you possibly eat all that chicken while missing so many teeth?"

"I lost another one this morning," Johnny replies with satisfaction. "They're dropping like flies. And the tooth fairy brings me five bucks every time. It's not a bad way to make a living."

The entire table busts up laughing at that, and Johnny smiles big, showing off his empty mouth.

"Millie," Zoey says, "I really love your dress."

"Oh, thanks," Millie replies. "I found it at Polly's place downtown."

"I *love* that shop," Mom and Zoey reply at once.

"I bought a bunch of stuff there today," Zoey adds.

"We had a lot of fun in there," Mom agrees.

"You mean *I* bought a lot of stuff in there today," Dad says with a scowl. "My girls are trying to break me."

"Oh, whatever, Dad." I smirk across the table at him. "Besides, you kept adding more things to the pile your-self. '*Megan, you'd look great in this. Zoey, this has your*

name written all over it. Erin, you can't live without this.'
You're the enabler in the family."

"Guilty," Dad says with a shrug. "I like to spoil my
girls."

"As it should be." Joy looks so happy, with everyone
gathered around the table, eating the delicious food she
spent all day preparing.

"Joy, you really outdid yourself today. This is delicious." I reach for more green beans. "I wish I knew how
to cook like this."

"I can teach you," Joy says.

"Make it a group lesson," Millie adds.

"I'm jealous that I won't be here for it," Zoey says.
"Maybe I'll come back, just for that."

And so it goes for the rest of the evening. Banter and
jokes and stories about football games played long
before I was born.

I love it. Our two families get along better than I
could have hoped for. Not that I thought they wouldn't,
but I was nervous.

And I see now that there was no need to be.

I glance up and find Rem watching me over the rim of
his water glass. "Hey, Doc," he says, "would you please
pass me the potatoes?"

"Sure." I pass the bowl to him, and he brushes his
fingers over mine, sending a little thrill through me. And
by the look in his eyes, he knows exactly what he's
doing.

"Doc?" Mom asks.

"The Seven Dwarfs," I reply.

"I need to hear how this all came about." Mom turns to Remington. "Spill it."

He looks at me, and I nod. "Go ahead."

"I used to go into the coffee shop every afternoon before I got the kids from school, and I saw Erin. I didn't know her name. Over time, she'd acted like almost every one of the dwarfs when I'd been there. Sleepy and happy and even dopey."

"I had a brain fart moment," I interject. "Just to be clear. Plus, I'm adorable and lovable."

Everyone nods, then turns back to Rem.

"Then, coffee spilled on my hand, and she fixed me up. So, I called her Doc."

"And I call him Grumpy," I add. "Because he *is*. Most of the time."

"He's been way less grouchy since you came to live here," Johnny says, surprising me. "He laughs more."

"And he gets to do stuff with us," Holly adds. "Like take us out on the horses and stuff."

"Well, I'm happy to hear that you like having Erin with you," Mom says. "I have to say, this spontaneous trip was exactly what I needed."

"We get to go on a trip, too," Holly tells her. "When do we go, Grandma?"

"In just a few days," Joy replies and turns to my mom. "John and I are taking the kids over to Spokane for a few days of shopping and eating in the city."

"And we get to see Aunt Melissa," Johnny adds.

"Oh, how fun," Mom replies. "Maybe someday, you two would like to see Seattle."

My gaze catches Remington's again, and he's simply watching me, listening to all the conversations going on around the table. Ryan and Brady are asking my dad a million questions about the team and being a famous football player. Chase, Millie, and Zoey are talking about crime, of all things. Which shouldn't surprise me because I'm pretty sure my sister is going to pursue a career in law enforcement after she graduates from college this spring.

I *love* the chaos and chatter happening around me. It reminds me of being with the rest of our family.

With everything else going on, this is exactly what I needed.

CHAPTER NINETEEN
REMINGTON

I need a break from the chaos. Dinner with everyone went better than I hoped, and I enjoy Erin's family, but I'm not used to the noise, and I just need a minute of solitude.

So, I sneak off while everyone's digging into my mother's chocolate cream pie and sit on the back deck, watching the sun set behind the mountains.

I'm falling in love with her. I've known it for a couple of weeks now, but I didn't acknowledge it. Tonight, watching her with her family and with mine, the way she so seamlessly balanced both broods, kept conversations running smoothly, and helped Holly when my little girl accidentally spilled her juice, only reinforced what I've known for weeks.

Erin is fucking incredible.

The door slides open behind me, letting the laughter and chatter spill out from inside. Will steps out and closes the door behind him, cutting off the noise once more.

"I saw you sneak off," he says as he passes me a plate of pie. "You can't walk away from pie. I think it's a federal law. Mind if I sit with you?"

"I don't mind at all," I reply as I accept the plate and take a bite. "My mom is one hell of a cook."

"Hell yes, she is." Will grins over at me. "Food is my favorite thing. Well, besides my wife."

"You're still so smitten with her." I frown when I realize that I said that out loud. "I'm sorry, I shouldn't have said that."

"Why not? It's true. I'm fucking *obsessed* with Megan. I have been since the day I met her, though she didn't like me back then."

"Why not?"

"Well, she worked on the pediatric floor of the hospital. She's a nurse and worked with *very* sick kiddos. She'd contacted my agent a few times, asking if I'd come by and cheer up the patients. I never got the requests because my *former* agent always declined them right away."

"That's kind of them."

"It was bullshit. Of course, I would want to go. So, when I found out about it, I got a few of my buddies from the team to go with me, and we took up a bunch of gear and merch for the kids and spent time with all of them."

"I bet that helped put you in Meg's good graces."

"It helped," he agrees. "She's also partial to chocolate cupcakes, and I had those delivered, too. The key is to pay attention. It sounds silly, but it's true. Anyway, I charmed her. And I can say with absolute certainty that my life wouldn't work without her."

"That's what everyone wants in the end. To find the person that makes their life better."

I feel him glance my way before turning back to the view. "I'm going to be brutally honest with you, Remington."

"That's the way I prefer it."

"I don't like your age difference. In my opinion, you're too damn old for my daughter."

"I would probably say the same thing if it was Holly in a similar situation." I nod and take a bite of pie.

"My opinion doesn't piss you off?"

"It's reasonable. That doesn't piss me off. Your daughter makes *my* life better. Not just because of how amazing she is with my kids, although that has to be a piece of it because Johnny and Holly are the most important part of my life."

"I get that."

"It's more than that. She doesn't give herself enough credit for how damn smart she is. She's witty and fun. She *loves* my home—not just this house, but the land it's on and Bitterroot Valley—and that's important to me. I didn't plan to fall for your daughter; it just sort of happened, and I'm grateful that it did. Sure, there's an age gap, but she's well into adulthood. She's not a kid."

"No, you're right about that. It would be a different story if she were eighteen or nineteen."

"I wouldn't have been interested in someone that

young, no matter how drop-dead gorgeous she is. Besides, I'm thirty-six, not seventy-six. It's not creepy or anything."

That makes him laugh.

"I can see with my own two eyes that you're good for each other," Will says at last. "I'm not blind. I like the way you've stepped up to protect her, and I can tell that you treat her, and all of your family, very well."

"My father would kick my ass if it were any other way."

Will nods thoughtfully. "Sounds like you were raised a lot like me. And I like that. Where do you see this going, Rem?"

"All the way." I blow out a breath, and Will reaches over to pat my shoulder. "Scares the shit out of me."

"If it wasn't real, it wouldn't scare you. Now, let's change the subject. Who's your favorite football team?"

"I've always liked Denver."

"And now you've fucked it up." He punches me on the arm, and then we laugh.

"It's so quiet with the kids gone," Erin says a few days later. Dad just drove away with a car full of kids and luggage and Mom in the passenger seat, on their way to Washington. "I mean, I know they're gone when they're at school, but this feels...*different.*"

"It always throws me for a loop," I agree and sling my

arm around her shoulders, tugging her against me. "I enjoyed spending time with your family this week."

"Me too," she says and smiles up at me. "I was sad to see them go."

"I have plans to keep you busy over the next few days so you don't think about that."

I grin at her and drag my knuckles down her cheek. I'd love nothing more than to spend every minute of those three days in bed with her.

"I know that look," she whispers. "We won't survive that."

"But it would be fun trying." I grin. "First on my list is a more thorough tour of the property. The tour we gave your family just skimmed the surface."

"*Yes.*" She pumps her fist into the air. "Yes, please."

"It'll take us all day, so we'll take some food with us. And lots of water."

"But there's a lot of water on the property. Streams and ponds and stuff."

I shake my head. "We'd need filters for that. You don't want to drink that water. You *could,* but there's likely bacteria from the cattle."

"Bottled water for the win." She grins and starts pulling stuff out of the fridge and cabinets. "I can make us sandwiches, and we have lots of protein bars and chips. Fruit."

"That's great, thanks. I'll go out and fetch a cooler from the garage to keep it all cold."

By the time I return with the cooler and empty all the

ice from the freezer into it, Erin has a nice pile of snacks for me to put in it.

"It's just one day," I remind her, eyeing all the food. "Not a week."

"I'm not taking any chances. I get hangry when I haven't had enough food." She grins and cuts the last sandwich in half before sliding it into a sandwich bag. "Okay, that's done. What should I wear?"

"Jeans, for sure. Hiking shoes or something similar. Layer the top. It might get warm this afternoon."

"I'm on it!" She runs through the house, and I finish packing the cooler and carry it out to the Jeep.

I'd much rather do this on horseback, but that would turn into a several-day tour, so we'll go motorized this time. Hopefully, someday, I'll get Erin on a horse and teach her how to ride and help her get over that fear.

Today is not that day.

I've just slid my own hiking boots on when Erin comes rushing back in. Her hair is up in a high ponytail, and she's dressed for an adventure in the woods. I can't see how her jeans hug her ass because it's covered by a flannel shirt that's open in the front, showing off a grey T-shirt. She makes outdoor gear look fucking hot as hell.

"You're staring," she says, looking down at herself. "Is this wrong?"

"No." I step to her and nudge her chin up. "It's perfect. You always manage to look amazing."

"Aww, you're just saying that because you're hoping for some forest sex."

"Counting on it." I laugh and step away. "Let's get this show on the road, Doc."

"Happily, Grumpy."

Once we're settled in the Jeep, we set off in the direction of my parents' house.

"I didn't know that there was a bunch of property this way," Erin says and rolls her window down. "I mean, I know your parents and Brady live over here, but I thought it was the edge of the property."

"No, we're pretty much smack in the middle of it. I thought I'd start over here because you haven't seen much of it."

"You're the guide," she says with a smile as she slides her sunglasses on. "Show me *everything.*"

When Brady's cabin comes into view, I point at it. "That's the oldest cabin on the property. Brady lives in it now. Before that, it was empty for a while. My mom and dad lived in it when they were first married."

"It looks tiny," she says.

"It is. But it works for one or two people." I follow the bend in the road. "And you've seen Mom and Dad's place."

"It's adorable." Erin smiles. "It's really perfect for them."

"I agree. It was a good move on Dad's part. Most of the property over here is wooded. We thought about clearing some of it out for more pasture, and that could happen in the future if we keep adding to our herd, but for now, we like the woods. They insulate the property during bad storms in the winter, and all the critters can live in there."

"Don't bulldoze Bambi's house," Erin says.

"No, ma'am. If local hunters ask for permission, we allow them to hunt in here, away from the cattle."

"Oh, good idea. Are you asked often?"

"Every year. They're regulars, been hunting here for a long time. But they always ask first, which we appreciate. There's a nice little lake back here."

Her eyes widen as I drive us over a little hill, and then there's a lake with the mountains in the background.

"Holy shit," she whispers. "Every time I think your land can't get any prettier, I see something new."

"The water is high right now because of the spring snow runoff. It's not big enough for motorized boats, but we like to take paddle boards and canoes out here in the summer. Sometimes, we fish."

"I would *love* to learn to paddle board," she says with excitement. "Is it deep?"

"In the middle, it's about fifty feet deep, so yeah. But the shorelines are shallow. The kids love swimming over here in the summer."

"We'll be out here every day."

I drive on, looping back around to the farmhouse and then past the barn and further out.

"I pointed out those old buildings that we don't use anymore, but I thought you might like to go explore them a bit."

"Uh, *yeah*." She bounces in her seat. "I *love* abandoned buildings."

"You do?"

"Hell yes. I like to think about who lived there before and what it looked like when it was new."

"Well, that was the first barn built on the farm."

"Why so far away from the first house?" she wonders.

"We don't know for sure. Anyway, my three times great-grandfather bought this land almost a hundred and fifty years ago. So, that structure would date back that far."

"Crazy," she says. "The walls are caved in."

"Yeah, we don't ever go inside. It's long past the days of being stable. But it's fun to walk around and look at. There are a couple of other smaller buildings, too. One was a feed shack, and we're not sure what the other was used for."

I pull to a stop and cut the engine.

"Wait here for a second. I need to make sure we're not disturbing any wildlife."

"Bears?"

"Among other things." I take my gun out of its case and walk around the perimeter, happy when I don't have any altercations with animals. I walk back to the Jeep and open Erin's door for her. After she steps out, I stow the gun away. "There's nothing here."

"Good." She walks over and peers through the door of the barn. "Wow, it just collapsed in on itself."

"Before I was born," I agree. "Dad always talked about using the barn wood for other projects, but he never got around to it."

"Are you *kidding me*?" Erin turns to stare at me. "This could be used for so many things. Flooring or furniture, jeez, anything. But it would make a really gorgeous floor."

"Do you hate the floor in the farmhouse now?"

"Not at all. But someone could use this. It's been all the rage for years now, Remington. Someone would pay a lot of money for it."

"Dad used some of it on their new house. We won't sell it or take it off the property. It stays here."

"That makes sense." She props her hands on her hips, looking in again. "Do you know if the wood was harvested from trees here on the property?"

"They likely grew right where we're standing," I confirm. "There's too much timber here to bring in wood from somewhere else, especially back then, when it was all by horse and buggy."

"Good point. I hope you find a project for it. Or you could even reuse it right here."

"How so?"

"Well, you could take it apart, board by board, and then rebuild it, adding in fresh lumber to keep it sound. Hell, use it for something. A guesthouse, an event space for weddings and big parties—heck, you could do anything. Weddings would be *huge* out here. With that view?"

She points to the mountains.

"Can you just imagine the photos? Holy shit, that's every girl's dream. A beautiful, rustic event space and this incredible view for the best photos ever. That's what I would do."

I can see it, plain as day. "It sucks that it's in the middle of one of my pastures."

"Could you move the pasture?" She taps her lips with her finger as she paces back and forth. "Fence off just this acre or two? So guests could still *see* the cows, but they won't wander into someone's nuptials."

"Yeah." I turn in a circle, mapping it out in my head. "That could work. It's a hell of a project."

"It would be big," she agrees. "And I'm just talking. It's none of my business if you use this or leave it as is, but man, it feels like a waste."

She's right. It does. I'll have to think it over and talk with my family about it. If we decide to move forward with something like that, I hope that Erin would be interested in helping. It's *her* vision.

"So, you don't know what this was for?" she asks, pulling me out of my own thoughts as she points at the smallest building.

"I'm pretty sure that was an outhouse," I reply and laugh when she pulls her hand back from trying the door. "If there was anything in it, it's long gone."

"Still, I'm good here. And that was the feed shack?"

"Yep."

"It has solid walls," she says as she just walks right inside. "You know, you could make this a little bigger and turn it into a coffee stand for events or a bar area. Or you could make it a bridal suite, where the bride can privately get ready for her big day."

"Not a bad idea," I murmur.

"So, *this* is the mystery building?" Erin points to the last building, farther away from the other two.

"Yes. It might have been used in the fall and winter to store meat after hunting season, but we don't know."

"Huh." She pokes her head in and then turns back my way. "This spot is fabulous."

"I've always liked it, too."

I can tell that her wheels are turning when she joins me, and we walk back to the barn.

"There's still a lot to see today."

"I could stay here all day, daydreaming," she admits and laughs. "But I definitely want to see the rest. I'll come back another time."

"Not by yourself."

She frowns up at me. "I don't think my stalker is hiding in the barn, Grumpy."

"It has nothing to do with that." I shake my head and open the door for her. "I don't want you to get hurt by an animal."

"Oh, yeah. Bears. Okay, deal."

I drive through some of the same terrain that we traveled the other day with Erin's family. I slow down at my family's favorite spot so we can take it in, and then I push on again.

"This ranch started out at fifty-thousand acres," I tell her as I drive. "Now, we're closer to eighty thousand. I bought the property next door. The former owners kept their house and barn and five acres for their horses, but they're done ranching and didn't have children to leave it to. They wanted the land to be worked and used, so we bought it."

"Are we on that property now?"

"Not yet." I grin over at her. "We're getting there. It's worked great for us because we also took over his cattle, and we now have more pasture space."

"So, you can continue to expand," she guesses correctly.

"That's right. Now, hold on, because I'm going to climb that hill over there."

"Like, in the Jeep?"

"Yep."

I put the Jeep in four-wheel drive and push on the gas to get us up the steep grade and then stop at the top.

"Uh, Grumpy?"

"Yeah, Doc?"

"Did I mention that I hate heights?"

I glance over, and her eyes are clenched shut, so I reach out and take her hand in mine.

"You're fine. We're not even getting out of the Jeep, I promise. Open your eyes."

"As soon as we get off this hill, I'll be happy to do so."

With a chuckle, I reach over and brush my fingers over her cheek. "Come on, pretty girl. The view into Bitterroot Valley is *insane* up here."

That gets her to slit one eye open, and then they both go round as she stares at the view.

"How is this possible? We're so far out of town."

"We're higher in elevation here, and it gives us the perfect view. It's pretty wild at night, with all the lights."

"I'm going to have to see that," she murmurs.

"There used to be a fire lookout up here," I continue. "The Forest Service paid to rent out this hilltop in the summer months, and they stationed a man to live up here and keep an eye out for fires."

"Why don't they do that anymore?"

"Technology. Some towers are still in use, especially in remote areas, but we have drones and satellites now."

"I think that would be a lonely job."

"Some people thrive in it. Okay, we have to go back down so I can take you to the next spot, where we'll have lunch."

"Oh, shit." She sucks in a breath and clenches her eyes shut again.

I shake my head, laughing. "Your confidence in me is awe-inspiring."

CHAPTER TWENTY

ERIN

"I have confidence in you," I insist, still clenching my eyes closed. "But I don't like the ascent or the descent. I think I must have died in a plane crash or something in a previous life. I'll have to ask my cousin, Haley, about that."

"Haley would know about your past lives?" He doesn't sound so sure.

"Maybe. I don't know. Are we down yet?" I do *not* want to have the first panic attack of my life sitting next to the man that I've fallen in love with while he's trying to show me his ranch.

"Almost," he murmurs. After a few minutes, I finally hear him say, "Yes. We're down."

I crack one eye open, and when I see that we're level again, I open the other one. "Whew."

"So, aside from a possible fatal plane crash in a past life, you don't know why you're afraid of heights?"

"Not really. There wasn't one specific incident or

anything, if that's what you mean." I reach into my pocket and pull out a peppermint and pop it into my mouth. "Mint?"

"Sure." He accepts it. "So, no specific scary heights incident."

"Nope. But I've known since I was little that I didn't want to go on the scary rides at the fair or at any of the amusement parks. They make me feel sick, and I don't like being up high."

"A lot of people get motion sick."

"I know, and it sucks. Anyway, I avoid it."

"How do you do in a plane? When you travel?"

"Not bad, actually. I just make sure I'm in an aisle seat toward the front of the plane. Did you know that if you're prone to motion sickness, it's not usually as bumpy toward the front of the plane when they hit that unexpected rough air?"

"I don't think I've heard that, but I *did* know that you're the safest in the middle of the plane."

"You know, I have a theory that if you're going down, there is no safest place to be. Other than the ground, that is."

I turn in the seat so I can look at him.

"Are you the thrill seeker type?"

"No." He smiles over at me. "Definitely not. But I don't mind roller coasters. Johnny loves them, too. The ones he's allowed to ride, anyway. However, Holly is just like you. They make her sick."

"Then she and I can eat funnel cakes while we watch you two risk your lives on a roller coaster." I stop and frown.

"What's wrong?"

"I shouldn't just assume that you'd invite me to a carnival or something. That's a huge assumption."

"Oh, we'd invite you," he assures me and reaches out to take my hand, pulls it up to his lips, and nibbles on my knuckles. "We like having you around, Doc."

"That's nice to hear. Holy shit!" I pull my hand out of his and point. "What is *that*?"

"What does it look like?" He puts the Jeep in park and turns off the engine.

"A hole in the side of the mountain, with a door."

"That's pretty much what it is." He smiles over at me, and then hops out and lifts the cooler out of the back. "I figured we could stop here and eat."

"Is something going to walk out of there?" I demand, still not moving from the Jeep.

"I hope not." He closes the back hatch and walks over to a level spot on the ground, spreads out a big blanket, and sets the cooler on the corner of it. Then he smiles over at me and gestures for me to join him.

He doesn't look particularly worried, so I decide not to worry about it either.

"This was a gold mine," he says as we sit on the blanket. "From the mid-1800s. Western Montana was full of gold rush people, mining for the stuff."

"Is there gold in there?" I ask as I accept a turkey sandwich from him.

"I doubt it. It was closed and sealed up about seventy years ago for safety reasons. Animals would live in there, and kids could get hurt when they were exploring shit they shouldn't. The mine was abandoned before my ancestors bought the property. It was deemed useless, so the story goes that the property was cheap."

"Do you know how much your many-times great-grandfather paid for it?"

"I've heard twenty-five dollars and a bottle of whiskey." He grins over at me. "I'd say it was a good investment."

"I'd say you're right. And when did the Lexingtons buy their land?"

Remington frowns over at me. "Why do we have to ruin a perfectly nice day by talking about them?"

"I'm curious."

"A year later," he replies.

"So, the Wilds were here first."

"Yes. We were. Their land is on the other side of that fence." He points to a wooden fence about a hundred yards away. "These days, there's no shooting at each other and shit like that. But I have cameras on this side, and they have cameras on theirs, just to make sure that nothing shitty happens."

"I think you're both paranoid," I reply, with a bite of sandwich in my mouth. "Sure, back in the day, with no TV or any forms of entertainment, maybe a family feud was the way to go, but come on, Rem. It's *way* in the future, and maybe you could let bygones be bygones."

He watches me and looks absolutely stunned that I'd even suggest something like that.

"Millie told me about Holden, and it sounds like he's

an upstanding kind of guy. I mean, he totally had her back with those horrible tourists and everything."

Rem sets his sandwich aside and holds up a finger. "Wait. *What* tourists?"

"Oh." I cringe and then take a huge bite of the sandwich so I can't talk while I try to think up a way to get myself out of this.

"Erin."

I hold up a finger, concentrating on chewing my food. I would have thought that between Millie and Chase, Rem would have heard about the horrible tourist situation.

Unfortunately not, I guess.

"It's nothing," I say at last. "Totally nothing to get worked up about."

"Do I *look* like I'm worked up?"

"You look like you're on the verge of it."

He laughs and takes a bite. "I guess I can piece it together. Some tourists were being obnoxious. Millie called them out on it, and when she might have gotten hurt, Holden stepped in on her behalf."

"Punched the guy right in the face," I confirm. "And, for what it's worth, she wasn't thrilled that it was Holden who stood up for her. But he did. So that tells me that their family isn't all bad."

"Holden just took over the business," Remington says. "Like mine, his dad retired. I don't have a beef with him."

"Good."

"But I don't like him, either."

I roll my eyes and dig into the cooler for the little apple tartlets that I included and break one open.

"You know as well as I do," Rem continues, "that there are players or teams that your dad didn't get along with. There were rivalries there."

"It's a *sport*," I reply. "That's not the same thing as despising your *neighbor* for the better part of two centuries, Grumpy. That's just stupid."

"Ah, well." He shrugs and grabs his own apple tartlet. "It's tradition."

He starts to say something else, but I stop him, listening.

"I think I heard something," I whisper. We're both still as we wait and listen, and then Remington stands, pulls me to my feet, and we hurry to the Jeep.

When I'm safely inside, he grabs the gun.

"You're not going back out there," I say.

"Hell yes, I am. You stay here, you hear me?"

"I'll stay. I don't want to get eaten by a bear or a mama moose."

"Me either." His face is grim as he walks to the back of the Jeep so he has a wider vision of our area, and then I see him hightail it to the driver's side and climb in. "It's a motherfucking grizzly bear."

"*What?*" My voice is a squeak. "Where?"

"It's still about twenty yards away. I can't let it eat our lunch."

"I don't mind sharing."

"No, I'll explain later, but just stay here."

Before I can protest, Remington jumps out of the Jeep

and runs to where we were just sitting, grabs all of our supplies in his arms, and runs back to me, tossing everything unceremoniously into the back and shutting the door. The bear stops on the grass, staring at Rem.

"He looks irritated at you."

"I'm sure he is. But he's not allowed to eat human food, or we'd have to have him put down."

"Oh, my God." I frown over at Rem before turning my gaze back to the bear. "Holy shit, he's a she, and she's a mama."

Two tiny, little fuzzy cubs come sauntering along behind her, bouncy and playful.

"We have to go," Rem says and starts the engine. That startles all three bears, and the mama rises up on her hind legs. "Jesus H. Christ, she's big."

"Could she get into the Jeep?"

"Easily," he confirms and starts to back away. "But she can't catch us. She won't want to. She just wants us gone."

"Happy to oblige."

Rem nods and then turns the wheel and takes off in the direction that we came. I look in the mirror and see that the mama bear isn't chasing us. She's standing with her cubs, watching us leave.

"I need to make sure I let the guys know she's out here," he says. "We'll need to keep an eye out. She'll eat my cattle if we're not diligent."

"I didn't even think of that," I admit with a sigh.

"They don't often. They'd rather eat fish and berries or smaller rodents. But if it was a harsh winter, and they're starving, they'll eat whatever they can get. I don't like that she's on my land. I'll call Fish and Wildlife and have her tracked."

"Good idea. Wow, my first bear in the wild. She was gorgeous. And her babies are just so adorable. Makes you want to hug them."

"Have you heard of the idiots in national parks who try to pet baby bison or pick up bear cubs?"

"Yeah. Even I know that they're ridiculous to think they can touch wildlife."

"The thing that breaks my heart is, they have to put the animal down after that happens. If they've been touched by humans, their mother will reject them, or even kill them."

"I didn't know that. God, that's awful."

"I don't want this mama to be put down; I just don't want her to try to pick off my cattle."

"Why don't you make a couple of calls now?" I suggest.

He nods and comes to a stop, and when I glance around, I realize we're at the special spot that Millie brought me to that morning. It feels like a lifetime ago.

While he talks, I step out of the Jeep and lean against the door, my arms folded over my chest, enjoying the magical view of the mountains. This *is* a special place. The whole ranch is, but this particular spot speaks to me. I'm sure it's the same way for Millie and her family.

A little fawn walks out of the trees and eyes me, his tail swishing.

"Don't worry, little guy. I'm gonna stay right here."

His mama steps out right behind him, chewing and cocking her ears. I stay perfectly still, watching them until they both march back into the trees.

"I love seeing all the animals," I confess to Remington as he joins me, his call obviously finished. "They add another layer of peace to this view."

"I spoke with Lucky and Fish and Wildlife. It's going to be taken care of."

"What do you mean?"

"They'll monitor her and the cubs. Make sure they stay away from the cattle. Chances are, they'll wander away from the ranch. They don't like people so much."

"I can't blame them."

We're standing side by side, arms crossed, staring at the view. I lean my head on his shoulder, and I feel him kiss the top of my head.

"If you want, we can eat some more," he offers.

"Not yet." I'm not usually the type to jump someone's body, but damn it, I want him. I turn to him and glide my hand up his chest and into his hair. "Rem?"

"Yeah?"

"I think it's time for that forest sex now."

His eyes spark and lower to my mouth before he frames my face in his hands and kisses the breath right out of me.

"I never stop wanting you," he growls against my lips. "It's a constant ache, a constant *fire* that rolls through me every single minute that I'm awake."

"That's actually really good to know because I thought maybe it was just me."

He laughs and kisses me some more, his clever hands unfastening my jeans and pulling my shirt out of them so his hands can roam.

"I'm not getting naked in the woods," I inform him.

"No need to," he says and turns me to face the Jeep. Suddenly, my jeans are around my knees, and Rem pulls my hips back, my hands braced on the side of the vehicle.

I want him to go fast, but he doesn't move fast enough. I can hear his zipper and the sound of his jeans being pushed down.

His hand glides down my torso and around the front of me to my pussy.

"You're already so damn wet for me." His lips are near my ear, his breath hot on my neck. "I never stop wanting all of you, in any way I can get you."

He takes one of my hands in his and guides it down to my clit, and with our fingers twined together, we rub that hard nub of sensation, making me moan in delight. He slides inside of me now, and it's almost too much to bear.

"God, listen to those sounds you make, the way you always meet me, thrust for fucking thrust."

"So good," I moan and look back at him, over my shoulder. "It's just so fucking good."

He kisses me and pushes me over the edge, into nothing but fireworks.

My body is *throbbing*, begging for relief, but also never wanting him to stop.

"I'm not stopping," he says.

I must have said that out loud.

"You're *mine*, Erin."

"God, yes." I'm tightening again already, and he must feel it because his thrusts grow harder, and finally, we're both falling over that delicious edge together, into oblivion.

He's breathing hard, his forehead resting on my back as we try to steady ourselves. When he's sure that we both have our feet under us, he pulls out, and before righting his own clothes, his first order of business is getting me straightened out.

"I'm okay," I say with a smile as I fasten my jeans. "I didn't think I'd enjoy outside sex."

"And now?"

"Ten out of ten stars. Would highly recommend."

"Oh, we can definitely do this under the stars sometime."

"That's not what I—" I stop when he just grins at me. "Yeah. Yeah, that would be fun. You know what I want to try next?"

"What's that?"

"The chairs on the front porch. They're so comfortable."

"Your wish is my command," he says before kissing my forehead.

CHAPTER TWENTY-ONE
REMINGTON

"You were right," Erin says as we climb the steps of the porch to the house. "It took us all day to see everything. And now, I'm dragging."

I grin at her as I unlock the door and open it, gesturing for her to go in ahead of me.

"I can't believe I saw a mama grizzly with her babies," she continues as she kicks off her shoes. "*Plus,* a mountain lion on the way home. Rem, that was crazy. Aren't you always afraid when you're out there?"

"No." I kick off my boots and hang my hat on the wall. "They don't come near the houses or the barn because they don't like people. Sure, we might have an animal walk through on their way to somewhere else, but they don't hang out here."

"It's scary," she murmurs.

"Hey." I tip her chin up and brush a stray piece of hair behind her ear. "You don't need to be afraid of the animals. Just keep your eyes and ears open and be alert, especially if you're by yourself. Besides, *you're* the one who heard the grizzly. You did the right thing."

She blows out a breath. "Yeah, you're right. Do we want dinner?"

I lift an eyebrow. "Are you hungry?"

"No, I'm *exhausted*." She chuckles and leans her forehead against my chest. "I want to go to bed, and it's only nine."

"Then we'll go to bed." After kissing the top of her head, I take her shoulders and push her away gently so I can kiss her forehead.

"Thank God," she says and sets off for her bedroom.

"Where are you going?"

She stops and turns to me with a frown. "To my bed."

"While the kids are gone, you'll be sleeping in *my* bed, Doc."

She blinks, smiles, and continues toward her room. "I just need to grab a couple of things."

While she handles her business, I make sure the house is locked up tight and pour us each a glass of wine. When I walk out from the kitchen, Erin's walking out of her bedroom with a tote bag full of things. She also changed out of her dirty clothes and into my old college sweatshirt. No pants.

"You look like you're going on a weekend trip. Well, one with no pants."

She laughs and then shrugs. "I guess I kind of *am*."

I pass her a glass of wine and take the bag from her and frown in surprise. "This thing is heavy."

"I needed a lot of stuff," she says with a careless

shrug and takes the lead up the stairs. I can tell that she's tired because the typical bounce in her step is gone. She trudges down the hall to my bedroom, as if her feet weigh fifty pounds each.

But those legs are *stellar*.

Erin sips her wine and turns to me. "You know, it occurs to me that in all the times we've managed to have sex, it's always been in my bed downstairs or against the side of a Jeep."

She smirks and glances at my bed.

"Which side do you sleep on?" she asks.

"The one closest to the door."

She nods and wanders around to the other side, setting her phone and wine on the bedside table.

"We need to check you for ticks."

Her eyebrows shoot up at that. "Excuse me?"

"Ticks. It's spring, and there are ticks."

"That might be the most unromantic thing anyone has ever said to me in my life." Her gorgeous eyes look terrified. "*Ticks?*"

"You probably don't have any." I keep my voice calm so she doesn't freak out. No one likes to think about those disgusting little critters, but we have to look. "Come here. We'll go into the bathroom."

I gesture for her to follow me and walk into my en suite, pulling a pair of tweezers out of the drawer just in case.

"Strip," I order her.

"*You* strip," she counters. "You're dirty, too."

With my eyes on hers, I have no problem taking it all

off and depositing it right into the hamper. Stark-ass naked, I turn to her and raise an eyebrow.

"Your turn."

She pulls the sweatshirt off, sets it on the sink, and does the same with her panties.

"You know, getting naked with you is a lot sexier when there aren't tiny insects involved."

"I can't argue with that. Turn around." I scan her body from head to toe, even checking in her hair, behind her ears, and between her legs.

"If a tick made its way into my cooter, you can just shoot me and put me out of my misery."

I chuckle and turn her around once more. "You're good to go. My turn."

"Ohhh, I get a turn." That pleases her, and her gaze roams all over me, and that just turns me on. "I don't see any ticks, but I do see that the idea of them turns you on."

"Wrong." I catch her wrist in my hand and yank her against me. "*You* turn me on."

"Coincidentally," she says, staring at my lips, "same here. But I'm freaking exhausted, and we had forest sex *twice.*"

"Let's each take a quick shower, and then we'll snuggle down and watch something in bed."

Her eyes light up at that idea. "*Yes.* That's perfect."

My body is trained to wake up at five every morning, even on Sundays, when I let the guys handle the ranch, and I spend the day with my kids. So, when my eyes pop open, and I see that it's so early, I'm not surprised.

It is, however, a nice reminder to find Erin cuddled up next to me, still sleeping soundly. The sun hasn't come up yet, but the first signs of light are coming to life outside as I turn to her and press a kiss to her cheek.

She doesn't stir.

We were both too exhausted after our showers to even watch TV, let alone have sex. I didn't know that was possible for me when it comes to Erin, but it seems even I have a point of exhaustion.

This morning, however, I'm feeling rejuvenated, and Erin is *in my fucking bed.*

I've wanted her here almost since the day she moved into my house. And if it wouldn't confuse things for my kids, I'd have had her here long ago.

But I have her here now. And I intend to enjoy every second of it.

My hand drifts up and down her side. She must have gotten too warm in the night because the sweatshirt is gone, and she's only wearing her little white panties.

Which will be gone momentarily.

Lazily, I drag my fingertips over her ribs and up to her breast, where her nipple comes to life and puckers for me.

Erin takes a deep breath, as if she's starting to surface from sleep, and I kiss her lips gently.

"Mm," she moans and leans in for more kisses. She

drags her leg up the outside of my own and drapes it over my hip, opening herself up for me.

But I'm taking my time here. I want to steep myself in her.

She still hasn't opened her eyes when I let my hand drift down between us, down her belly, and farther still, until I'm cupping her.

That wakes her up.

She tries to straddle me, but I shake my head and push her back onto the mattress.

"Lazy this morning," I say, just barely brushing my fingertips over her folds. "There's no hurry."

She sighs and kisses my shoulder and then my neck. Her hand runs down my arm, and she links her fingers with mine in a sweet gesture that makes my heart stutter.

"You're so sweet," I whisper before kissing her lips once more, still keeping the tone light and lazy. I could do this with her all day.

But Erin is a little more impatient and scoots herself even closer to me, rubbing her core against my erection, and that's all it takes for me to reach down and guide myself to her slick center.

With the slightest of thrusts, I push inside of her and cup her ass, drawing her tightly against me. We're on our sides, facing each other, watching each other intimately in the dim light of dawn.

"Oh, Jesus," she groans and bites her lip. "This angle."

I can't help but move just a little faster now, holding

on to her ass as I push and pull, completely hypnotized by this woman and the way she makes every inch of me crave more while chasing a finish that I know will blow my mind.

Erin cups my cheek and kisses me long and slow, her tongue dancing against my own, and I feel the tightening, the adrenaline, and then there's no stopping the orgasm from sweeping through me.

Her pussy is like a vise around me, contracting and milking me dry.

And when her eyes, still heavy-lidded from sleep, meet mine, she smiles slyly.

"Well, that was a good way to start the day."

"I think it's my new favorite," I agree. "You should go back to sleep."

"So should you."

"I have to work for a little while. I like going, knowing that you're burrowed in my bed, with the scent of what we just did hanging in the air."

"God, you're good at the dirty talk. It's always the grumpy ones."

I laugh and push her flat on her back, kissing the hell out of her again.

"I fucking *love* the way you look here, in my bed, in my room. Naked and still buzzing from having my cock inside of you."

"Keep it up and you'll be late for work," she warns me.

"I'll be back," I promise her. "Just a few hours, and I'll

be back. And then we're not leaving this bed for the rest of the day."

"I'll hold you to that."

———————

"I HAVE NEWS," Chase says as he walks through the front door, as if he still lives here. "Where's Erin?"

"I'm here," she calls out from the kitchen. "Just getting the kids dinner."

"Before we go in there," I say to my brother, "is it good or bad news?"

"It's great news," he replies with a grin and walks into the kitchen.

It's been a month since the kids went out of town with my parents. A month since my few days alone with Erin.

And it's been damn peaceful.

No flowers sent, nothing that would make any of us think that the asshole stalker is around Bitterroot Valley anymore.

And that's just the way I fucking like it.

"Hey, you guys," I say to the kids. "How about I let you have your dinner in your bedroom, just this one time?"

"Does this mean that we don't get to hear the news?" Holly asks with a frown. "Because I wanna know what it is."

My daughter will make an excellent gossip when she's an old woman.

"This is grown-up talk," I tell her. "Go on up and play with your Barbies, okay?"

"Can we sit on your bed and watch TV?" Johnny asks.

"Yes, but please be careful with your drinks." I suspect this is a bad idea, but I don't want them to hear about Erin's stalker. I don't want them to be afraid.

"I'll help them get settled," Erin offers, loading up a tray with their plates, silverware, and drinks that she's already put into tumblers.

She thinks of everything.

Johnny and Holly follow her up the stairs, talking a mile a minute as Chase walks to the sink and looks out the window, then turns back to me.

"You're going to marry her." It's not a dare, not an accusation. It's just a simple statement.

"Yeah." I push my hand through my hair. "I am. Haven't asked her yet, though."

"When I walked in here, it was as if this was always the way it's been. The four of you. And I don't mean that to sound disrespectful to Jess; you know I liked her."

"I get it," I reply. "I know what you mean. And yeah, it fits. The whole thing just fits perfectly, and part of me wonders when the other shoe will drop, and I'll realize that it actually doesn't fit the way it should, but then I decide to stop borrowing trouble."

"You're giving yourself good advice," he says with a smile, but then he turns serious again. "Your kids are way invested in her."

"I know that. Didn't plan on it, but I don't think it's a bad thing."

"I'm happy for all of you," he says, just as Erin hurries back in.

"Okay, they're settled, and there should be no spillage on the bed. Just in case, I put an extra blanket over the comforter to catch any crumbs."

"You're pretty smart," I reply with a smile. "And handy to have around. Thanks. Okay, Chase, what's up?"

"Well, I just got off the phone with the parole officer in Washington. The asshole hasn't missed even one appointment. From what we can tell, he's in Washington. So far, we can't prove that the flowers came from him, but when we do, he'll likely go back to prison for fucking up his restraining order. But the best news is, he's not in Montana."

"Thank God," Erin says with a relieved sigh. "I can start work again at the coffee shop."

"Let's not get ahead of ourselves."

"Why not?" she counters. "I *miss it*. And it's only on Sundays because your mother has claimed that day as her grandma day with the kids. It works."

"She's safe," Chase says to me.

"I need this." Erin crosses to me and takes my hand, pressing it to her cheek. "I'm an independent person, Grumpy. I need to be able to go back to my job, see my friends without a chaperone, *all* of it. The ranch is not a prison for me. I love it, but I need the rest of my life back."

"That was a damn good speech," Chase says with approval.

"Go away, Chase."

"See you later!" He waves and leaves the kitchen. I hear the door shut behind him, and then his engine roars to life.

"Okay," I say at last with a gusty sigh. "We'll still watch your back."

"Oh, yeah, I won't do anything stupid. I'm so *excited.*" She bounces and then throws her arms around my neck and kisses me hard. "Thanks, Grumpy."

"You're welcome, Doc."

"I CAN'T BELIEVE the school year is over," Erin says as she puts the finishing touches on Holly's pretty braids for her kindergarten graduation ceremony. "This spring just flew by."

"Don't forget," Holly says, as if she's the parent, "we have seats saved for you and Daddy and Johnny."

"I won't forget," Erin promises. "What about the rest of the family?"

"They'll have to sit in the back," Holly says. "There are too many of them."

I laugh and usher everyone out to the Suburban so we can drive into town for the ceremony at the elementary school.

Speaking of time flying by, how is it possible that Holly's going into the first grade next year? My kids are growing up too quickly.

"I was invited to Aurora's birthday party on Saturday," Holly reminds us for the fifth time today. "At two o'clock."

"We won't forget," I reply.

"Okay. I hope some of the others come to my graduation. Like Grandma and Grandpa and Aunt Millie."

"Don't worry about that."

There's already a shortage of parking when we arrive, so I take a space a block away. I take Holly's hand, and Johnny takes Erin's, and we're off.

Holly has to go join her class, so I lead the others to our seats with the other families. And when I look behind us, my mouth drops open.

"They *all* came," I whisper to Erin, who only grins at me.

"I know."

Everyone is here. Not just my parents and my siblings, but all of my ranch hands, too, and they're waving at us. When I glance back over at Erin, she's holding up her phone, and her parents, along with Zoey, are on FaceTime.

"You look pale, Rem," Meg says through the phone. "You have to breathe."

"Ladies and gentlemen," the principal says into the PA system, "please take your seats so we can begin."

"I owe them," I murmur so only Erin can hear. "I owe them all."

"No, you don't. This is what family does, Rem."

CHAPTER TWENTY-TWO
ERIN

"What are you up to?"

I look up from my desk in surprise and see Rem leaning against the doorjamb, watching me. Since I've completely taken over the bookkeeping from Joy, Remington gave me his desk to use, since he does so much work at his office in the barn.

And so far, that's worked just fine for me.

"It's too late for you to be working," he says as he pushes off the doorjamb and slowly walks toward me. "The kids are in bed."

"I'm not working on the bookkeeping," I admit. "But I *am* figuring out the summer schedule."

"Schedule? The kids just got out of school yesterday."

"I know, but I think it's a good idea for them to still have a routine. A schedule. And I'll be with them most of the time, so I'm juggling things around. See." I turn the calendar his way. "For example, on Mondays, Holly will have dance, and then Johnny's taking karate classes right after. But in the mornings, I want them to read a book of their choosing, and before their classes, we'll go to the library so they can trade them in. On Tuesdays, we'll start with math, and then after lunch, we'll go to that amazing lake you showed me for swimming or paddle boarding."

"Wow," he murmurs, looking it over. "You're giving them riding lessons?"

"Of course not." I smirk at him. "But one of the new ranch hands you hired volunteered to give them an hour a week. They already know *how*, but they don't get a lot of practice, and this way, they will."

"Which kid?"

"Kyle?"

Rem nods with approval. "I'm glad I found Kyle. I can get behind that. What's this?"

He points to the yellow star on Sundays.

"Grandma day," I reply with a laugh. "And I haven't written in my day at the coffee shop yet, but I will."

"And what day do *you* get off?"

I blink up at him. "What do you mean?"

"Between the bookkeeping, my kids, and the coffee shop, you haven't scheduled a day off for yourself."

"Rem, I count my coffee shop day as my day off."

"Fuck that." His voice is mild, but his eyes say, *I won't back down on this.*

"If I take another day off, it leaves you in a lurch. Besides, I *like* this schedule."

"I'll only agree with this if you take a day, every other week, to yourself. You can go to the spa or go hang out with Millie or, shit, I don't care if you go sit in that fancy condo on the ski hill all day, but you'll have some time for yourself. With the kids out of school, there won't be any of that, and you'll need it."

"Okay." I nod slowly, looking over the schedule. "I'll figure it out."

"Good. I like it. You're right, they do best with a routine."

"I do, too," I admit with a smile. "Without it, it's nothing but chaos, and I can't deal with that."

"Are you about done in here?"

"For now." I stand and turn off the desk lamp, then circle the desk and walk into Rem's arms for a big hug. The two of us have gotten into our own routine with each other, and this is part of it.

After the kids go to bed, and the house is quiet, Remington seeks me out, and I get the best bear hug the world has ever seen.

It's almost as good as the sex, and that's saying a lot.

And the hug almost always leads to the sex.

"I *LOVE* the pretty Barbie doll and clothes we got for Aurora," Holly says from the back seat. She's so freaking cute in her pink dress, totally appropriate for the pink-themed party and dress code that came on the invitation.

Her hair is up in braids again, which seems to be her go-to these days. I don't mind. It gives us some time to chat and be together without any of the boys. Pink ribbons are tied at the bottom of the braids, and the big, pink gift bag is on the seat next to her.

"I like that one, too," I agree. "She's pretty."

"Maybe I'll add her to my birthday wish list."

"When *is* your birthday, Holly?"

"June twentieth."

That's just a couple of weeks away. How do I not know their birthdays?

"And when is Johnny's?"

"December twenty-third. He thinks it's lame because people try to combine his birthday and Christmas gifts into one gift."

"Yeah, that's kind of lame. Have you thought about what you want for your birthday party?"

"I want a princess party," she says with excitement. "I want my friends to wear pretty princess dresses. And we can ride a horse from the barn."

"I think that's hard to do in a princess dress, but I like the idea of seeing if we can get the ranch hands to help us give rides, if it's okay with your friends' moms and dads."

"Yeah! And we can have a pretty princess cake and flowers and balloons."

I should have started planning this a month ago. I can't *believe* I never thought to ask when their birthdays are.

With the help of GPS, I find my way to Aurora's house and park on the street. I help Holly out of the back and pass her the gift so she can be the one to give it to her friend.

There's a sign that says to walk around to the backyard, so that's what we do, and I've never seen anything so adorable. There's a photo booth that looks like a Barbie box, where the girls can stand in it and look like a Barbie themselves.

The cake is, of course, a Barbie cake, and all the people here, big and small, are dressed in bright pink.

Even I found a cute pink top at Polly's shop for the occasion.

"Oh, it's so pretty," Holly says with excitement and then runs over to Aurora to offer the girl her gift.

"We'll add that to the table," Aurora's mom, Christine, says with a smile. "Thank you so much for this beautiful gift."

"You're welcome," Holly says shyly, and then Aurora takes her hand, and they run off to play.

"Hi, I'm Erin."

"Oh, yes, it's good to see you, Erin," Christine says with a big smile. "Thanks for bringing Holly. Aurora just adores her."

"So do I. What can I help with?"

"Nothing right now. We're just serving a light snack before the cake so the girls don't end up with too much of a sugar high. Come on, you can join the other moms."

"I'm not—"

"Close enough," she interrupts. "Would you like something to drink? I have lemonade and bottled water."

"I'd love a lemonade." I'm suddenly as nervous as I always was on the first day of school. What if these people don't like me?

"Everyone, this is Erin. Most of you probably know her," Christine says. "I'm going to grab her a drink."

Everyone smiles and says hello.

So far, everyone is warm and welcoming, and none of their faces register any kind of mean girl tendencies, so I relax a little and take a seat next to a beautiful blonde.

"I'm Abbi," she says with a smile. "My daughter is Daisy, the one who claimed she just had to be flight attendant Barbie."

I follow her gaze and smile when I see the little girl playing with Holly and Aurora.

"She's beautiful. Personally, I always loved that Barbie."

"Isn't this party great?" Abbi asks. "I mean, that photo booth is ingenious. I never would have thought of it."

"The best part about it," Christine adds as she passes me my drink, "is that it raises and lowers, so we can all be Barbies, too."

"That's always been my dream," I reply, making the others laugh and setting myself more at ease. "This is maybe the cutest party I've ever been to, and I have been to a *lot* of birthday parties. How did you come up with it?"

"I'd like to say that it was all my idea, but I used Pinterest."

"Fair enough."

"Excuse me, ladies, while I go check on the snacks." Christine walks into the house, and I smile over at Abbi.

"I'm surprised that I haven't run into you before this. I'm usually the one to pick Holly up from school and stuff."

"Oh, Daisy and I just moved to town a few weeks ago," she replies. "I'm a single mom, and I needed a fresh start, if I'm being totally honest."

"I get it. I've only been here for about six months or so, and it was the best move I ever made. Everyone in Bitterroot Valley is so nice."

"I'm discovering that." Abbi grins and watches her daughter with the other kids. "How long have you and Holly's dad been married?"

"Oh, we're not. We're seeing each other, but we're not married. I'm the nanny. Is that weird?" I cover my face in embarrassment and peer out between my fingers.

"No, it sounds like a juicy story that I want to hear," she says with a laugh.

"I'm sorry, but I couldn't help but eavesdrop." I look over to see a woman smiling at us. "I'm Bella, Simone's mom, and I've known the Wild family all my life. Did you say you're seeing Remington?"

"Yes?" I don't know for sure if this is a trick question.

"Well, it's about damn time someone scooped that man up," Bella says and raises her glass to mine. "He is one hot tamale."

"You're not wrong." I laugh and search the yard for Holly, relieved when I see her playing with other girls at a ring toss game. "He *is* hot. And he's a really good dad. Why is that so sexy?"

"Because not all dads are good," Abbi says ruefully. "So, when they *are*, it's hot as hell."

"I went on a date with Remington once," a woman named Helena says smugly. "We had fun, but there was no spark. Of course, that was more than fifteen years ago, and we were practically babies, but yeah. He's hot."

I can't help but laugh at that. I'm going to have to ask Joy if she can show me photos of Rem when he was about twenty. I'd love to see them.

"Okay, everyone," Christine announces, pushing a cart loaded with snacks. "Let's eat!"

HOLLY IS fast asleep in the back seat when I pull up to the farmhouse. I don't want to disturb her, so I shoot Remington a text.

Me: Sitting in the car with Holly, running the AC. Nothing's wrong. She's sleeping, and I don't want to wake her.

Five minutes later, I see Remington walking toward the car in the rearview, from the direction of the barn.

Not wanting to wake Holly, I slip out the door and carefully latch it shut.

"Hey," I say in a low voice. "She's all tuckered out. I don't mind sitting out here to keep an eye on her while she naps."

"How did it go?"

"I think Holly and I both had a blast," I reply with a grin. "I made a couple of new friends, and the whole party was just really fun. Also, I met your old flame, Helena."

He looks confused for a second. "Helena Brown?"

"It's Ryerson now."

"I think we went on one measly date." He shoves his hands into his pockets, clearly uncomfortable, and I laugh.

"It made an impression. Everyone was nice, but that seems to be the norm for this town. Holly had a blast. And she informed me that her birthday is in a couple of weeks, and I haven't even started planning the party."

"We don't usually do parties," he says. "We just have family dinner and cake."

"She's in school now. That won't work. She deserves to have a party with friends, Grumpy. She's a good kid."

"Yeah, yeah, okay. We'll do a party."

"It's too bad the old barn hasn't been transformed into that event space we talked about. That would be a *killer* party."

"You know, I've been thinking about that," he says as he leads me to the steps of the porch. We sit down, side by side. "I think it's an excellent idea, and I'd like to take it to the rest of the family. I know that I'm technically in charge now, but it's a family ranch, and they should have a say."

"I love you."

My eyes go wide, and I slap my hand over my mouth

in shock. Did I really just blurt that out like that? When he's talking about his family?

"I mean—" I clear my throat, but before I can say anything else, Remington pulls me into his lap, and as I straddle him, he kisses me silly.

"I love you, too," he whispers against my lips. "Madly. Stupidly. Irrevocably. I'm wild for you, Doc."

"Oh, thank God. I thought I'd really made things awkward there for a minute."

He laughs and cups my face. "No. You didn't."

"It's awkward timing," I admit. "But damn, Grumpy, I love how much you love and respect your family and the legacy of this ranch. I *love* it. I didn't know if I'd ever meet someone who had a similar family dynamic as mine, but I did. And it's one of the things that's always attracted me to you."

"I know," he says and brushes my hair over my shoulder. "And I feel the same."

"You were saying you're going to talk to your family about the old barn?"

"Yeah. And I want you to be there because if it's going to happen, you're going to be in charge of it."

"What?" Stunned, I sit back and stare at him. "Why me?"

"Because it's your vision, and I want it to be exactly the way you picture it in your head."

"Wow. Okay. Sure, I can do that."

"I know you can," he says simply before kissing me again.

"Why are you kissing?"

We break apart at the little voice, and I shimmy off Rem's lap. Obviously, Holly woke up and got out of the car without either of us hearing it.

"Because I like to kiss her," Rem says to his daughter. "Did you have fun today?"

"Yes, and Erin says that she'll help me plan the perfect party for my birthday."

"I'm sure she will."

I just don't think that life gets any better than this.

I'm *finally* back at work at Bitterroot Valley Coffee Co., and it feels amazing. Millie's working with me today, and we're having a great time, switching back and forth between the one taking the orders and the one making the coffee.

We work so well together.

Remington brought the kids in this morning for a treat, and that was a fun surprise. And every single person I've waited on today has been happy and in a good mood.

Today is *my* day.

"Hello."

I turn and smile at Clay. "Oh, hey. How's it going?"

"Fine." He doesn't look as friendly as he used to, but maybe he's not having as good of a day as I am. "I'll just take a caramel mocha."

"You got it." I finish the transaction and smile at Clay. "I'll bring it out to you when it's ready."

"You can just set it up here. I'll come get it," he says and walks away, his face already glued to his phone.

Alrighty, then.

"Remington told me he loves me yesterday," I whisper to Millie as I walk up beside her to give her the order to make.

"*What*?" She almost spills hot milk on herself, and I quickly grab a towel to help her.

"I said it first," I clarify. "I couldn't help myself, and then he said it back, and it was really sweet."

"Holy *guacamole*." Millie wraps her arms around me and hugs me tightly. "That's the best news I've heard in years. You do realize that if you marry him, you'll be my sister."

"No one has talked about marriage."

"He will. Rem isn't an alley cat; he's a one-girl kind of man. Oh, my God, this is so exciting. I mean, I practically picked out my own sister-in-law."

"Yes, this is all about you."

Millie laughs and hugs me again.

"What's going on back there?"

We both turn at the sound of Chase's voice. He's standing at the counter, grinning at us.

"Rem told Erin that he loves her," she says in a mock whisper that's loud enough for the whole world to hear.

"'Bout time," Chase says with a nod. "He's slow, but he's loyal."

I snort at that and set Clay's coffee out for him to pick up, then walk over to take Chase's order just as Summer walks in, holding a gorgeous bouquet of yellow daffodils.

Their trumpets are just gorgeous, and when she sets them down in front of me and says, "These are for you, Erin," I can't help but sigh.

"Those are *not* ugly red roses," Millie says.

I hear the sound of a chair scraping angrily on the floor and look up in time to see a very angry Clay stomp out of the shop.

Boy, something crawled up his butt today.

Not that I care as I stare at these gorgeous flowers.

"The card," Summer adds, passing me the envelope. She turns her attention to Chase. "How are you, Chase?"

"Can't complain, thanks. And you?"

"Oh, I'm as busy as a spider spinning daydreams," she replies with a pretty, bright smile. "And that's just the way we like it. I have to hurry back to the shop, but I wanted to get these to you right away."

"Thank you so much," I call after her, and then watch as Chase watches Summer leave.

When the door's closed behind her, I grin at Chase and cross my arms over my chest.

"What?" he asks when he turns back around.

"You *like* her."

"Summer? Sure, she's nice."

"And flat-out gorgeous," Millie adds. "Not to mention, a great businesswoman and an all-around nice person. Oh, and Chase has had a crush on her for, like, three years."

"I have not."

"Wow. Three years is a long time. Maybe you should ask her out."

Chase's eyes narrow. "Is my coffee done yet?"

"Here you go," Millie says sweetly and passes it to him. "Erin, are you going to read that card?"

"Oh, yeah." I open the envelope and take out the card.

Hey, Doc,

You deserve your favorite flowers every day.

Love,

Grumpy

"Awwww," Millie says and covers her heart with her hands.

"Boy, Rem can be sappy when he wants to be," Chase puts in.

"It's not sappy, it's romantic," I counter. "Now, go ask Summer out on a date."

"I'm outta here," Chase says and takes his coffee right out the door.

"I love pestering my brothers," Millie says with a happy sigh. "It means I'm using my sister powers for evil, rather than good."

I laugh at that and then feel my phone vibrate with a text. Frowning, I check it because no one ever pings me when I'm at work.

"Oh, it's Roger." I read the text and feel my heart speed up. "Oh, God, he's hurt. He needs me. Mill—"

"Go," she says immediately as I untie my apron and shove my phone into my pocket. "Just go, I've got this."

I hop into the Suburban and drive faster than I should the short distance to Roger's house. I've barely turned the engine off when I'm sprinting up the sidewalk to the front door and use my key to get inside.

"Rog?" I call out, my heart in my throat. "Where are you, Roger?"

"Oh, he's not here."

I freeze at the sound of that voice.

I *know* that voice.

CHAPTER TWENTY-THREE
ERIN

This can't be happening.

That's all that keeps running through my mind as I stare at Clay. This *can't* be happening. Because that voice doesn't belong to Clay; it belongs to Steven Turner, the man who made my life a living hell before he was put in prison.

"Clay?" I ask, my mind whirling as I try to figure out what to do. "Where's Roger?"

"I don't care," he says and shoves his hands into his pockets. The southern accent is nowhere in sight. "He's not *here*. And don't call me Clay. Clay is a pussy role I played to get close to you."

"I didn't even recognize you," I murmur. I'm shocked that I can hear anything over the pounding in my ears. "You're supposed to be in Washington."

"I'm *supposed* to be wherever the fuck you are!" His voice is hard and loud. "Of course, you didn't recognize me. I made sure of it."

He pulls the contacts out of his eyes and drops them to the floor. He peels off a little mustache and even pulls a teeth prosthetic out of his mouth, dropping that, as well.

A damp washcloth appears from his back pocket, and he wipes makeup off his face. And now, aside from the lighter hair, I can see that it *is* Steven.

"You're such a fucking slut." His eyes are wild. Crazy. "You promised you'd wait for me. I did everything right."

He takes a breath and calms his voice.

"I figured out how to make the guards and warden like me. I got a job in the computer lab, and I finally figured out how to hack into all kinds of servers. I changed my release date. I deleted any mention of victim's rights so your family wouldn't have to know. I changed the way I looked. JUST LOOK AT HOW MUCH I DID FOR YOU!"

I take a tiny step back and lick my lips.

"Oh, no. You're not going anywhere." He tsks, shaking his head like I'm a kid who's been bad. "You *mocked* my flowers. MY FLOWERS! They're beautiful. They're your favorite."

"They used to be. You ruined that for me."

His face pulls into a sneer. "Fuck that. You love them. You stopped working at the coffee shop, so I didn't get to see you anymore, and that pissed me off. Hurt my feelings. I've had to drive back and forth to fucking Washington. Do you have any idea how inconvenient that is? How long it takes? I don't have a private jet that I can just fly around in at my whim."

Oh, God. What do I do? I don't know what to do.

"How did you find me in Bitterroot Valley?" I need to stall him, keep him talking.

"Please." He rolls his eyes and then looks at me like I'm a child that needs placating. "It's not like you changed your name or something. You even got a Montana driver's license. I hack into computers, remember? I tried to chat with you on social media, but you wouldn't reply to my messages."

I frown, and then it dawns on me. The spam I deleted. It was from *him*.

"The only good thing that happened is that I got your old apartment and your old furniture." His face splits into a sick, perverted smile. "I fucked you on every surface in that apartment."

I'm going to throw up.

"And you *loved* it. You wanted more and more. You *begged* me to marry you."

"No." The word comes out strong and hard. "That didn't happen. It's not true, and it'll never be true."

"Shut the fuck up!" He storms over and backhands me, making me see stars. "You're a motherfucking liar, you whore."

"I'm not lying."

He hits me again and then pushes me down into a chair. It's one of Roger's kitchen chairs. My cheek throbs, and I feel nauseous again, but I realize that he's tying me to the chair.

"You're not that stupid fucking rancher's," he mutters over and over again as he ties the knots. "He can't give you what I can. He can't love you like I do. In for a penny, in for a pound. In for a penny, in for a pound."

He keeps repeating odd phrases, over and over. He's mentally insane.

And he's going to kill me. Oh, my God, he's going to kill me, and Roger will find me here. Sweet Roger, who wouldn't hurt anyone.

Remington and the kids need me. My whole family needs me, and this monster is going to take me away from them.

"Your dad told you," he says, looking me right in the eyes. "He told you that he wanted you to marry *me*. Because he knows. He's smart, and he's famous, and he *knows*."

"What does he know?" It comes out in a whisper.

"That I'm the only one for you." He calmly reaches up to drag his fingers down my cheek, and then he grips my mouth, bruising my face on either side. "*I'm* the one who loves you. I would have treated you so fucking nice, but you just wouldn't listen to me. No, you had me put away. But you can't stop a love like ours, Erin. When it's meant to be, it works out. And we are meant to be."

"No," I whisper and earn another slap across the cheek.

"You shut your whore mouth!" he screams in my face, spittle hitting me. His breath stinks like old coffee, and he has something stuck in his teeth. I must be in shock because that strikes me as funny. "Don't you laugh at me."

"This whole thing is laughable," I reply. He's going to kill me anyway. I might as well be honest. "What, are you going to take me up to your apartment and keep me hostage there?"

"Not hostage," he says. "Our home isn't a jail for you, my love. No, it's your safe place. Roger told me that you bought that furniture for us. You've already made it our home. That's where you belong."

"I don't belong anywhere near you."

He stands and paces away from me, pushing his hand through his hair. Then he rounds on me and punches me with a closed fist, and everything goes black.

CHAPTER TWENTY-FOUR
REMINGTON

"Hey, Dad?" Johnny asks as we walk down Main Street.

"Yeah, buddy?"

"Maybe we could just stay in town until Erin gets done at work, and then we could take her out for dinner. We haven't done that in a long time."

"Yeah!" Holly agrees. "We could get BBQ!"

I stop and look down at the two of them. They're staring up at me with excited eyes, and I know that there's no way I'll say no.

"Best idea I've heard all day. We should definitely do that. We don't spend much time in town, do we?"

"Nah, but there's lots to do out at the ranch," Johnny reminds me. "Sometimes, it's fun to come to town, though."

"Let's pop back by the coffee shop," I say as Holly slips her hand into mine, "and we'll make sure that Erin doesn't have other plans."

"If she was gonna do something with Aunt Millie, she can come with us, too," Holly suggests. "Then it'll be even *more* fun."

"We can invite Aunt Millie if you want."

We're just about to walk inside the coffee shop when I hear someone call out my name.

"Rem!"

I look behind us and see Brooks striding our way. "Hey, Brooks. How's it going?"

"I'm well," he says and shakes my hand. "Surprised to see you in town. How are you guys?"

Brooks grins at the kids and ruffles Johnny's hair.

"We're going to see Erin at work to invite her to dinner," Holly says with a grin. "Do you want to go to dinner?"

Brooks grins. "Not today, but I'll take a rain check. Thanks for asking me."

"You kind of look like my daddy," Holly adds with a shy smile.

Brooks and I share a glance, and I shrug. "She's a kid."

"She's an adorable kid. Anyway, I have a guy on my staff who should be on *your* staff."

I raise an eyebrow. "Why?"

"All he talks about is horses and ranching. He's nineteen, and he's a good kid. Horrible with an engine, but he has a strong work ethic, and I think he'd thrive out at Wild River Ranch."

"Give him my number. I need more help for the summer, and we'll take it from there."

"Thanks." Brooks nods. "Have a fun dinner, you guys. See you later."

After a wave in Brooks's direction, I push through the door of the coffee shop and blink in surprise.

At the counter, Holden Lexington is grinning at my sister.

And she has her arms crossed over her chest, trying not to smile back.

"Where's Erin?" Johnny demands as we approach.

"Oh, she just had to run and check on Roger real quick. She should be back soon." Millie turns back to Holden. "Do you need anything else?"

"This coffee is delicious," Holden says idly, as if he has all day to lean on the counter and ponder over his coffee. He looks over at me and nods. "Rem."

"Holden." I nod back. "Have you met my kids?"

"Sure, but I haven't seen them in a long time. Jenny and Cameron, right?"

Johnny and Holly laugh.

"No," Holly says. "I'm Holly, and he's my brother, Johnny."

"That's right." Holden glances back up at me with a wink and then turns back to Millie. "Thanks for your time, Miss Wild."

"You're not welcome," she mutters, making Holden smile more as he takes his coffee and walks out of the shop. "He's a moron."

"He's not as bad as his father," I reply.

"You hate him," she reminds me. "And you were *nice* to him."

I remember what Erin said to me when we were by the mine.

"Bygones," I reply with a shrug. "You said Erin went to check on Roger?"

"Yeah, the poor guy. He—"

She's interrupted by the sound of the door, and Chase strides in, looking good and irritated.

"Forgot my wallet," he says as Millie holds it up for him.

"That's what you get when you run away from the truth," Millie says as she starts making something in small cups. "Do my two favorite kids want some hot chocolate?"

"Yeah!" both kids say together.

"I'm not avoiding the truth," Chase mutters darkly.

"What truth is that?" I ask.

"He's hot for Summer," Millie says. "The woman, not the season."

"You are?" I blink in surprise. "Well, she's pretty and nice. And a good businesswoman."

"That's what I said," Millie agrees.

Chase just shakes his head and pulls his hand down his face. "Everyone shut up about it."

"I like Miss Summer," Holly says. "She has pretty flowers."

Chase looks down at Holly mournfully. "Not you, too."

Before she can answer, Chase's phone rings.

"Wild," he answers, and suddenly, his body tightens, his face goes blank, and I know that something is wrong.

"When? Is he there now? Tell him to stay outside, and I'll be there in three minutes. Send backup."

He ends the call and looks at me.

"Erin's in trouble."

"I've got the kids," Millie says immediately. "Go."

My adrenaline has never been higher as we run out of the shop and over to Chase's cruiser.

"Roger called 9-1-1," Chase says as he cranks the engine. "He just got home and heard someone yelling, so he didn't go in. He looked in the window and saw a man yelling at Erin."

My hands close into fists. "Stalker?"

"That's the only thing I can think of."

Blind fury pulses through me. "If he's laid a hand on her, I'll kill him."

"You can't say shit like that to me," Chase mutters in frustration. "We don't go in until backup arrives."

"Fuck that."

"You listen to me, Rem. I only brought you because I knew you'd go on your own anyway, and because she'll need you, but I'm in charge here, and there are protocols when it comes to circumstances like this."

"Fuck your protocols."

"Don't make me cuff you and keep you in the car."

"I'd like to see you try." I glare over at him, but he doesn't back down.

"I'll do it. Don't think I won't. If you fuck this up, it could fuck up the whole investigation, so you'll do what I say."

He parks a couple of houses down, and we immediately run for the house. Roger's waiting for us on the sidewalk.

"There's a man in there with Erin," he says immediately. "He's yelling nonsense at her. I think he hit her."

"No," Chase says, gripping my arm. "Are you sure he hit her?"

"Yes," Roger says. He's beside himself, shaking in fear. "That poor girl, we have to get in there and help her. I don't know what I'd do without her."

"You did the right thing," Chase assures him. "As soon as backup arrives, we'll go in."

Without a word, and with the sound of sirens behind me, I set off for the house. I'll be damned if I'll let her sit in there alone while a maniac has his way with her. He could be doing *anything* to her in there, and I will not have her in there for one more second.

Just as I bust through the door, I see him pull his fist back, and he punches her, square in the face.

I don't stop. I run for him and tackle him to the ground, and with him on his back, I punch him in the face myself.

"You like to hit women, you piece of shit?" I hit him again, satisfied when blood spurts out of his nose. Men swarm into the room, and I'm pulled off of him. "You just got a death sentence," I yell out.

"Stop," Chase says, yanking me by the shoulder. "Take care of *her* and leave him to us."

"She wanted it," the asshole cries. "She loves me. I'm her soulmate, and we're going to be together forever."

"Get him out of here," I snarl and then crouch next to Erin.

She's out cold and tied to the chair, so I quickly untie her, lift her into my arms, and lay her on the couch.

"Wake up, baby." I kiss her hand. "Come on, Doc, you have to wake up for me."

"Don't you touch her like that!" They're leading him out, and he's struggling to reach us. "You take your filthy hands off my wife!"

"Jesus Christ, *I'm* going to punch you in the face if you don't shut the fuck up," Chase says as he muscles the man out the door.

"I'm so sorry," Roger says as he lays a cool washcloth on Erin's forehead. "I don't know how that man got into my house."

"It's Clay," Erin whispers, and I turn to her in relief. She's *awake*. "Well, he was *pretending* to be Clay. He's really Steven, and he pretended to be Clay so he could get close to me."

"Shh." I kiss her hand again. "Don't talk, baby. How badly did he hurt you?"

"Some smacks to the face," she says as she fights to sit up but falls into my arms, clinging to me, and the tears start to come. "I was so scared. I thought he was going to kill me and that I'd never see my f-f-family again, or you and the k-k-kids."

"Shh, it's over, baby. It's over." I rock her back and forth as she sobs, letting it all out. "It's okay. I'm right here."

She continues to cling to me, and I kiss her head, rubbing my hands up and down her back.

"You're going to the doctor," I announce, and she nods in agreement.

"Yeah." She looks over at Roger and smiles softly, wiping tears from her cheeks. "Are you the one who called for help?"

"Of course, I did." Roger takes her free hand in his. "I'm sorry, my sweet girl."

"I'll be okay. At least now we've caught him." She looks back up at me with those swimming green eyes. "I have so much to tell you and Chase."

"You'll tell us," I promise her, relieved that she seems to be fine. "But right now, I'm taking you to the doctor."

CHAPTER TWENTY-FIVE
ERIN

"I'm *fine*," I insist for the sixtieth time. "I'm not dizzy. I just have a hell of a headache."

"Hmm." The doctor, a pretty woman named Emily Peabody, doesn't say much as she shines a light in my eyes. "Follow my finger."

I do, and she says, "Hmm," again, and makes notes on her computer.

"Dr. Peabody," I repeat. "I'm *fine*. I just need to go home and lie low for a day or two."

"I agree," she finally says, and I glance at Remington triumphantly.

"Told you."

"The X-rays don't show any fracture where you were punched. You're going to have one hell of a black eye for a while, but that'll heal. I suspect the psychological trauma will take longer, though." She turns to me with kind eyes. "I can recommend a good therapist if you'd like."

"Yeah." I swallow hard and grip Remington's hand. "Yeah, I think I would."

She nods and stands. "I'll write it on your discharge papers. Take ibuprofen for the pain, and get some rest."

"Thank you," Rem and I say in unison as she leaves the room.

"Scared the shit out of me," Rem says as he leans in to kiss my cheek. "My God, when I saw you there, unconscious, I...it was a bad moment."

"I thought for sure he'd kill me," I admit softly and brush my fingers through Rem's hair. "His eyes, they were crazy. He's not mentally right."

"He's going back to jail," he says with certainty. "Chase will have some questions for you."

"I'll talk to him now. Where is he?"

"I told him to wait until you're feeling better."

"Remington." I roll my eyes and then flinch at the pain. "I have to talk to him right away. I'll go over to his office when we leave here."

"No driving," Dr. Peabody announces as she walks back into the room. "Not for today, anyway. Let your handsome fella here chauffer you around. Take it easy."

"Thanks." I stand, and Rem slides his arm around my waist to keep me steady.

Which, right now, I need.

"Let's go," I murmur. "I hate hospitals. Did anyone call my parents?"

"Chase did," Rem replies. "He texted me. They're on their way."

"What?" I frown up at him as relief floods through

me. I *really* want my mama. "They don't need to come out here. I'm *fine.*"

"Maybe if you keep saying that, you'll talk yourself into it." He spares me a mild glance. "They're worried about you and want to see you. And I can see by the look on your face that you're relieved. You don't always have to be the badass, you know. Also, Chase will meet us at the house. You're not going to his office."

"Did he say that?"

"No, *I* said that. I'm taking you home, Doc. No arguments."

I don't feel up to arguing. "Oh, shit! The kids! Where are the kids?"

"Millie took them home," he says.

"Okay, good."

He leads me to the Suburban, buckles me in, and then circles around to the driver's side. My head is spinning a little, so I close my eyes and lean on the cool glass of the window.

"I know you want me to tell you everything. But it's just easier if I say it once, when Chase is with us. I don't have the energy to go through it several times."

"That's fine," he replies and reaches for my hand. Since I woke up in Roger's living room, Rem has had his hand on mine in some way. He's been close to hold me and reassure me, and I'm so grateful. "I know the most important piece, and that is that you're safe."

"You get swoony in an emergency." God, every piece of my body is so *sore.*

He chuckles. "Most people call it pushy."

"I like that you're protective and that you take control in a crisis. It's hot. Pull over so we can have some car sex." I can't keep my eyes open.

"As tempting as that is, I'm going to pass for the time being. I'll take a rain check, though. Baby, you're so tired." He kisses the back of my hand.

"You never call me baby." I open one eye and peer over at him. "Like, *never*. But I think I kind of like it."

"I'm feeling particularly tender toward you right now," he admits. "Are you sure you shouldn't be monitored in the hospital overnight?"

"Don't tell me you've never taken a punch to the face."

"I've had my share."

"And did *you* spend the night in the hospital?"

He doesn't say anything, and I close my eye again.

"See? I just need a nap and some ibuprofen. Part of me thinks I should call my parents and tell them to stay home, but the other part kind of wants my mommy, so I won't."

He pulls off the freeway and through the gate, and when he stops in front of the house, I frown.

"Your *entire* family is here."

"Looks like it."

"Why?"

He turns and stares at me like I'm suddenly stupid. "Because that's what family does, Doc. They're worried about you."

"That's really sweet."

Before I can walk up the stairs, Rem picks me up and carries me up to the door, which is opened by Millie.

Her eyes are red and puffy from crying, and both Johnny and Holly flank her sides, their faces covered in worry.

"Oh, Erin," Millie says with a sniffle. "Are you really okay?"

"I'm fine." I feel like it's the eightieth time I've said it. "Really, I am. I just have a cool shiner. I'm not sure why I'm being carried."

"Because it makes me feel better," Remington replies and sets me down on the couch. There are questions and worried faces, and finally, I hold my hand up and everyone stops talking.

"And because you have an owie," Holly informs me and sits up on the couch next to me. "Daddy always carries me when I have an owie."

"That's very nice of him." I kiss her brow and smile at Johnny as he watches me with concern furrowing his brow. "Everything's okay, buddy. I look a lot worse than I feel. Honest."

"You have a bad black eye," he says as he steps closer, standing right in front of me. "Does it hurt?"

"A little." I swallow hard, really wanting my own mother right now. I reach out for Johnny's hand, wanting to comfort him. "I know you're worried, but I'm going to be just fine."

Johnny steps into my arms and hugs me tight. "I love you."

"Aw, sweet boy, I love you, too." I kiss his head and

then his cheek. I glance up at Remington. "Does anyone know how far out my parents are?"

"They're in the rental car, on the way here," Chase replies.

"You're kidding. That was *fast.*" I accept a glass of water from Joy and take a drink as Johnny sits on the other side of me. "I'll tell you everything when they get here so I don't have to repeat it."

"That's fair," Chase says, his face grim. "I will tell you now that he's going back to prison on the original charges, but now we've added kidnapping, trespassing, assault on an officer, and a whole host of other things. He's going away for a very long time."

"Good. That's good."

"There was a bad guy?" Holly asks with a tremble in her little voice, and I close my eyes. I wish with everything in me that these two babies wouldn't have to see me like this or hear this story. I love them both so much.

"There was a bad guy, but your uncle Chase got him, and he can't hurt me or anyone else ever again. Isn't that awesome?"

She frowns and crawls up in my lap, snuggling against me. "I'm sorry."

"Me too, baby." I kiss her brow and cuddle her and then smile when Johnny takes my free hand in his. These two little loves mean the world to me.

John and Brady are pacing the room, and Joy sits across from me, her face lined in worry as she watches me with the kids.

Finally, I hear a car pull up outside, and Remington walks over to open the door.

"Where is she?" Mom demands. "Erin?"

"Everyone's in the living room," I hear Remington reply.

"Oh, my baby," Mom says and breaks into a fresh bout of tears. "My girl."

"Mama." She folds me and Holly both into her arms, and I break down into tears again. All the fear and emotions from the past several hours just bubble up and out, and I can't control it.

When the tears finally slow down, I glance around and find everyone watching me, including both Holly and Johnny.

"Sorry." I wipe at the tears, sucking in a breath when I rub my hurt eye too hard. "Ouch. Okay, Chase, get your recorder ready because I'm about to spill my guts. Wait, should the kids be here for this?"

"Hey, you two, let's go out to the barn and see if we can talk Lucky into taking us all for a ride on the horses," Millie says.

"I want to stay," Johnny says, shaking his head and crossing his arms over his chest.

"I'll talk to you and Holly later, and tell you the story," I promise, running my hand over his hair. "I promise, I will. But for now, I have to tell the adults, and I think it's best if you and Holly go have fun, okay? I love you, buddy. It's going to be okay."

Johnny firms his lower lip and looks like he's going to

be stubborn, but he glances over at his little sister and reluctantly nods.

"Okay. Come on, Holly."

Holly hugs me tight, kisses my cheek, and then joins her brother and Millie.

When I hear the front door close, I take a deep breath and let it out slowly, take another sip of water, and then nod. "Okay, so I was working with Millie..."

"It's my birthday party day!" Holly announces as she runs into my bedroom and bounces on my bed, still in her Cinderella jammies. "My friends are coming, and we're going to have a real castle!"

"Yes, I'm aware," I reply with a laugh as she wraps her little arms around my neck and hugs me close, snuggled down in my bed. Over the past two weeks since the incident, as I've now come to think of it, the kids have become more and more comfortable coming to hang out with me in my room, especially in the morning. "I'm the one who ordered the castle."

"When do your parents get here?" she asks.

"In a couple of hours." Even though they were just here two weeks ago, they made it clear that they wouldn't miss out on Holly's party. "They'll be here before the party starts."

"Good." She reaches up and pats my cheek. "Erin?"

"Yes, love."

"When do you think it would be okay if I called you Mommy?"

My heart catches, and my throat wants to close up. Jesus, I want that more than I thought I ever would. I smile at her and brush her pretty hair off her cheek.

"Oh, sweet girl. You're so precious to me. You know that, right?"

"Uh-huh."

"Maybe we just need a little more time."

"Where are you guys?" Johnny pokes his head in and grins, then runs over and jumps on the bed. "What are you talking about?"

"I want to call her Mommy, but she said no."

Johnny frowns over at me, and I shake my head.

"I didn't say no. I said we need more time."

"Why?" Johnny wants to know. "We love you, and you love us, so what's the problem?"

"Because it's not just up to me," I reply and tap him on the nose. "But I love you both, too. We'll talk about this later, okay? We have a lot to do today."

"My *party*," Holly agrees and smiles at her brother. "Are you excited?"

"Not really," he says with a shrug, but I see the excitement in his eyes. Why do older siblings always have to give their younger siblings a hard time?

"Erin, will you make the pretty fishtail braids in my hair?" Holly asks.

"You bet."

"You kicked ass with this party," Millie says as she joins me at the cake and ice cream table. "The kids are having a blast. Even the adults are. That cake was delicious."

"I must admit, this was my first time throwing a kid's party, and I didn't do half-bad." I glance over and frown when I spot Remington walking with my dad. "What are those two talking about?"

"I wouldn't know," Millie says.

"That means you do know."

She laughs and shakes her head as Rem breaks away from my dad and heads our way. "No, it doesn't."

"You're amazing," Remington says as he walks up and wraps his arms around my middle. "I don't recall ever seeing Holly smile as big as she did when she saw that we bought her her very own horse for her birthday."

"To be fair," I reply, "I didn't have anything to do with the horse. But something tells me they're going to be good friends."

"While the kids play," Rem says, "I was wondering if you'd come have a chat with my family?"

Millie grins and nods.

"Am I in trouble *again*?"

"No." Rem laughs and kisses my cheek. "Come on, you'll see."

He takes my hand, and Millie joins us, walking over to where Rem's parents and brothers are gathered together. I notice there are two empty chairs where my parents were sitting.

"Where did Mom and Dad go?"

"They're playing with the kids," Joy says with an

inviting grin. "Remington was telling us about your idea regarding that old barn out in the pasture. He mentioned it a few weeks ago, actually, but we were just having a conversation about it."

"Oh, okay. I wasn't trying to overstep," I say as I sit in one of the empty chairs. "The idea just came to me when Remington and I were out there, and I ran with the idea."

"We kind of love it," Millie says. "It's a great idea."

"Really?" Surprised, I raise my eyebrows and look at each member of the family. "You like it?"

"It's genius," Ryan confirms. "It will be profitable, while maintaining some history of the property. We just have one stipulation."

"What's that?"

"That you're in charge of overseeing the project." Remington takes my hand. "It's your vision. Of course, we're all here to help, but we want this to be your project. And once it's built and underway, you'll be the CEO of that business."

Stunned, my mouth opens and closes, but no sound comes out because I'm not sure what in the hell to say to that.

"Again, we can help," Millie adds. "And you'll hire staff."

"But my whole job here is to take care of the kids." I frown over at Remington. "They're a full-time job."

"It's going to take a while for the construction of it— the landscaping, hardscaping, everything. Likely at least a year, maybe more. The kids are in school most of the year, remember?" He smiles over at me. "You won't be bored, that's for sure."

"Think about it," John says kindly. "You don't have to jump in right this minute. Give it some thought."

"You'll have a whole family here to help you," Joy reminds me with a wink.

"Wow." I take a deep breath and let it out slowly. "I'll admit, it sounds like such a fun project. I'd love to do it, but I have no experience in anything like this. I have lots of family who do, and I know I could consult with them, but this is way out of my comfort zone."

"Comfort zones are lame," Brady says with a grin. "I figure, to get experience, you have to jump in and figure it out."

"Like I said," John adds, "give it some thought. Now, I'd like to go check out that new horse."

They all get up and go off to play with the kids or check out the horse, and I'm left alone with Remington.

"I don't know if I'm really the person you'd want for that big of a project."

He calmly reaches over to tuck my hair behind my ear. "I think that you need to start giving yourself more credit. But if you don't want to do it, no harm, no foul."

"Who am I kidding? I want to do it."

He grins over at me. "I figured you might."

"Wake up, Doc." Remington's voice is smooth and sexy in my ear, lifting me out of the hardest, most delicious sleep ever. "I have to show you something."

"Time is it?"

"It's early, but I need to show you something. Come on."

Yesterday was exhausting. Who knew that a kid's party could take it completely out of you? I feel like I could sleep for a week.

"Do I have time to pee and brush my teeth?" I ask as I push my hair off of my face.

"Absolutely," he says and steps away from my bed. "I'll meet you in the kitchen."

"Oh, one more thing." I grab his shirt before he can pull out of arm's reach. "I love you."

His lips curve in that staggering smile. "Back at you, Doc. Come on. Let's go. You won't want to miss this."

I stretch and then pad into the bathroom to take care of business. Once I'm dressed, I find Remington in the kitchen.

He passes me a to-go tumbler of coffee.

"Are we going somewhere?"

"I can't get anything past you," he says with a wink and takes my hand. "Come on. I'm not telling you where we're going. It's a surprise."

He doesn't have to tell me. We're going to the special spot with the view of the mountains. I don't know how I know it. I just do.

And I'm not wrong.

He pulls the Jeep to a stop and climbs out, then

hurries around to open my door for me, and with our coffees in hand, he leads me to a little spot that already has a blanket spread out on the grass.

"When did you put this here?"

"About an hour ago," he replies with a satisfied smile before taking a sip of his coffee. "I couldn't sleep last night, so I came out to set up something nice for you."

"Why couldn't you sleep? What's wrong? After that wild party yesterday, I slept like the dead."

"Nothing's wrong." He kisses my fingers, and then we sit on the blanket, snuggled up together. My coffee is delicious, and the sky is starting to turn pink as the sun climbs up behind the mountains. "I wanted some alone time with you in a special place before the sun comes up."

"I'm glad your parents came for Holly's party," he says and sips his coffee. "It's convenient that we're only an hour's flight away from Seattle. When I spoke to your dad yesterday, he said he'd never miss his granddaughter's birthday party."

The words start to sink in, and I turn my gaze up to his. "I know I haven't had much coffee yet, but—"

"I love you," he says, his voice perfectly calm. His amazing eyes are full of happiness and hope as he stares down at me. "I never believed in love at first sight, but I took one look at you at that coffee shop, and I knew I was a goner. Why do you think I went in every single day? I can get plain black coffee at home."

I press my lips together, determined to soak in every word of this and not ruin it with questions.

"I've done the marriage thing before, Erin." He sighs and brushes my hair back behind my ear. "I'm not sure that I was any good at it. I made a lot of mistakes, and I can be a bear to live with sometimes. Just ask my kids."

"You're not selling this very well."

He taps the tip of my nose with his finger and grins. "I know that I'm a lot to take on. I have two children and a ranch that demands a lot of my time. But I want to make a life with you here. I want to marry you, share my home and my kids with you."

He pulls a ring out of his pocket and offers it to me. It's a simple solitaire diamond, but it has to be at least three karats.

"Whoa." My heart leaps into my throat, and I'm swamped with emotion.

"Will you marry me, Erin Montgomery?"

I search his face and eyes, and I can see the love there, radiating back at me. And I know, without a shadow of a doubt, that I want to marry this man, and be the mother to his gorgeous kids. I want this life with him.

"Without hesitation." He slides the ring onto my finger and then kisses it. "I love you and the kids and this place more than anything. When I came to Montana, I was so lost. I didn't know for sure what I wanted or even who I was. But I found it with you, and with Holly and Johnny. This is absolutely where I'm supposed to be. And the kids are champing at the bit to call me Mom, which just melts my heart every time they ask. They're the sweetest, and I love them with my whole heart. Not just because they're a packaged deal with you, but because of who they are as people. I hope their mom would approve of me stepping in on her behalf."

Remington swallows hard and nods. "She'd like you, Doc. And I know my kids are crazy about you because they've also been hounding *me* to ask you to marry us so you can finally be their mom."

"So, you gave in to peer pressure?" I giggle and then moan as he kisses me, soft and slow.

When we finally come up for air, he whispers, "Look at the mountains."

I turn my head and gasp. The sky is on fire, in red and orange, as the sun is just starting to come up behind the peaks.

"It's the most beautiful thing I've ever seen."

"Heart stopping," he agrees, and I glance to him and find him looking at me.

"There's that swoon again."

"This is only the beginning, Doc." He kisses my nose and pulls me closer to him, and I know that this is just the beginning of an incredible life here in the wilds of Montana.

EPILOGUE
CHASE WILD

I hate the Fourth of July. Not because I'm not patriotic, but because as a cop, I spend the entire week responding to disturbing the peace calls because people can't seem to understand that lighting off fireworks is against the law within the city limits.

Kids like to get into trouble on this holiday, as well, stealing fireworks, drinking...pretty much any trouble they can find.

And I should know. Once upon a time, *I* was that kid.

I've just left the home of one such teenager, one that I'm sure is about to be grounded for the rest of the summer, when I get another call.

"Wild," I say, responding to dispatch.

"I need you to respond to four-three-three Sixth Avenue. Attempted robbery report."

"On my way, two minutes out," I reply and hit my siren. I know that house.

That's where Summer Quinn lives.

I pull up to a stop, hurry to the front door, and ring the bell. When Summer flings it open, her blue eyes are full of tears.

"Oh, God, Chase." She sniffs and wipes at a tear. "Someone tried to break into my house."

"Tell me what happened."

"I heard someone jiggling my door handle." She gestures to the front door. "So, I grabbed my gun and yelled at them."

"Wait, you *what*?"

"I'm no victim," she says and firms her chin. Jesus, she's gorgeous with those tears in her blue eyes yet looking so fierce. "I scared them right off."

"Do you have video on your front porch?"

"No." Her face crumples again. "I'll get it installed in the morning, for sure. It's probably just kids, right? Because Bitterroot Valley is so safe. I've never heard of anyone breaking and entering around here, and I've been here for almost five years."

"It doesn't happen often," I assure her. "And yeah, probably kids."

I'm not so sure, but there's no reason to scare her even more than she already is.

"Are you okay to stay here tonight? I'll dust for fingerprints and look around outside, but without video, I don't know how much I can do."

Summer swallows hard before nodding. "I can stay with a friend tonight."

I almost blurt out that she can stay at my place, but I refrain.

"Don't worry," I assure her. "It's going to be okay."

"I'm sure." I pat her shoulder, and she visibly shrinks out of my reach. It makes me wonder who hurt her, and it also makes me want to punch the dude in the face. "You get your things, and I'll get those prints."

"Thank you." She sniffs again and looks like she wants to say something else, but then changes her mind. "Thanks."

She offers me a brave smile and turns to go pack her things.

I'm determined to figure Summer out. Because as strongly as I denied it to my sister, I *am* drawn to her, and I can't seem to shake the urge to be with her.

Summer Quinn is irresistible.

I don't know who would want to break into her house, but I'll get to the bottom of it. I'm determined to keep her, and Bitterroot Valley, safe.

THE END

Don't miss the next installment in The Wilds of Montana series! Get all the information on Chasing Wild here:

https://www.kristenprobyauthor.com/chasing-wild

. . .

Turn the page for a preview of the origin story for The Wilds of Montana, Merry & Wild. This novella is John and Joy's story! You can download it for FREE here:

https://www.kristenprobyauthor.com/merry-wild

MERRY AND WILD PREVIEW
JOHN

"I'm only going to this thing because I feel sorry for you."
I glance over at my baby sister and watch as she twists
her hands together in her lap as Prince sings about a red
Corvette over the radio in my truck. "And because I don't
want you driving on these roads."

"I was born and raised in freaking Montana," Melissa
says, rolling her eyes. "I can drive in a little snow."

"I look after the women in my family," I remind her,
and she stares over at me.

"Dude, it's 1986, not the fifties. I don't need you to
look after me." But then she softens and pats my arm.
"But I appreciate the moral support. I don't know why
I'm wigging out over this. It's just a Christmas party at
the fire hall. It's not like this is the first time I've gone to
one."

"Because *he* will probably be there, and you don't
want to see him. You just broke up with him last week."

Melissa is still in high school and has been dating a

guy named Pete for about a year. It was serious enough that he spent *last* Christmas with the family at the ranch. But after what he pulled, it's safe to say he won't be invited again this year.

Or any year.

"I don't care if *he's* there," she insists, firming her chin. "He can just kiss my little white butt. He's totally grody."

"Right. Well, Kendra will be there, right?"

"She's my best friend. Of course, she'll be there."

"Then you're safe. And if he pulls anything, I'll shoot him, and they'll never find the body."

That makes her laugh as we enter town. Our ranch is about fifteen minutes from the city limits of Bitterroot Valley, Montana, a tiny little ski town nestled in the Rocky Mountains of the western part of the state. Our family has owned the Wild River Ranch for a hundred years, and we intend to own it for a hundred more.

At least.

My father is about to retire since Melissa is about to graduate from high school. She's the youngest of the family, and he's ready to hand the operation over to me.

The eldest and only Wild son.

I'm excited as hell and scared out of my mind.

"There's not much parking left," Melissa mutters as I turn into the parking lot. "All the snow makes parking hard."

"People definitely don't park well in it," I agree and find a spot at the end of a row. "Hold on. I'll help you out. You should have worn boots."

"I'm not wearing *boots* with a holiday dress," she says for the fifth time tonight as I climb out of my truck and walk around to hold her hand as she slides out to the snow-covered ground below. "There, see? I'm fine."

"You're going to bust your ass."

"I am not," she says with a laugh and almost slips with the first step. "Whoa!"

"Hold on to me, damn it." She grips my sleeve and holds on as I lead her to the covered entrance to the hall, where she lets go and stomps the wet snow off of her shoes. "Okay, we're here. Now stop babying me. Sometimes it sucks being ten years younger than you."

"Stop whining," I suggest, and open the door for her. She's off like a shot, looking for her friends so she can dance and mingle with other teenagers.

And now, I get to wait for her to decide that she's ready to go home. It's not a big deal, since I know pretty much everyone here, and I can do some mingling of my own. But there's a storm blowing in, and I'd like to get back to the ranch so I can check on the animals and make sure they're ready to hunker down through the worst of it.

"John Wild?"

I turn at the voice and smile down at a face I remember from high school, but I can't place her name. "Judy?"

"Joy," she corrects me. "It's been a long time."

"A *long* time," I confirm with a nod, and take the offered punch in her hand. "Thanks. I thought you moved away after high school?"

"I did." She shrugs and taps her foot as Madonna starts to sing about dressing up. "But I'm back. It's funny because I thought I wanted to be a city girl, but it turns out the city isn't all it's cracked up to be. It was fun for a while, and I like to visit, but Montana has my heart."

I nod and can't help but notice that Joy looks amazing in a simple green dress, her feet in heels, and her dark hair pinned back on one side with a clip. Her green eyes are happy and flirty, and it's all starting to come back to me.

Yeah, Joy was always pretty as a teenager. But now, she's absolutely beautiful.

"I'm glad you're home," I reply, and clink my glass to hers.

"Are you still out at the ranch?" she asks casually.

"Oh, yeah. I was born there, and I'll probably die there. But that's not a bad thing. What are you doing these days?"

"I'm a bookkeeper," she says. "For Bitterroot Pediatrics. It's not a bad thing, either, really. I like the doctors."

"Is Doc Simpson still there?"

"He is, and he's about a hundred years old."

I laugh with her and notice that Joy isn't wearing a ring on an important finger. "No husband?"

"Nah, I'm single. What about you? Are you still with Sandy?"

"No." I shake my head, thinking about my high school girlfriend. "We broke up not long after graduation, actually."

"So, you're single, too, then."

I nod, and Joy's smile spreads. "That's pretty convenient, because I have a confession to make."

"I can't wait to hear what it is." I wave back at a friend from across the room and then give Joy my undivided attention. "Spill it."

"I've had a massive crush on you since the sixth grade."

NEWSLETTER SIGN UP

I hope you enjoyed reading this story as much as I enjoyed writing it! For upcoming book news, be sure to join my newsletter! I promise I will only send you news-filled mail, and none of the spam. You can sign up here:

https://mailchi.mp/kristenproby.com/newsletter-sign-up

ALSO BY KRISTEN PROBY:

Other Books by Kristen Proby

Single in Seattle Series
The Secret - Vaughn & Olivia
The Scandal - Gray & Stella
The Score - Ike & Sophie
The Setup - Keaton & Sidney
The Stand-In - Drew & London

Check out the full series here: https://www.
kristenprobyauthor.com/single-in-seattle

The With Me In Seattle Series

Come Away With Me - Luke & Natalie
Under The Mistletoe With Me - Isaac & Stacy
Fight With Me - Nate & Jules
Play With Me - Will & Meg

Rock With Me - Leo & Sam

Safe With Me - Caleb & Brynna

Tied With Me - Matt & Nic

Breathe With Me - Mark & Meredith

Forever With Me - Dominic & Alecia

Stay With Me - Wyatt & Amelia

Indulge With Me - Shawn & Lexi

Love With Me - Jace & Joy

Dance With Me Levi & Starla

You Belong With Me - Archer & Elena

Dream With Me - Kane & Anastasia

Imagine With Me - Shawn & Lexi

Escape With Me - Keegan & Isabella

Flirt With Me - Hunter & Maeve

Take a Chance With Me - Cameron & Maggie

Check out the full series here: https://www.
kristenprobyauthor.com/with-me-in-seattle

Huckleberry Bay Series

Lighthouse Way

Fernhill Lane

Chapel Bend

The Big Sky Universe

Love Under the Big Sky

Loving Cara

Seducing Lauren

Falling for Jillian
Saving Grace

The Big Sky
Charming Hannah
Kissing Jenna
Waiting for Willa
Soaring With Fallon

Big Sky Royal
Enchanting Sebastian
Enticing Liam
Taunting Callum

Heroes of Big Sky
Honor
Courage
Shelter

Check out the full Big Sky universe here: https://www.
kristenprobyauthor.com/under-the-big-sky

Bayou Magic

Shadows
Spells
Serendipity

Check out the full series here: https://www.
kristenprobyauthor.com/bayou-magic

ALSO BY KRISTEN PROBY:

The Curse of the Blood Moon Series

Hallows End
Cauldrons Call
Salems Song

The Romancing Manhattan Series

All the Way
All it Takes
After All

Check out the full series here: https://www.
kristenprobyauthor.com/romancing-manhattan

The Boudreaux Series

Easy Love
Easy Charm
Easy Melody
Easy Kisses
Easy Magic
Easy Fortune
Easy Nights

Check out the full series here: https://www.
kristenprobyauthor.com/boudreaux

The Fusion Series

Listen to Me

Close to You

Blush for Me

The Beauty of Us

Savor You

Check out the full series here: https://www.
kristenprobyauthor.com/fusion

From 1001 Dark Nights

Easy With You

Easy For Keeps

No Reservations

Tempting Brooke

Wonder With Me

Shine With Me

Change With Me

The Scramble

Cherry Lane

Kristen Proby's Crossover Collection

Soaring with Fallon, A Big Sky Novel

Wicked Force: A Wicked Horse Vegas/Big Sky Novella
By Sawyer Bennett

All Stars Fall: A Seaside Pictures/Big Sky Novella
By Rachel Van Dyken

Hold On: A Play On/Big Sky Novella
By Samantha Young

Worth Fighting For: A Warrior Fight Club/Big Sky
Novella
By Laura Kaye

Crazy Imperfect Love: A Dirty Dicks/Big Sky Novella
By K.L. Grayson

Nothing Without You: A Forever Yours/Big Sky Novella
By Monica Murphy

Check out the entire Crossover Collection here:
https://www.kristenprobyauthor.com/kristen-proby-crossover-collection

ABOUT THE AUTHOR

Kristen Proby is a *New York Times*, *USA Today*, and *Wall Street Journal* bestselling author of over seventy published titles. She debuted in 2012, captivating fans with spicy contemporary romance about families and friends with plenty of swoony love. She also writes paranormal romance and suggests you keep the lights on while reading them.

When not under deadline, Kristen enjoys spending time with her husband and their fur babies, riding her bike, relaxing with embroidery, trying her hand at painting, and, of course, enjoying her beautiful home in the mountains of Montana.

facebook.com/booksbykristenproby

instagram.com/kristenproby

bookbub.com/profile/kristen-proby

goodreads.com/kristenproby

Printed in the USA
CPSIA information can be obtained
at www.ICGtesting.com
LVHW042008280124
769923LV00010B/330